A Dangerous Game

LUCINDA CARRINGTON

Black Lace novels contain sexual fantasies.
In real life, make sure you practise safe sex.

First published in 1999 by
Black Lace
Thames Wharf Studios,
Rainville Road, London W6 9HT

Typeset by SetSystems Ltd, Saffron Walden, Essex
Printed and bound by Mackays of Chatham PLC

ISBN 0 352 33432 0

A Dangerous Game

Jacey surveyed her reflection in the mirror. You look like a tart, she thought, amused at her image. She knew this was exactly what Nicolás wanted. In this game he wanted a woman who would do as she was told.

I'll act the part for him, she thought. She smiled. There was something Nicolás did not suspect. She was playing games too – with him. But her game was no fantasy – and in it she was the one in control.

Chapter One

Jacey Muldaire could see Anton lying on the bed, a sheet twisted loosely round his knees. His cock was limp now, but still an impressive size. It gave her a thrill of pleasure to look at him, half-naked, and asleep. He was always sleepy after making love.

She sighed, knotted the sash of her black silk kimono, and switched on the kettle. Anton O'Rhiann, she thought. French mother, Irish father; an explosively gorgeous combination. A body like an athlete and dark eyes that could melt steel. Most of the nurses were drooling over him, envying anyone who was able to get close to him, and certainly envying her. And I didn't even try to hook him, she remembered. If he hadn't questioned me when we were doing the ward rounds, I probably wouldn't have even noticed him. Then she smiled. Well, maybe that's not quite true, she thought. I would have noticed him, but I wouldn't have encouraged him. He did all the chasing. And I did warn him. I told him I wasn't into permanent relationships. He didn't believe me then, and he doesn't believe me now. Neither does anyone else. They can't see why I

1

don't grab him with both hands while I've got the chance.

The water boiled and the kettle switched off. She took two red mugs from the cupboard and glanced through the open door again. Anton shifted lazily, turning on his side, displaying his neatly rounded buttocks. He's attractive in bed, and out, she admitted to herself. He always gives me an orgasm. And if we run out of small talk we can always discuss work!

She knew that gossip at the hospital had already decided they were a perfect couple. The nurses were probably taking bets on when she would announce her engagement, and Anton's friends were deciding what kind of embarrassing tricks to play on him on his stag night. They don't understand, she thought. And Anton doesn't understand either. She knew that he was hurt by her constant refusal to consider any kind of permanent relationship. He felt it was an insult to him.

'You can carry on working,' he had often told her. 'I'm not suggesting you give up your career, for God's sake. In fact, I'm proud of you, Dr Muldaire! Beauty and brains; it's a very sexy combination.'

He often told her she was beautiful. She glanced at him again. His eyes were closed and his breathing was steady. He had been on duty before coming to see her. It seemed a shame to wake him when he was so tired, just to give him a mug of coffee. She left the mugs on the table and walked over to her full-length mirror. Beauty and brains? Well, I made it through university without too much trouble, she mused. But beauty? She had never considered herself beautiful. She liked the deep burnished red of her hair, a colour you could never find from a hair-dye, but although she knew she had good cheekbones, she thought her face too square and her lips too full to be described as beautiful. Striking perhaps, she conceded. She had

2

a dancer's legs, long and slim, and a dancer's supple grace. Her breasts were OK; not huge, but at least visible. She had never liked her bottom, and she thought her hips were too narrow. It was then that she heard a soft wolf-whistle behind her and turned. Anton was sitting up in bed.

'I thought you were asleep,' she said.

'All good doctors sleep with one eye open,' he said. He grinned. 'Stop posing. You know you're gorgeous.'

'I'm not.' She twisted to look over her shoulder. 'My bottom's too small, and it looks like a man's.'

Anton laughed. 'No one's ever going to mistake you for a man.'

'I played Romeo in a school play,' she said. 'I was very convincing. I got good reviews.'

'And how old were you?' he scoffed. 'Twelve? Thirteen? Flat-chested and spotty? You wouldn't fool anyone now. You're all woman.' He patted the bed. 'Lie down and enjoy it.'

She gave a theatrical gasp of surprise. 'Already? Your powers of recovery are remarkable, sir.'

'With you to inspire me I could be a six-times-a-night man.' He glanced down at his now semi-erect cock. 'See? Just thinking about you is making me hard. Come and use that lovely mouth on me and inspire me a little bit more.'

She shook her head and backed away. 'No. I'm going to make coffee.'

When she reached the kitchen she glanced back and saw that Anton had stretched out on the bed again, his eyes closed. She smiled and went into the living room, where most of Anton's clothes were scattered. She picked up his denims and tugged them on, surprised to find that they were quite a good fit. His soft, leather bomber jacket was too large but it disguised her breasts. She dragged her hair back as severely as she could and pushed the pony tail under the jacket collar. Then she found an old baseball cap which someone had given her one day when it was raining. She pulled it on, walked back into the bedroom and shook Anton roughly. 'Wake up, big boy,' she growled. 'Fancy some action?'

She saw the bemused expression on his face as he opened his eyes. It was momentary but it satisfied her. 'Fooled you!' She pirouetted in front of him. 'And I wasn't really trying. Think how much better I'd look in a man's suit.'

He grinned lazily. 'I've seen pictures of Marlene Dietrich in a suit. She looked very sexy. But she didn't look remotely like a man. And you wouldn't, either.'

Jacey struck a camp pose, one hand on her hip. 'Well, handsome, d'you want me or not?'

He caught her wrist and pulled her down on the bed. 'I don't know,' he said. 'I'll have to inspect what you're offering.' He deftly unzipped the jeans and slipped his hand inside to discover that she wasn't wearing panties, and that she was wet and aroused. His fingers explored her. 'Well now, young man,' he murmured. 'Something seems to be missing here.'

'There's nothing missing,' she teased back. 'Everything's there. It's just a question of size.'

He captured her clitoris and tugged it gently. 'You mean you think you can satisfy me with this?'

She leant back on the bed and opened the leather bomber jacket. Her nipples were already erect and the cool air tightened them even more. She knew he enjoyed seeing them like that, small and hard. 'Oh yes, I can satisfy you,' she promised.

His eyes took her in admiringly. 'That's cheating,' he said. 'And if you were a young man I'd be interested in your arse, not your chest. Turn over.'

She turned lazily, and felt him pull the jeans down

4

to her knees. 'You'd be the butch one, would you?' she murmured.

'Well, we've just established that you haven't got what it takes,' he agreed. He straddled her suddenly, pinning her down. 'But I have.' She felt the warmth and weight of his body and the growing strength of his erection against her buttocks. 'I could take you as if you were a boy,' he whispered, close to her ear. 'Would you like that?'

The suggestion excited her. She had never tried sex that way before. She could feel his body trembling in anticipation; the idea obviously also appealed to him. She found that surprising. They had discussed some mild sexual fantasies before, and played out some of them – Anton's included watching her doing a strip-tease, and oral sex in unusual places, including the storeroom at the hospital – but he had never mentioned this one.

He dragged the jeans off completely and she pretended to resist him, laughing, struggling and kicking. She knew she could have escaped from him quite easily; in fact, she guessed, he would probably have been shocked at how easily. But now she let him push her down roughly, his hand on her back. 'Behave yourself,' he growled. 'Or you'll get a spanking first, and then a fucking!'

She was startled at this unexpected piece of play-acting, and by her own hot rush of excitement at the aggressive way he was treating her. The fantasy of being at his mercy was highly stimulating. She would love it if he indulged in a little erotic spanking. No man had ever spanked her before.

But instead he turned her on to her stomach, man-handled her into position, and pulled her legs open even wider. She felt the end of his cock probing her anus. She was not sure if she would like this new experience but she was aroused enough by now to want to try it, and to try it there and then! She wanted to feel him push his way inside her. She wanted to feel him come, even if she didn't have her own pleasure. She knew he would satisfy her afterwards with his mouth or his hands. But having started his unorthodox advance, Anton hesitated. He still clasped her tightly, holding her captive, but he seemed reluctant to penetrate her. Hoping to tempt him into behaving in a more forceful manner, she pretended to struggle again.

She realised, too late, that it was a mistake. He pulled back at once. 'Don't worry,' he murmured, close to her ear. 'I won't hurt you. I wouldn't do anything you didn't like.'

'Don't be stupid!' she muttered, angry now. 'Fuck me!' She reached backwards and gripped his cock. She heard him groan as she tightened her hand around it and tugged. 'Put this thing in me. Do it now!'

'All right.' She could hear the excitement rising in his voice now. 'You want it! You can have it!'

His cock slid out of her grasp and nudged between her legs. She was already very wet, and he slid vigorously against her, anointing himself with her musky secretions. He probed again, searching for her entrance, then, just as he was about to plunge into her, quickly withdrew. 'I'm sorry,' he muttered. 'It'll hurt you. I can't –' He rolled away from her on to his side, with his back to her. She knew he wouldn't go on now, and didn't bother to try and encourage him. She also knew that he was embarrassed at his behaviour. She reached out and touched his shoulder.

'It's OK,' she said softly.

'I shouldn't have started this,' he began.

'I wanted it. Truly.'

'Perhaps another time,' he mumbled.

But she knew it was a cover-up. He would not try

6

anything unorthodox again. Mr Nice Guy, she thought ruefully. What a pity I'm not your Mrs Nice Girl. He shifted on to his back, and she realised that he had lost his erection. Reaching down, she caught hold of his cock. 'Bet you I can make you come in two minutes flat?' she challenged.

He smiled rather wanly. 'Do you really want to?'

'Oh, Anton,' she said briskly, 'stop trying to turn me into a bloody martyr. It's not my style.' She twisted round on the bed, and moved her lips over him, licking him lightly with the tip of her tongue. 'Two minutes,' she said. 'Time me.'

'I can't see the clock,' he said.

'Tough,' she said. 'You'll have to trust me.'

She enclosed the tip of his cock in her mouth, and felt him push upwards. Moving with him, grasping him lightly with her teeth and letting them scrape over his sensitive skin in a way she knew he enjoyed, she brought him to the edge of orgasm much quicker than she expected. Anton never came in her mouth. He pulled away from her and held himself as the spasms of orgasm shook him. Then Jacey heard a contented sigh.

'I won,' she said.

'I believe you,' he said. 'What do I do? Pay a forfeit?'

'Buy me a meal maybe?' she suggested.

He propped himself up on one arm. 'I was going to.'

She swung her feet off the bed. 'You fibber. When?'

'Next week.' She stood up and walked away from the bed, taking off his leather jacket as she went. 'Where are you going now?' he asked.

'To make coffee,' she said.

'I can make coffee too, you know. How come you never let me?'

'I've tasted it,' she said.

'My coffee isn't that bad.'

'You coffee is appalling.'

He grinned. 'Actually, my mother would agree.' He paused. 'I'm sure you'll get on well with her.'

She stopped and turned. She had an idea where this was leading. 'Anton, I haven't time to take a holiday in France.'

'You don't need to,' he said. 'Mother's coming over here.' She stared at him blankly. 'You'd forgotten,' he accused. 'I told you, mother is coming over for my birthday. My sister's coming down from Leeds. We're all going for a celebration, a slap-up meal. You too.'

She had forgotten. His birthday, she thought, I forgot about his birthday. How could I? Easily, she realised. I often forget my own, but I can hardly tell him that.

'You'll see what a nice family I have,' he teased her. 'And they'll see what a nice girlfriend I have. I've told them so much about you.'

She wondered if her expression betrayed her feelings. The last thing she wanted was a family reunion with Anton's mother. 'I'm not your girlfriend,' she said.

His expression changed. 'Then what are you? We've been together for eight months. Doesn't that mean anything to you?'

'It doesn't mean I'm your property,' she snapped, more sharply than she intended.

'Oh, for God's sake! Whoever said it did?' His uncharacteristic flash of temper disappeared as suddenly as it had come. 'Marriage wouldn't make you my property either. It'd make you my partner.'

'I told you when we started this,' she said. 'I'm not the marrying kind.'

He relaxed back on the bed again, smiling. 'So you keep saying. But wait until you meet my mother.

8

You'll love her. And she's determined to have you as a daughter-in-law.'

I don't need this, Jacey thought, I really don't need this. How can I get out of it?'

As if on cue, the phone rang. And when she picked it up she knew that she might have found her answer.

Major Fairhaven was exactly as Jacey remembered him. The immaculate hair, the immaculate suit, the little enamel badge in his buttonhole that discreetly announced he had been in the Royal Marines. She could never imagine him as a marine. But then, she thought, I can't really imagine him as a young man. I can't imagine him as anywhere else except sitting in this boring office, with its cream walls, government-issue furniture and framed print of the Queen on the wall.

The major smiled at her across his desk. 'Good of you to come, Dr Muldaire.' He paused. 'Actually, I wasn't sure you would.'

She shrugged. 'I'm curious. Why me? It's two years since I worked for you. And I seem to remember telling you when I left that I wanted to make a new life for myself. A quiet life so that I could pursue my profession.'

'You did,' he agreed. 'And I respected your choice.' He leaned back, linked his fingers together and looked at her benignly. 'Are you enjoying yourself as an over-worked and underpaid factotum in the Midland General?'

'I get job satisfaction,' she said.

'I'm sure you do.' Another pause. 'Dr Anton O'Rhiann is a good-looking young fellow, I'm told. And a combination of Irishman and Frenchman must make for some interesting . . . evenings.'

She knew Major Fairhaven far too well to be angry. Instead she laughed. 'I'm not impressed. Any junior

9

nurse could have told you that much. Just tell me why you called me, after all this time.'

He leaned back in his chair. 'Ever heard of Techtátuan?

'No.'

'Not many people have,' he admitted. 'It's in Guachtàl, in central South America.' He handed her several sheets of paper. 'Read this.'

She read fast, then looked up. 'Lots of rainforest, a few villages, and one major town. The original native people are of Inca descent, the ruling classes are Spanish, descended from the Conquistadors. They field a good polo team, host the occasional second-rate film festival, and probably throw lavish parties and get riotously drunk on the local vino.' She scanned the second page. 'And the economy is crooked. Well, that is a surprise. Nazi gold deposited when the SS generals began to lose faith in the Thousand Year Reich, some money-laundering and a nice line in business addresses for tax evaders.' She looked up at the major. 'And no free elections, of course. So who's the boss in Guachtàl?'

The major slid a photograph across his desk. Jacey saw a tubby man wearing a bemedalled uniform and a broad smile. He was holding both arms in the air in a victory salute, and was flanked by armed soldiers.

'That's Generalissimo Hernandez,' the major said. He smiled briefly. 'With his bodyguard.'

'A bully boy?' Jacey guessed.

'Surprisingly enough,' Fairhaven said, 'Hernandez is quite popular. He has a good military record and the army is solidly behind him. Some of those medals are genuine too, although they were won when he was a young man. I gather he was the kind of soldier who was too stupid to recognise danger when it was staring him in the face. But the fact remains, he won

10

the gongs, and lots of people think he's some kind of war hero.'

'And a financial genius too?' Jacey was sceptical.

'No.' The major grinned faintly. 'But this gentleman is.' He tapped the photograph again and Jacey noticed the group of civilians behind Hernandez. 'Señor Nicolás Schlemann. A very clever fellow. He's quite happy to let Hernandez parade around in front of the crowds, but he controls the purse-strings, and that makes him the real power behind the throne.'

The civilian faces were out of focus. Nicolás Schlemann looked like a blurred shadow. Jacey could make out dark hair and a dark suit but that was all.

'A German?' she asked.

'German father,' Major Fairhaven said. 'Spanish mother. His father arrived in Guachtàl in 1945, and by the early 1960s he'd doubled the illegal fortune he brought with him. Nicolás has probably trebled it since.'

Jacey glanced at the anonymous face again. How old would this man be? Thirty? Thirty-five? You couldn't tell from that smudgy, black-and-white image. A crooked wheeler-dealer who kept a small-time dictator in power. She didn't think she would like Señor Nicolás Schlemann.

'And he knows how to spend as well as save,' Fairhaven added.

'Wine, women and song?' she asked. Her voice was cool.

'Women, women and women,' the major asserted.

A dissolute womaniser, too? Nicolás Schlemann went even further down in her estimation. She pushed the photograph back towards the major. She was beginning to understand why he had called her. But do I want this? she asked herself. I need to get away but is this the answer?

'When I worked for you I was part of a team,' she

said. 'We trusted each other. This would be different. I don't think –'

'Wait a minute,' Major Fairhaven interrupted gently. 'This isn't anything like last time.' He smiled at her. 'The hospital at Techtátuan needs a doctor, preferably one who speaks Spanish and English. It's all above board. You can even use your own name.' His smile was warmer now. 'They call it La Primavera because it was built in the spring, and it's supposed to be symbolic of new growth, a new beginning. It's a beautiful place, so I'm told, and I don't think your duties would be too arduous. You'd have plenty of time to enjoy yourself and to socialise.'

'Oh, come on,' she said, with undisguised sarcasm. 'You're beginning to sound like a tour operator. If you're not planning to remove the crooks who're running Guachtàl, why do you want me to go out there?'

'At the moment we need a barometer,' Major Fairhaven said. 'One that we can trust. We want you to talk to people. Listen to the gossip. And then send us the occasional, er, weather report, so to speak.'

She smiled. 'Now you're making sense. You're expecting storms in Guachtàl?'

'Let's just say we want to know which way the winds will be blowing in the near future,' the major said. 'South America is opening up. They're cutting roads through the jungle right now. Guachtàl's main resource is the rainforest. They haven't done much with it yet but that could change quite soon.'

'They could start destroying it, you mean?' Jacey said.

The major smiled. 'You're not turning eco-warrior on me, are you?'

'It seems a shame to destroy something irreplaceable.'

The major shrugged. 'If your country was in debt,

12

and the people starving, you might not feel so senti-mental about a few trees. But that's also what we want you to find out. How do the people of Guachtàl see their future?' He linked his fingers and leant forward. 'Or to put it more accurately, how does Hernandez and his clever friend Schlemann see it? It would give us a chance to make our own plans.' He smiled. 'An occasional report, that's all we need.'

'And if I say yes,' she said, 'what about my job at the hospital? I can't just walk out.'

'If you say yes,' the major said, 'we'll organise a replacement for you, don't worry.'

She gave him a long, hard stare. 'I bet you've got someone lined up already.'

The major laughed. 'It's a nice assignment,' he said. 'More like a holiday.'

'When do you want my decision?'

He shrugged, still smiling. 'Go home and think about it. Let me know by the end of the week.'

After Jacey had left, Major Fairhaven picked up the phone and dialled an internal number. He listened for a moment and then said pleasantly: 'Oh, she'll go. Yes, I'm sure of it.' He paused, listening again. 'Oh no, nothing they do in Techtátuan could shock Dr Muldaire. She's a very liberated lady. And the perfect choice for this assignment. Of course, she doesn't realise exactly how perfect she is.'

On the plane Jacey felt ashamed that she had been such a coward. She had posted a letter to Anton, telling him that she hated tearful goodbyes. By the time he read the letter she would be on the way to a new job in South America. She reminded him that she had never been interested in marriage – although she knew he was – and that her decision to leave England would prevent them from reaching the inevitable painful break-up. Hopefully he would remember her with affection and not bitterness. She left out details of her new address.

When she arrived at Techtátuan there was a modern car waiting for her at the tiny airport. The driver looked as if he would have been too young to hold a licence in England.

'Dr Muldaire? I am called Paulo. I have been instructed to take you to the hospital.' His smile was friendly and his darkly tanned face looked as if it had been carved from smoothly polished wood. It was an unusual face, she thought, and rather beautiful. His Spanish had a distinct accent that she realised must be typical of the indigenous population. 'Don't worry,' he added solemnly, as he helped her load her bags into the boot. 'I am a very safe driver.'

She discovered that this was true, although there was very little competition on the roads. Most of the other mechanised vehicles were old, rickety-looking trade vans. She was surprised by how bright and clean the town looked. The buildings were white walled, with vibrant splashes of colour coming from window boxes and gardens. Paulo turned to her and started to make conversation. 'This is a pleasant town. You'll be happy here.'

'Were you born here?' Jacey asked.

'No, I was born in the village of Matá. My family has lived there for generations.' He paused. 'Long before the Spanish came.'

'So why did you leave?' she asked, guessing the answer.

'There's no work in Matá,' he said. 'The villages are dying.'

'Doesn't the government help?' she asked.

'The government does not help Indians.' She noted the bitterness in his voice. 'I came to Techtátuan to earn money for my family.'

'And you've been successful?' she guessed.

14

He shrugged. 'I have adapted. I learnt to read and write, and to drive a car. I don't mind speaking Spanish, or using a Spanish name.' She heard his voice change. 'But I have not forgotten my heritage. I will never do that.'

The car cruised down an avenue of trees and Jacey noticed large posters pinned to some of the trunks, all depicting the same crudely drawn portrait: a man with bulging, fanatic's eyes glaring from a gaunt, bearded face. His tangled hair was topped by a military-style fatigue cap. One word stood out in large print, a word she did not understand: LOHÁQUIN.

She tapped Paulo on the shoulder. 'Who's the man on the posters? And what does Loháquin mean?'

There was a brief pause before Paulo answered. 'You want to make a lot of money? Find that man and hand him over to the police.'

'He's a criminal?' Jacey guessed.

Paulo laughed shortly. 'Many would say so. Loháquin lives in the rainforest. It protects him. He wants to change things here in Guachtàl.'

'Loháquin?' Jacey repeated. 'That doesn't sound Spanish.'

There was another pause. 'It's the old language,' Paulo said. 'My language. Loháquin means a sort of ghost, but not the ghost of a dead person. More like a spirit, a spirit who lives between two worlds, our world and the invisible world. It's difficult to translate.'

Interesting, Jacey thought. A ghostly rebel, with a large reward on his head? Someone was obviously taking this 'spirit' very seriously indeed. Why didn't Major Fairhaven mention this mysterious character to me, she wondered. Clearly the situation out here isn't quite as simple as he pretended. She leant back

15

in her seat again. 'Does this Loháquin have much support?'

Paulo shrugged. 'Who can say? If anyone supports him, they don't talk to strangers about it.'

Well, Jacey thought, that's put me in my place. Don't ask the wrong questions, Dr Muldaire, because I won't answer them. 'But no one's claimed the reward?' she persisted. 'Obviously Loháquin has friends who protect him.'

'The rainforest protects him,' the boy said. 'I don't know of anyone who claims to have seen him.'

'Someone drew the picture,' Jacey observed.

Paulo laughed. 'There are plenty of people with good imaginations. I have heard that Loháquin has green skin like the trees, and that he is seven feet tall. Also that he is quite small. Women like to dream that he is very handsome, and will come to them in the night and make love to them. Who knows the truth?'

Someone must know, Jacey thought, making a mental note to find out more about the elusive Loháquin. The car drove along the side of a high, white wall and stopped by a pair of ornate but solid-looking iron gates. Paulo hooted. A man in uniform opened the gates, and closed them as soon as the car had passed through.

'Rather heavy security for a hospital,' Jacey commented lightly.

Paulo shrugged. 'There are some very important people here. They need to be private and peaceful when they're ill. Even Generalissimo Hernandez comes here.'

'And Nicolás Schlemann?' she asked.

'You know Señor Schlemann?' Paulo's voice was suddenly wary.

'No,' she said. 'I've heard of him, that's all. He's as important as Hernandez, isn't he?'

'He's very powerful,' Paulo agreed after a moment.

16

He glanced at her. 'No doubt you will meet him in due course.'

'Oh, I don't expect I will,' Jacey said brightly. 'Why would he want to meet me?'

The car halted outside a large white building. 'Because Señor Schlemann likes beautiful women,' Paulo said.

'I'm here as a doctor,' Jacey said, 'not as entertainment for Nicolás Schlemann.'

'Señor Schlemann considers all beautiful women are for his entertainment.' She was surprised at the sudden note of concern in Paulo's voice. 'You should be careful not to offend him, Dr Muldaire. Señor Schlemann is used to getting his own way.'

'I won't offend him if he doesn't offend me,' Jacey said curtly. Nicolás Schlemann was someone she liked less and less. A jumped-up bully, she thought, who uses his position to tyrannise women and anyone else too frightened to fight back. Paulo still looked worried, so she smiled brightly. 'Don't worry, Paulo,' she reassured him. On an impulse she kissed her fingers and tapped the kiss lightly on his cheek. His skin felt smooth and warm. 'I can look after myself. Believe me.'

Later that night Jacey lay in bed, recapping on the events of the day, her mind too active for sleep. Her room was spacious, air-conditioned and cool, pleasantly different to what she had been expecting. The staff quarters were set apart from the main hospital building and looked like an expensive apartment block. She had a living room, bedroom, bathroom and a small kitchen, plus a balcony crowded with brightly flowering plants. A smiling young nurse had previously shown her the staff canteen (as luxurious as a first-class restaurant), the gym, a sports hall and a swimming pool.

17

The hospital's senior doctor, Garcia Sanchez, had officially welcomed her. A charming, elderly Spaniard, he complimented her on her Spanish. He told her he was not born in Guachtàl, but had lived there for fifty years. 'It's a fine country with nice people. You'll enjoy working here, Dr Muldaire.'

'I'm looking forward to it,' she said. 'Perhaps tomorrow someone can explain what my duties are? I'm anxious to start work.'

Dr Sanchez laughed. 'There's no rush. We have emergencies, of course, but most of our patients come in for routine check-ups and minor problems. All we ask is that you wear your pager when you're in the hospital and carry your mobile phone when you go out. I'll get Dr Draven to explain how we do things here. You'll like him; he's English too. Until then you must relax. Recover from your journey.'

What kind of hospital is this, she wondered, as she lay in the semi-darkness. It was the first time she had ever been told to relax at the beginning of a new job. She was certain that Major Fairhaven had not been honest with her about La Primavera. From what she had seen so far, the place looked more like a health spa than a hospital. And if the major was interested in weather reports, why hadn't he told her about Loháquin? She recalled the gaunt, fanatical face on the posters. This man was obviously keen to change the political climate of Guachtàl. I'll have to check him out, she thought. And I think I know someone who might help. I'm sure Paulo knows more about Loháquin than he pretends.

She suddenly remembered the warmth of Paulo's tanned skin when her fingers had touched his cheek. She remembered his slim body, loose-limbed and leggy as a young colt. Exactly how old was he? Sixteen? Seventeen? Was he a virgin? Somehow she knew he was. It was strange, but she found she could

18

think of him as sexually attractive, without actually desiring him. He was a sweet boy. Sweet and innocent. Her memories stirred. Appearances could be deceptive. She turned restlessly on the wide bed. Don't think about it, she told herself. But her mind was already forming the pictures, unwinding them like a film. And she watched, even though it hurt.

A beach. Golden sand and palm trees, a picture-book exotic location. A girl with auburn hair, sunbathing, eyes closed. On holiday. Her first holiday abroad, without her parents. Jacey remembered that it had taken sustained nagging to get her parents to allow her to join a group of friends for that trip. And some lying. Their destination was a singles-only holiday camp and her friends were determined to sample the local talent. She had not told her parents that, but had justified the deception by telling herself that she had no intention of behaving immorally. She simply wanted a holiday where she could do as she wished without considering anyone else. Get up when she wanted, go to bed when she wanted, laze about all day on the beach without being told that too much sun was bad for you.

Behaving immorally? Jacey thought. She had actually used words like that when she was eighteen, when she was still a virgin with her body and her ideals untouched. Apart from daydreaming wistfully over the glossy, flattering photographs of a couple of good-looking actors, her main interest in her teenage years had been sport. Any sport, the more dangerous and athletic the better. Men were simply companions, or sometimes rivals. She rode, did martial arts and went rock-climbing. Her father taught her to shoot. She raced Go-carts and learned to glide.

She realised later that she had been lucky. As an only child she had been thoroughly spoiled by her proud parents. Life was easy. Her parents were delighted when she told them she wanted to study medicine. She did well academically, and this holiday was her reward, a chance to relax prior to university. She had made it clear to her friends that she was not interested in man-hunting, so while they were, in their own words, 'looking for a good fuck', she swam, read a book, did some lazy shopping, dozed in the sun. And enjoyed it, she remembered. For seven of the ten days. And on the eighth day everything changed.

The memory was as sharp as reality. She could almost feel the sun that had warmed her as she dozed on the beach in a secluded spot that she had discovered earlier that week. She remembered how the sand had shifted slightly, and she knew someone had stopped in front of her. If I hadn't opened my eyes, she thought, what would my life have been like? How different would it have been? But I had to be nosey. What a fool I was.

She remembered her first view of Faisel. He was looking down at her. He wore a bright red, silky bathing slip, so brief it was almost a posing pouch. It was tied at both sides and did absolutely nothing to disguise the bulge of his sexual parts, a bulge made even more impressive because his hips were jutting forward and his legs were slightly apart. He was reed-slim and the sun had enhanced his natural tan. His hair was jet black, and his eyes, which captured hers as soon as she opened them, were liquid brown. She gaped at him in startled amazement.

'Hello,' he said politely, and added in perfect English: 'You have the most amazingly beautiful hair.'

Today, faced with such an opening compliment, she would have retaliated with something like 'And you have the most amazingly beautiful body', but at eighteen her repartee was limited by shyness. She remembered saying, 'Thank you'. She remembered that he squatted in front of her with easy grace, smiled, his white teeth contrasting with that beautiful brown skin, and asked her name.

'Jacey?' he repeated. 'That's unusual.'

'It's really Jane Catherine,' she explained. 'Jacey is from the two initials. No one calls me Jane.'

'Well, that's sensible,' he said. 'You shouldn't be called Jane. Plain Jane, don't they say?' He sat down and relaxed next to her. 'You're not a plain Jane, are you?'

His eyes wandered over her body, and she felt flattered and confused. She was strangely aware of his closeness, and his almost indecent near-nakedness. His skin was surprisingly hairless and his nipples were clear, dark aureoles on his smooth chest. Why did she feel so disturbed when she looked at him? There were plenty of other young men on the beach in brief bathing slips and many of them had bodies more muscular than his. Some of them had already tried to pick her up. A girl on her own in a tourist area known for its singles-only holidays was an obvious target for locals and fun-seeking tourists. But she hadn't felt anything except slight irritation when they had stopped, posed, and tried to chat. They did not interest her. So why did this dark-haired boy make her feel both awkward and excited at the same time?

He told her he was an Arab, his name was Faisel, and he had been educated in England. He knew London very well and had an apartment there. He had recently graduated from Cambridge and intended to work in his father's business. That surprised her. She told him she had assumed that he was her age. He laughed. 'I look young, do I? That's because I lead a blameless life. I don't smoke. I don't drink. No vices at all.' He captured her eyes again. 'And no girlfriend, either.'

21

She remembered giggling like a silly schoolgirl. And that's what I was, she thought. A silly, inexperienced virgin schoolgirl, bowled over by her first taste of sheer physical lust. Lusting after that beautiful, soulless bastard, and thinking that lust was love.

'And how about you?' he had asked, smoothly. 'No boyfriend?'

'No,' she said.

'I find that amazing.'

'It's true.'

'So it's OK if I ask you out tonight? For a meal at the Gala Hotel?'

The Gala was the most expensive hotel in town. She had seen the guests arrive, the men in dinner suits, the women in long gowns. 'Oh, but I couldn't,' she said. 'I haven't anything suitable to wear.' She knew now that she had responded exactly as he'd planned. How could she have been so pliable? So stupid?

'That's not a problem,' he said. 'We'll go shopping.' He stood up, and again she studied the outline of his penis and the curve of his balls beneath the thin, silk bathing slip. 'Tell me the name of your hotel, and I'll come and collect you.'

It had been a perfect afternoon and a perfect evening. Faisel had been attentive, funny, and generous. He bought her a beautiful white silk dress and a gold chain, plain and tasteful. The meal was excellent but when it was finally time to go home, she felt suddenly nervous. Now he's going to expect his payment, she thought. He hasn't spent all this money on me for nothing. And although the idea excited her, she was afraid she would disappoint him. He might not have a girlfriend but he would certainly have had other women. Maybe even professionals, who would have entertained him with their repertoire of exotic

22

tricks. What could she offer? She'd never touched a man in a sexual way in her life.

But it didn't happen like that. Clever bastard, she thought, turning on the bed, the pictures clear in her mind. Taking me home, kissing my cheek. Thanking me for a wonderful evening. Waiting a moment, then kissing me gently on the lips. Treating me like the romantic innocent that I was.

She remembered lying in bed that night, drowsily listening to her friends talking about their conquests.

'And then he said, open your legs, I'm going to put my tongue right in there and lick you. And he did.'

'What did it feel like?'

'Nicer than having them stick their cocks in. I came so fast, I couldn't believe it. And then he made me do it to him.'

'Suck him, you mean?'

'Yeah.'

'Urgh! I couldn't.'

'Did he come?'

'You bet he did. I'm good.'

'Kinky cow! You'll be asking them to pay for it next.'

'Good idea. Maybe I will. It'll pay for my next holiday.'

Jacey remembered feeling sorry for them as they giggled together. They made sex seem sordid and cheap. She had something special, something they would not understand. A man who wanted her for herself and not just for what he could get from her. But the crude descriptions her friends were bandying about sparked up pictures in her own mind. She imagined Faisel's glossy head between her legs, his tongue working, giving her the same kind of pleasure that she gave herself sometimes with her own fingers. The idea excited her but it embarrassed her, too. What an innocent I was, she thought. I was unreal.

I thought he would give me a nice clean, romantic orgasm, wrapped up in tissue-paper like a pretty gift. We'd make love differently to everyone else because we were special. We were in love.

She remembered her first time. They had spent the day on the beach then she had gone back to her apartment to change before meeting him for a meal. She told him she was flying back to England the next morning. He had reacted with a suitably shocked expression, and had reached across the table and taken her hand. 'Will I see you again in England?'

'If you want to,' she said. She felt her heart beating. 'I'd like us to be friends.'

His fingers had tightened round hers. He tugged at her gently, forcing her to lean towards him. 'I want more than that,' he said. 'But we can be just friends, if that's what you prefer.'

She remembered that she had actually blushed. No, she had told him, it wasn't what she preferred. She wanted more than that, too. She had expected him to look grateful but he simply smiled and said: 'That's what I thought. I have rooms here, you know? We can go up after our meal and you can stay as long as you like.'

Thinking back on it now she realised how mechanical his love-making had been. She let him use her because she did not really know what to expect. And he had known that, had counted on it. She forgave him all the things she did not like. She convinced herself he was the kind of lover she wanted and ignored the truth.

He had undressed her and encouraged her to undress him. Her hands shook when, as his clothes came off, her fingertips touched his skin. She wanted to linger, to caress his chest, his nipples, the hollow of his neck. Kiss his ears, his eyes, his lips. But he seemed uninterested. He hurried her on, pushing her

24

hands to the buttons of his shirt and the waistband of his trousers. He said very little until they were both naked. She noticed that although his penis was large, he was not erect. Because she was so inexperienced, she thought he was deliberately holding back so that he did not rush her. When he pushed her on to her back she was startled but compliant. When he straddled her and pushed his limp penis into her mouth, she struggled briefly.

'Do it.' He put his hand under her head and lifted it slightly. 'For me. Do it for me.'

She was not even sure what to do. His penis filled her mouth. She tried to suck, to nibble and caress. He moved his hips and she felt him swell and heard him gasp. 'Yes, good. It's good.'

She was pleased because he seemed pleased. When he was hard, he groaned, pulled out of her mouth and pushed her legs open. 'Are you ready for me?' She felt his hands on her pussy and shuddered with unexpected pleasure. He made no attempt to excite her, but simply inspected her quickly. 'Yes,' he muttered. 'You're ready. Now I'll make a woman out of you.'

He entered her quickly, thrusting with rapid movements, and she felt a keen sense of disappointment. She wanted to be touched and kissed. She would have liked to feel his lips explore her secret places. She would have liked a slow build-up to the final pleasure. Instead he came with a violent jerking of his hips and a groan of relief, and immediately pulled away from her and lay on his back. She felt nothing. No pain, no pleasure. And even then, she remembered, she did not blame him. She thought this was how it should be, the first time.

'Was that good?' he asked.

'Yes,' she lied.

He knew very well it wasn't good, she thought,

25

remembering. And when I lied, he knew I was his. He'd baited the hook with pretty words, some pretty gifts and a couple of nice meals, and he'd landed his prize. A silly, besotted, sexually ignorant teenager. Just what he wanted. The bastard!

She made a determined effort to shut off the film that was running through her mind. Why do I still think about the past? she wondered. Why torture myself? She turned restlessly in the bed. She knew why. She blamed herself for everything that had happened to her, for every horrible detail. And after ten years, it still hurt. It hurt like hell. Especially at times like this, at night, in the darkness, when she felt alone. She felt her teeth clench with anger and frustration as she thought about Faisel. Bastard! I didn't know what hate was until you taught me!

And yet I can still be turned on by a beautiful young body, she thought, after all that Faisel did to me. I must be crazy. Although I don't think I'd fuck Paulo, even if he asked me to. From now on I'm sticking to adults, men who want the physical fun without the emotional baggage. Men who don't want to get married. She stretched out under the light sheet that covered her. Men like Nicolás Schlemann.

The thought jolted her. Why the hell am I thinking about him? she wondered. She remembered Paulo's warning. She had no doubt that he was right. Nicolás Schlemann was clever, ruthless and powerful. He was used to getting his own way and he considered all beautiful women were available for his entertainment. He probably also thought they would feel honoured to perform for him. Was that really the kind of man she needed? No, she decided, it wasn't.

Dr Peter Draven turned out to be a pleasant surprise. For some reason she had been expecting someone middle-aged, not a loose-limbed young man with a

26

charming smile, casually dressed in jeans and an open-necked shirt. His shock of blond hair and tanned skin made him look slightly Scandinavian, she commented. He laughed. 'My grandmother was Swedish. The hair missed a generation and decided to favour me. My mother has never forgiven me. Do you want coffee before I show you round?'

They sat in the spacious staff room, which over-looked a garden full of exotically colourful shrubs and flowers, and swapped stories about their student years. By the time he decided to show her the hospital, Jacey knew a great deal about Peter Draven's hopes and ambitions. He had no steady girlfriend, and she suspected that he would jump at the chance of sex with her if she gave him the slightest encouragement.

Well, why not? she thought, as she followed him into the airy corridor. He could be just what I need. We already have a lot in common. He has a sense of humour and he's not bad looking; nice smile, nice eyes, and nice hands. We can have some fun and games, just as long as he doesn't want a long-term commitment. She hung back and let him lead her down the corridor. Nice bum, too, she noted.

Her tour of La Primavera confirmed her suspicions that this was no ordinary hospital. It was incredibly well-equipped, with beautifully furnished private rooms. Many of them were empty and the occupants that she did see looked more like guests relaxing on holiday than patients suffering from any kind of disease. Mostly middle-aged men, they lolled comfortably on their beds, reading magazines or sleeping.

Peter Draven led her into an operating theatre so clean and sparkling that she doubted if it had ever been used. She turned to him. 'This place must have cost a fortune to build, and I bet it costs a fortune to run. Where does the money come from?'

He shrugged. 'Who cares? There's plenty of it.'

'It's the most under-used hospital I've ever seen,' she observed. 'All this fantastic equipment. It seems such a waste.'

'The patients here want privacy,' Peter said, echoing Paulo's comment. 'And they're willing to pay through the nose for it. We just do our job, and don't ask questions. And the operating theatres do get used, believe me.'

'I've been told Hernandez comes here,' she hinted casually.

'Lots of people come here,' Peter said. He was standing in front of her now, and she felt the edge of the operating table brushing against her thighs. 'Important people.' He was almost touching her. 'If you play your cards right you can have a very nice time.'

'If I'm nice to the right people, you mean?' Her voice was cool. 'Like Hernandez?'

He smiled back. 'You mean you'd fancy Hernandez? Mind you, he is the Numero Uno around here, and they do say power is a potent aphrodisiac.'

'I'd need more than a potent aphrodisiac to fancy Hernandez,' she said. 'Anyway, I thought Nicolás Schlemann was the real power behind the throne?'

'Oh, you fancy the tall, dark and handsome Nicolás, do you?' Peter nodded. 'Well, I'm not surprised. Lots of women do.'

She put her hand on his chest and pushed him back. 'No, I damn well don't fancy Schlemann, whether he's tall, dark and handsome or not.'

'Nicci will certainly like you,' Peter said. His eyes wandered quickly over her body in an unashamed sexual appraisal, and then back to her face. 'But then he always did have very good taste.'

28

She was not immune to the compliment and Peter Draven's body, close to hers, was beginning to have an effect. The more she looked at him, the more comfortable she felt with the idea of a nice, no-strings affair.

'If we had known each other a little longer,' she said, 'I would think that was a pick-up line.'

He stepped forward. 'You'd be right,' he said. His blue eyes held hers. 'You fancied me the first time you saw me. Admit it.'

'That's your diagnosis, is it?'

He put his hands on her shoulders, and then let them slide down slowly to her breasts. 'My expert opinion,' he agreed. His fingers began to unbutton her blouse.

'I don't think this is the time or the place for a medical examination,' she said but she made no attempt to rebuff him.

'Actually,' he leaned closer to her, 'it's exactly the right time and place.'

She felt his hands exploring her skin, and saw him smile with approval when he realised that she was not wearing a bra. 'Easy access,' he said. 'I like that.' His hands cupped her breasts, his fingers exciting her nipples. He kissed her on the lips lightly, then harder. Suddenly she felt both his hands move down over her thighs towards her knees. He grasped the hem of her skirt and yanked it up and the lightweight material rucked up to her hips. He caught her round the waist, hoisted her into a sitting position on the operating table, and stood between her legs. 'Lie back,' he murmured.

She felt his tongue caress her ear, felt his fingers tugging at her lacy briefs. She tried to push him away. 'Not here, for God's sake. Someone might come in.'

'No one will come in,' he muttered. He had

managed to slide her panties down and the surface of the table felt cool under her naked bottom. She saw the round theatre-lights above her and fantasised that they would suddenly illuminate, displaying her to an audience of first-year students, who would stare down at her, eager to watch her making love. It was a surprisingly arousing fantasy. Her body tingled with the need for sex.

Peter was lying on top of her now, struggling with his jeans. His erection was so large and urgent that he was having trouble pulling down his zip. She felt her hands tangle with his as she helped him, sensed him wince as the metal teeth scratched his skin. He gasped, half with laughter, half with desire. 'Jesus, you're in a hurry, aren't you?'

He entered her strongly, and she moved her hips towards him, tightening her muscles to pull him deeper. He began to match her rhythm, his breathing now more regular. The tension was building deliciously. And then suddenly his body jolted, out of control, and he came with an explosive groan. For a moment she felt his full weight on her. After a while he propped himself up on his elbows and eased himself off her. 'I'm sorry,' he said. 'I'm really sorry. I just couldn't help myself.'

She lay on her back for a moment, wondering if he was going to use his mouth or his hands to satisfy her. But to her disappointment, he simply slid off the table and zipped up his jeans.

'That's never happened to me before.' He smiled rather sheepishly. 'You shouldn't be so damn sexy.'

Is that supposed to be a compliment? she wondered. Or is he blaming me? Frustrated sexual tension made her feel shaky. And irritable. She stood up and tidied her clothes.

He watched her. 'I didn't expect that to happen. I'll make it up to you next time, I promise.'

30

'What makes you think there'll be a next time?' Her voice was distinctly frosty.

He looked at her anxiously. 'Come on, I'm only human.'

'So am I,' she said. 'And I like to have an orgasm, just like everyone else.'

'Sorry,' he repeated inadequately. She turned and walked towards the door, and he added dolefully: 'Haven't you ever been overcome with passion?'

Despite herself, she smiled. 'Peter, stop talking like a bad film.'

'Well, what would you prefer to call it?' he persisted. 'Love?'

Her smiled disappeared. 'You're not trying to tell me you're in love with me, Peter?'

'No,' he said. He hesitated. 'But you never know what might happen later on.'

'I do,' she said. She stopped and turned to face him. 'Let's get one thing straight. Sex can be a lot of fun, but romance is out. I'm just not interested.'

'Fun and games, but no commitment?' He smiled. 'Well, I won't argue with that. With you as a playmate, few men would. Very well then.' He held out his hand solemnly. 'Our relationship will be strictly sex, without the hearts-and-flowers stuff. I'll never mention passion, or love, again. Do we have an agreement?'

She tapped his hand away lightly, and laughed. 'Maybe,' she said. 'Now, how about finishing our tour?'

'I think I've shown you everything,' he said.

'Except where I'm supposed to report for duty in the morning.'

He laughed. 'The most important thing of all. You'll have your own office. Come and see.'

The office was carpeted, decorated in pastel shades, with a huge window with slatted shutters opening

31

out on to the hospital gardens. Peter tapped the brand-new computer on the glass-topped desk. 'You can access all the medical files and the hospital library.' He tapped the modem. 'And if you get bored, you can surf the Net. We'll get you fixed up with an e-mail address.'

'Great,' Jacey said. She sat down and switched the computer on. 'Can I send an e-mail right now? My friend Chris is waiting to hear from me.'

'Chris?' He smiled. 'I'm jealous.'

'Chris is a girl.'

He shrugged, still smiling. 'I could still be jealous.'

'Chris has three children and a loving husband,' Jacey said. 'Definitely not my type. But I told her I would keep in touch. I promised.' She logged on and typed a message: Hi Chris. I'm here. The weather isn't quite what I expected, but at least one of the natives is very friendly indeed, blue eyes and blond hair! Got to go – he's waiting for me!

Make what you like out of that, Major Fairhaven, she thought. If you knew about this mysterious Loháquin, you'll guess what I'm talking about when I mention the weather. And if you didn't, that should keep you guessing until I find out more.

By the end of her first day on duty Jacey began to understand a great deal more about what went on at La Primavera. The first clue came when she was doing her morning rounds. She found the middle-aged and affable Señor Valienté – who was under observation for bronchial problems – dictating letters to a startlingly attractive blonde in a very short skirt, who looked as if she would be more at home on stage as an exotic dancer than in an office. The air smelled of expensive cigar smoke. Señor Valienté smiled at her, flashing several gold teeth. 'Just catching up with a little business, doctor. It keeps my mind active.'

'You've been smoking,' Jacey accused.

The improbable-looking secretary laughed, and crossed her long legs, displaying dark stocking-tops and suspenders. 'He's a naughty boy,' she said, in a husky voice.

When Jacey closed the door she heard them both laughing. The woman's giggling was abruptly silenced. Jacey strongly suspected that if she found an excuse to go back into the room again she would find her patient and his so-called secretary engaged in something very far removed from dictation. It was Señor Valienté's body that was being exercised and not his mind.

From then on she began to look more closely at the steady stream of hospital visitors. As all the rooms were private, people arrived at any time during the day. Many of them were obviously family members, often with neatly dressed children obediently in tow. Others were young businessmen in smart suits. But quite a few were ladies who did not fit into any conventional category. Immaculately dressed, they arrived in large, chauffeur-driven cars. They exuded sexy confidence and seemed popular with all the staff, from the cleaning women upwards.

That evening Jacey went to Peter Draven's office. 'Why didn't anyone tell me that this hospital also functions as a brothel?'

Peter looked up from the report he was writing. 'Who says it does?'

'Oh, come on!' She sat down opposite him. 'No wonder there are so many healthy-looking patients here. They just check in for a medical so they can fuck in comfort.'

He grinned. 'Elegantly put. But their money keeps this place running, and pays your wages too.' He

33

signed his report and pushed it aside. 'You're not trying to tell me you're shocked?'

'Surprised,' she said. 'Why don't these men just visit the local cat-house?'

Peter shrugged. 'Because they're members of a strictly traditional society. As long as they behave themselves in public, everyone turns a blind eye to their private weaknesses.'

'Everyone?' she enquired acidly. 'Including their wives?'

Peter leaned back in his chair, and smiled. 'What makes you think their wives don't know what's going on? They probably even know which women are servicing their husbands. The women who come here are some of the highest paid whores in Techtátuan. They're discreet and they're clean. If you were married, wouldn't you rather your husband used someone like that, instead of the local brothel, where anything goes?'

'Is that supposed to make it acceptable?' she enquired coolly. 'I'm cheating on you, dear, but don't worry, I won't catch anything nasty.'

He laughed. 'Do you think it's all one-sided? Have you seen the elegant young man who comes in to visit Señora Atriega? The one she calls her nephew?'

Jacey nodded. 'I met him in the corridor.' Señora Atriega's nephew had given her a soulfully lingering look as he went on his way to his aunt's room. 'At first I thought he was trying to flirt with me.'

'He probably was,' Peter said. 'Having you as a client would be mixing business with pleasure in a big way.'

'You mean he's a whore?' She was genuinely startled.

'Of course he is,' Peter said. 'One of the best, I'm told.'

She laughed. 'Well, I suppose that's one kind of

equality.' She glanced at Peter mischievously. 'He was rather nice. Perhaps I'll try him out.'

'You wouldn't be able to afford him,' Peter said. He leant forward conspiratorially: 'And just between the two of us, I've given him a couple of check-ups, and I can tell you that there isn't much to choose between him and me when it comes to size.'

She grinned. 'But perhaps he has better control?'

'Ouch. I suppose you think I deserved that?'

'Yes,' she said. 'Don't you?'

'Maybe,' he agreed. 'But first impressions can be deceiving. Are you going to give me a chance to redeem myself?'

She shrugged. 'I suppose I could be persuaded.'

'Tonight?' he suggested. 'I'll take you out for a meal. Is that a date?'

'Dates are for girlfriends,' she said. She grinned. 'This is a more of a trial run.' She smiled. 'When are you going to pick me up?'

He smiled back. 'About eight.'

It had been an enjoyable meal, and Jacey was pleased when Peter hinted that he was not going to push her into any follow-up. I can do without sex, she thought, but it would be pleasant to have someone to share my off-duty time with. Peter is good company. I'm sure I can educate him into being more accomplished in bed, given a little time. It might even be interesting.

She accepted Peter's invitation for a nightcap in his apartment. Together they finished a bottle of wine. When Peter planted his first kiss on her, it soon became apparent that her services as a tutor would not be needed. This time he was in no hurry. His mouth moved gently over her face, lingering on her lips. With the tip of his tongue he drew patterns on her throat and neck, then moved up to circle her ear.

His hands on her blouse were so light and gentle that she did not realise he had unfastened the tiny buttons until the tips of his fingers touched her nipples, pinching them gently, arousing them even more.

She lay back and allowed him to undress her, moving languidly to help him. The air felt warm on her flesh. He peeled away her blouse and took off her flimsy bra. She wriggled her hips as he removed her skirt, and returned the compliment by tugging down the zip of his trousers. But he seemed far more interested in taking off her clothes than having her take off his. He laughed softly when he discovered that she was wearing suspenders and stockings. With his fingers he traced the dark circle of her stocking tops, and pulled gently at the lacy suspenders. 'I like these. I thought all modern women wore tights.'

She smiled. 'When we want to turn someone on, we try a little harder.'

'You're trying to turn me on, are you?'

She reached for him. He was already hard. 'Looks like I've succeeded,' she observed.

'You didn't really have to try,' he said. 'The sight of you is enough.'

When she was finally naked, he pushed her back and, as she remembered his last hurried finale, she thought, maybe that's it? Playtime's over? But he knelt across her, smoothing his hands down to her thighs, following their exploratory caresses with his mouth and tongue, until he was nuzzling the dark red bush of her pubic hair. He pressed his palms against her inner thighs, encouraging her to spread her legs, and his fingers parted her secret lips. He bent over her, letting his tongue find her swelling clitoris, and circled it. She loved this most intimate of kisses. He licked her, gently at first, but with increasing pressure, until she felt her whole body trembling

36

with the need for release. He looked up at her. 'You're ready for me, aren't you?'

She pushed his head down again. 'Don't stop,' she ordered huskily. 'Please don't stop.'

Peter laughed softly, enjoying her pleasure, and went to work again, his tongue sliding and probing her folds. She writhed with delight, feeling the sensations mount to their inevitable, explosive climax. Her body convulsed and she clutched at Peter's head, digging her fingers into his scalp, pulling him in close. He waited until her tremors had subsided, then shifted his position.

'I've got to have you,' he muttered, hoarsely. 'Right now.'

He entered her easily. His thrusting prolonged her fading orgasmic spasms, encouraging her to yet another peak of pleasure, this time more gentle than the first, but equally potent. Her sigh of delight escaped at the same moment as his own deep groan of fulfilment. Afterwards, as they lay drowsily together on the settee, she wondered idly why he'd had such trouble controlling himself the first time they made love. Surely he hadn't been worried about being discovered? He had been the one to instigate the action, after all. It was hard to equate that performance with the one which had left her so sated today.

Perhaps he was just nervous, she thought. And then another unbidden thought came into her mind: why? She shifted her position and felt his warm body move comfortably with hers. Stop asking questions, she admonished herself sleepily. You're not working now.

But she couldn't stop the doubts nagging at her mind.

Chapter Two

*J*acey soon settled into a pleasant and undemanding
routine. After only two weeks she was seriously
bored. She was working in conditions that would
have turned her friends back at the Midland General
green with envy and yet she felt a growing sense of
frustration.

She knew there were plenty of people in Techtátuan who could have benefited from her medical
knowledge, people who could not afford to come to
La Primavera. These were the people she should be
mixing with and talking to. If Major Fairhaven
wanted an accurate 'weather report' she ought to find
out more about Loháquin, and she certainly wasn't
going to discover anything worthwhile from her rich
and idle so-called patients. Why had the major sent
her to this particular hospital? She would learn
nothing of value here.

Her sense of frustration made her irritable, and
although she was too professional to allow it to affect
her work, she found it increasingly difficult to be
sociable with people like Señor Valienté and his ever
present 'secretary', or Señora Atriega. When she was

38

accosted during her morning rounds by a young man in the corridor, asking her where he could find the Señora, she could barely contain her annoyance. Another nephew, she thought, irritably.

He was attractive, she had to admit. With his large, brown eyes, dark, brown hair that seemed to glint with a hint of gold, and a beautiful smile, he was almost too perfect. She liked a little irregularity in a man's features, something that added individuality to his face. This boy looked as if he had employed a plastic surgeon to turn him into a text-book gigolo. He was smaller than average height, but his body was perfectly proportioned, and he moved with the grace of a dancer. I bet he's practised every gesture in front of a mirror, Jacey thought crossly. Posing and preening, and calculating the effect it would have on any woman who cared to watch him. Well, it won't have any effect on me.

She treated him to her most frosty smile. 'Señora Atriega is in Room Fourteen,' she said. 'I really think you should check details like that before you arrive.'

He looked slightly surprised. 'But I only flew in from London this morning. I came straight here to see dear Julia, and give her all the gossip. She's not in terrible pain, is she?'

'Hardly,' Jacey said coolly. 'Terribly bored, most likely.'

'I'll cheer her up.' He smiled disarmingly. 'Isn't that what friends are for?'

Jacey was getting irritated by his pretensions. Just flown in from London? Did he really expect her to believe such a stupid story? 'Well, "friend" is a new name for it,' she observed acidly. 'But it's probably more honest than calling yourself the Señora's nephew.'

He looked momentarily puzzled and then his smile broadened. 'That's what they all say, isn't it?

Nephew, or cousin, maybe? But I'm not like the others.'

'You look just like them to me,' she said.

'Really?' He stepped back and his brown eyes wandered over her body. It was an impudently sexual appraisal, and she suddenly felt glad that she was covered by her straight-cut, white doctor's coat. 'Well, you certainly don't look just like any doctor I've ever seen.' He struck a pose, one hand on his hip. 'Would you like to give me a thorough medical? I'm sure it would be very arousing for both of us.'

What would it be like to make love to a professional, she wondered suddenly. A man who was being paid to please her? Would it excite her? Or would she feel cheap and maybe slightly ridiculous? Would she wonder what he was really thinking while he used all his skills on her body, and murmured his standard repertoire of compliments? She had read that female prostitutes switched off their emotions when they were working. It was all mechanical for them: get it up, get it in, and get him out of the door. Would male prostitutes be equally dispassionate? Surely a man would have to think about something to turn himself on, particularly if his client was unattractive.

'So, do you want to make a booking?' She came back to the present with a jolt. He was still smiling at her. 'I'm very clean, very discreet, and very imaginative.'

'And no doubt very expensive, too?' she said, curious to know how he would respond.

He hesitated for a moment. 'A thousand dollars. American dollars, of course.'

She stared at him for a moment and then laughed derisively. 'Are you crazy? No man in the world is worth a thousand dollars, and certainly not second-hand goods like you.'

'It's for a whole night.' He sounded slightly piqued.

'I wouldn't pay that for a whole week,' she scoffed.

He shrugged. 'Then I'll just have to go and be nice to Julia.'

And more fool her, if she parts with that kind of money for sex, Jacey thought, watching him walk down the corridor. He does have a nice tight little bum, she thought, and then checked herself crossly. I bet he knows it, too, conceited little brat.

But she did have a sneaking sympathy for him, and others like him. Even her brief experience of Guachtàl had shown her that the majority of people there were poor; for most of them there was probably no escape from their poverty except to sell their bodies. Could she really blame that beautiful young man for cashing in on his assets?

What would I have done, she wondered, if I had been born here? Would I have married, produced a dozen children, and been worn out by the time I was thirty? Or would I have sold myself to the highest bidder? After all, men use us, so why shouldn't we use them? The thought prompted a memory. A memory she did not want, which had a habit of resurfacing when she least expected it.

A man in an elegantly tailored suit, looking incredibly sexy and desirable. And a wide-eyed girl standing next to him, dressed in white, her burnished, red hair piled up and held in place by a circlet of tiny, white flowers. My wedding day, she thought. Supposedly the happiest day in any woman's life. What sentimental crap.

Despite the fact that she was married in a registry office, she had wanted to wear white. Faisel had promised her a religious wedding when she returned home with him. She did not question why he wanted a civil ceremony in England first. Her parents had attended, looking unhappy because they disapproved

41

of Faisel and the way he had steamrollered her into a quick marriage. They were also unhappy that she was going to fly back to the Arab States with him that evening.

It's a holiday, she had told them. A honeymoon. And I have to meet his family. She repeated all the lies Faisel had told her. We'll be back in London soon. Faisel is going to work in his father's City office. I'm going to apply to London University to study medicine.

Faisel had seemed only a little concerned at her parents' misgivings. It was natural, he said. They felt they were losing their only daughter. When he returned to England with Jacey he would make a special effort to win her parents' approval. And I believed him, she remembered. I believed all his lies.

The time that passed between her marriage ceremony and her arrival at Faisel's home was still a blur in her mind, a jumble of images: the bustle of the airport; the boredom of the flight (Faisel slept for most of it); and the oven-hot air that engulfed her when she finally stepped out of the plane. Faisel's father was in America. His mother, a stunningly elegant woman in a white, linen designer suit, greeted Faisel with theatrical emotion, but eyed Jacey coolly, offered her a slim hand and a frosty smile, and then ignored her. Jacey spent the next three days on her own, in a plushly furnished apartment, attended by servants, but isolated by her lack of Arabic and her inability to ask where her husband was.

When Faisel finally appeared, he did at least apologise. It was, she recalled, probably the last time he ever did so. He had been obliged to visit a variety of relatives, he said. These things were expected of him; he had a large family. He sat next to her on the large

42

settee. It was the first time they had been alone together since their marriage.

How would I describe what happened next? she thought. In those days, I could still pretend that we were making love. But she knew now that Faisel's actions had nothing to do with love. He copulated with me, she thought. It had hurt because she wasn't ready or aroused. He had wanted her to use her mouth but she wanted him to put his arms round her and kiss her. She remembered his irritation as he unzipped his trousers and pushed her head between his legs. 'Make it hard,' he ordered. 'Suck me.'

'I don't want to.' She vividly recalled the strength of his hands on her head as he tried to push her down over his lap. 'Not yet. Let's talk.'

'Talk?' He turned it into a swear word. 'You're my wife. Behave like a wife.' He managed to push her down. He was not even partially erect and his penis felt flaccid against her lips. 'Do your duty,' he said. 'Service me.'

She had started to cry, and he let her go, muttering something in Arabic under his breath. He took hold of himself and masturbated. It was the first time she had ever seen a man do that. He achieved his erection quickly, and turned to her. 'Open your legs. You want me, don't you?'

She had wanted him, she remembered, but with tenderness and love, not the crude speed of a rutting dog. When he had satisfied himself and rolled off her, he added the final insult. He stood up, zipped up his trousers, and left.

And I forgave him, she recalled bitterly. Those first few times I forgave him. I even thought I was being noble and understanding by forgiving him. And I thought it would get better as we got to know each other. What a little fool I was. What a dewy-eyed, empty-headed, fucking little fool. I deserved

43

everything I got. Didn't I? No, she thought, I didn't. No one deserved what happened to me.

Why am I remembering this? she wondered. It was twelve years ago. She did not want to think about the time that had elapsed either. It's over and finished. Forget it. But she knew that she never could. It's made me what I am, she thought.

An ex-boyfriend had called her hard when, easily and without regrets, she had broken up with him because he had kept talking about marriage. Hard? she thought. She preferred the word 'strong'. Strong enough to resist male flattery and promises. Strong enough to discard a man when he started to expect more than she was prepared to give.

She walked purposefully down the corridor towards Peter's office. She liked Peter Draven. He was good company and – apart from that odd first incident – he always satisfied her in bed, or anywhere else he decided was a suitable venue for sex. She didn't think he wanted anything more than a light-hearted, fun affair, but if he did start to become possessive, she knew she could break off the relationship without regrets. At least Faisel gave me that much, she thought. He taught me not to let silly, romantic notions about love screw up my life.

Peter was updating his computer records when she entered the room. He glanced at the clipboard she was carrying. 'Here, give me that. I'll put it on file for you.'

'You might as well repeat my last reports,' she said, unable to keep the irritation out of her voice. 'Nothing's changed.'

He grinned. 'You don't want your patients to get worse, do you?'

She shrugged and managed a slight smile. 'It would make me feel useful. At the moment I feel like a social worker, walking round with a big smile, handing out a few vitamin tablets and saying good morning, all for sex maniacs like Señor Valiente and Señora Atriega.'

Peter pushed his chair back and spun round to face her. 'Do you really miss being a house doctor? The long hours, the night calls, the senior consultants who treat you like an idiot, and the patients who do contrary things, like dying in spite of all your efforts to save them? Do you miss the smell of blood and guts, and disinfectant and excrement and –'

'Yes,' she interrupted. 'Stupid and illogical as it sounds, I miss it all. The blood and guts and excrement, and the wonderful feeling when you tell a patient the operation was a success, and they're going to be all right.'

'And little Johnny will play the violin again?' He smiled. 'Yes, I know. Our job does have a few perks. So, how would you like to recapture the glamour and excitement of being a real doctor again for a couple of days a week?'

She looked at him curiously. 'Tell me more.'

'I do voluntary work downtown, at a hospital you've probably never heard of. El Invierno,' he said.

'The Winter Hospital?' she translated. 'Odd name.'

'That's what everyone calls it,' he said. 'And if you think it's a dig at La Primavera, you're right. El Invierno is under-funded, understaffed, the equipment's ancient and they're so short of beds they usually ask patients to bring their own mattresses and park them on the floor. Money was poured into La Primavera. The staff at El Invierno have to grovel for crumbs. But it'll certainly satisfy your craving for the lovely smell of blood, urine and disinfectant.' His smile disappeared. 'And it's all most of the poor sods in Techtátuan have got when they get ill. The senior doctor is Filipe Rodriguez. He's five foot nothing, irascible and brilliant. He might even be some kind

45

of saint. I'm sure the locals think so, anyway. You'll like him. He'll probably like you, too.'

'Sounds great,' she said. And she meant it. Not only would this give her an opportunity to use her medical skills, but it might also provide her with a chance to find out more about Loháquin. 'But will I get permission to have a couple of days off?'

'Of course you will,' Peter said. 'Leave it to me. I'll arrange it.' He grinned. 'I have friends in high places. And talking of friends, I've been invited to a party. Have you heard of Carlos Márquez?'

The name was familiar. It had been on Major Fairhaven's briefing sheet. The Márquez family were very rich, and friends with Generalissimo Hernandez and Nicolás Schlemann.

'Isn't Márquez the name of a legal firm?' she asked casually.

'The biggest and the best in Techtátuan,' Peter said. 'Which means the biggest and the best in the country. They have money and influence. Alfonso Márquez started with nothing and ended up a millionaire. He died a couple of years ago from a heart attack and his three sons inherited the business.'

'Are they all lawyers?' she asked.

Peter laughed. 'Carlos practises. Raoul is qualified, but he hasn't decided yet whether he wants to be a lawyer or a polo player, or an actor, or whatever else takes his fancy. Leonardo is still in diapers.' He saw her expression and grinned. 'Well, not literally. He's the baby of the family, though.'

'Who's throwing the party?'

'Carlos, ostensibly. It'll be very conventional to start with, then Carlos and his wife will go home, followed by the more traditionally minded guests. After that things will probably hot up a little.' He glanced at her. 'Well quite a lot, actually. We can go before that happens, of course.'

'It turns into an orgy, does it?'

He looked at her quizzically. 'Would that interest you?'

'No, it wouldn't,' she said sharply. 'I'm fussy who I share my body with, and I've never been into group sex.'

He smiled. 'Don't worry, we'll leave before anyone starts taking off their trousers, and if you're harassed by a randy young stud, I'll protect you.' He picked up his clipboard. 'I have a couple more patients to check and then we can go for a coffee. Wait here for me, I'll be right back.'

She sat in one of the comfortable swivel chairs, and spun herself round gently. Protect me, would you? she thought. Thanks for the offer, but I think I can protect myself. She remembered her schooldays and the first book she had read on judo. When one of the boys had tried to grab her bag, she had used a throw, pulling him off balance and sweeping his ankle, to tumble him to the ground. She still remembered the expression of surprise on his face. It had probably equalled hers, she thought, because she had never expected the technique to work. But success had excited her and she talked her parents into letting her join a judo club, achieving her black belt in the minimum period allowed. She had hoped to take her second Dan, but working for her A-levels, she had no spare time.

The memory of her examinations automatically triggered a picture of Faisel. If I hadn't passed with such good grades, I wouldn't have gone on holiday, she thought. My life would have been so different. I was able to take care of myself physically but Faisel overpowered my mind with a few lies and a beautiful smile. Talk about the world's most deadly weapon. Sexual attraction, masquerading as love, takes some

47

beating. It certainly turned me into a weak-kneed victim.

She had never gone back to judo but before she qualified as a doctor, the deceptively gentle elegance of aikido had intrigued her. She studied it for two years before the pressure of exams, and then the pressure of work, made it impossible to continue training. When she began working for Major Fairhaven, many years later, she found herself being taught methods more suited to dirty street-fighting than a martial arts dojo. But her past skills, and her natural sense of timing, had given her a definite advantage over some of the others in her class.

Peter's desk phone rang suddenly, bringing her back to the present. She picked it up and heard an authoritative, masculine voice on the other end, a voice she did not recognise. 'How much longer are you going to keep me waiting, Draven?'

'Dr Draven isn't here,' she said coolly. 'This is Dr Muldaire. Can I help you?'

'Muldaire? You're the new woman, aren't you?' There was a pause. 'Are you properly qualified?'

Jacey bit back a sharp rejoinder. 'Yes,' she said abruptly.

'Come to Room Six. Now.' The last word was an order issued in a tone of voice that was guaranteed to infuriate her. Before she could respond, the phone went dead. She hesitated for a moment, then stood up. This was obviously one of the patients Peter had been planning to see. She was tempted not to answer the abrupt telephone request but there was something about the voice that made her want to go and see who this man was, and put him in his place.

With her temper almost under control, she stalked down the corridor. She knew that Room Six was a small consulting room in the general accident wing. But the man on the phone did not sound as if he was suffering from anything other than a severe lack of good manners.

When she opened the door she saw her prospective patient standing by the window, looking out. He turned when she entered, smiled charmingly, walked towards her and held out his hand. 'Dr Muldaire? I'm Nicolás Schlemann. I'm delighted to meet you at last.'

Jacey wasn't often lost for words but this tall, dark figure in his immaculate suit effectively managed to both silence and disorient her. She shook hands without thinking. His grip was warm and firm. His dark brown eyes surveyed her. 'I'm afraid I was rather abrupt on the telephone,' he said.

His German patrimony could be seen in his narrow face, and his features were attractively angular. His Spanish mother had given him a natural tan and his glossy, straight black hair was beautifully cut, with sideburns just long enough to be discreetly fashionable and a fringe irregular enough to look rakish, without being untidy.

She realised that she was still holding his hand. Annoyed with herself, she pulled away from him and stepped backwards. 'Yes,' she said. 'You were rather impolite.'

'I am in rather a hurry.' He began to take off his jacket. 'I have a meeting with Generalissimo Hernandez.' He was unbuttoning his shirt now and she realised that he had a bandage strapped round his ribs. She also noted that he had the body of an athlete, and moved with the grace of a dancer. His hand touched the bandage. 'This is becoming irritating. Surely I can dispense with it now?'

'What happened?' she asked.

'I fell off my horse,' he explained. Again that charming smile. 'My fault entirely. I was pushing him too hard. I broke two ribs.'

'Sit down,' she said. She unwrapped the bandage and pressed his ribs gently. 'Does that hurt?'

He winced slightly. 'No,' he said.

'Señor Schlemann,' she said, 'I don't believe you.'

'It's doesn't hurt – much,' he qualified. 'And the bandage is damned uncomfortable.'

He flexed his arms and shoulders and she saw his muscles move sinuously. She was reminded of a cat preening, a cat which was well aware of the effect it was having on her.

What effect? she thought, almost guiltily. This is the man I was certain I was going to dislike. A womanising crook. Am I really attracted to him? Yes, she thought, just a little, but only physically. It's a purely biological reaction. He's an agreeable-looking man. What a pity his character doesn't match his body.

'Please keep still,' she said. She inspected his ribs. His skin felt warm and smooth under her fingers. She prodded him a little harder than necessary but this time he hardly reacted at all. She stepped back. 'You seem to have healed very well.' She kept her voice neutral. 'You can throw the bandage away. You don't need it.'

'Thank you.' He stood up gracefully, reached for his shirt, shrugged it back on, and buttoned it. She was certain he made the actions take longer than necessary. He unzipped the top of his trousers and tucked his shirt in, hesitating just long enough, she felt certain, for her to admire his sharply defined abdominals. 'Are you happy working here, Dr Muldaire?'

'Yes,' she said simply.

He knotted his tie and put on his coat. She watched him silently. 'I imagine you're very popular with the patients,' he said.

'If you're ill, you tend to like someone who makes you feel better,' she said.

He smiled. 'And if that person is very beautiful, that's an added bonus.' He moved his body experimentally. 'It still hurts a little,' he said.

'I'm sure you'll learn to live with the pain,' she said dryly.

He reached the door, opened it, and turned. 'If it gets really bad, I'll come back and see you.' His smile was briefly inviting. 'I'm sure you'll be able to make me comfortable.'

She walked past him. 'Come back and see Dr Draven,' she said. 'You're his patient. He's properly qualified too, you know.'

'Well, the notorious Señor Nicolás didn't waste much time checking you out,' Peter commented. He lay sprawled across Jacey's bed. The sunlight, filtering in through the shutters, striped his naked body with shadows. 'What did you think of him?'

'Conceited,' Jacey said. She switched the kettle on and searched in Peter's cupboard for the coffee jar. 'Sexist.' She smiled. 'A typical male animal.'

Peter watched her lazily. 'And he didn't attract you at all?'

She turned crossly. 'What's that supposed to mean?'

Peter sat up. 'Come on,' he said. 'You know exactly what I mean. Nicci's not bad looking, if you like them tall with black hair. And I'm told he can be very charming, when it suits him.' He smiled. 'Does the thought of having sex with him excite you?'

Jacey smiled back. 'What an odd question,' she said, sweetly. 'Does the thought of me having sex with him excite you?'

Peter lazed back on the bed. 'Maybe. I think it could be great fun to watch you perform. To watch

51

Nicci undress you slowly, and go to work on your mouth, and your neck and your nipples, and then go down and warm up your clitoris with his tongue. I'd like to see you panting and losing control, and bucking and writhing, until he gave you the kind of climax you deserve.'

'You're a closet voyeur,' Jacey accused.

Peter shrugged. 'Most men are.'

She had a sudden suspicion. 'Schlemann didn't suggest anything like that to you, did he?'

Peter laughed. 'No. But I wouldn't mind betting he'd go along with it if you were the star performer.'

'Not a chance,' Jacey said. 'I'm not an exhibitionist and I've got no intention of jumping into bed with Señor Nicolás!'

But was that really the truth? Jacey asked herself, as she tried to decide what to wear to the Márquez party. Unwanted thoughts about Nicolás Schlemann were distracting her. She was not vain but she was sure Peter was right about Schlemann's intentions. If he considered all beautiful women to be candidates for his bed, he was probably planning to add her to his list of conquests. Thinking back on their meeting, she realised how cleverly he had played his hand. It was a variation of the Mr Nasty and Mr Nice Guy interrogation technique. He had made her angry, and then totally disarmed her by being the opposite to what she had expected.

Clever bastard, she thought. I was determined not to like you and you almost persuaded me to change my mind. But although you didn't know it, you started off with a few advantages. I always did have a soft spot for tall, slim, dark-haired men. But fancying you, and going to bed with you, Señor Schlemann, she admonished him, are two totally different things.

She held her favourite little black dress against her naked body and surveyed her image in the mirror. Too short? Too sexy? Her other choices included a silver, beaded gown, with a high neck and a very low back which was more suitable for a nightclub, and a sedate, designer ball-gown, which hugged her figure just tightly enough to be discreetly provocative but which she felt was too formal for the kind of party Peter had described.

It has to be the little black number, she thought. She hadn't worn it for some time and so slipped it over her head just to check that it still fitted in all the right places. The hemline came just above her knees. She turned. The skirt fitted neatly over her behind, and the cut of the bodice lifted and held her breasts so well that she had no need for a bra. Just right, she thought. Sexy but nice. She was sure Peter would approve. Another thought teased her. Would Nicolás Schlemann be at the Márquez party? She had a feeling that he would be. She turned again, looking at her reflection. She did not look much like the professional, white-coated woman he had met. She lifted her arms and released her hair, letting it tumble to her shoulders. Because the dress was not properly fastened, the movement lifted her breasts upwards and for a moment her nipples were visible. She smiled and adjusted the neckline decorously. Well, Señor Schlemann, she thought, if you're at the party, sorry, but this is all you're going to see!

On the day before the party Jacey arranged to go to El Invierno for the first time. Some of the staff at La Primavera had expressed surprise that she was visiting the hospital, let alone intending to work there. But when he came to collect her, Paulo was delighted. 'Where you're going, the people need you, Dr Muldaire. Not like the patients here.'

'Some of the people here are ill, Paulo,' she said.

'They are more seriously ill at El Invierno,' he answered.

She soon discovered he was right. She had been prepared for overcrowding and antiquated equipment, but the reality of El Invierno appalled her. Peter had not been exaggerating when he told her patients brought their own mattresses and slept on the floor. She picked her way carefully over sprawled bodies and family groups who were camping out next to their sick relatives. When she found Dr Rodriguez he was swabbing an open wound on a young boy's arm. He looked tired and hot.

'Dr Muldaire?' His eyes assessed her without welcome or enthusiasm. 'Are you willing to get your hands dirty?'

'I'm a doctor,' she said crisply. And added, with the trace of a smile, 'Just like you.'

She did not get a smile back. 'Not like me. You get paid ridiculously high wages at La Primavera, and I guess that you do very little.' He thrust a swab at her. 'Here, carry on with this. Don't take too long. There's a queue of people outside who need attention.' He glanced at her white blouse and pale, linen skirt. It was a totally impersonal appraisal. 'I hope you've got an overall in that expensive bag of yours. Those fashionable clothes won't look so good with blood all over them.'

She refused to take offence. 'I've got an overall,' she said. 'And I've also got some antibiotics.' She saw no change of expression in his dark eyes and added hastily, 'I didn't steal them. They're a gift, from Dr Draven and the staff at La Primavera.'

'I wouldn't give a damn if you had stolen them,' he said. For a moment she thought he almost smiled. Then he turned to go. 'Thank Peter, and the others,' he said abruptly.

54

Thrown in at the deep end, she looked at her first patient. Two mournful brown eyes stared up at her. Quickly she found a new swab and started work on the boy's arm. His mother watched her as she worked, her face as smooth as a carved mask. 'There you are,' Jacey said, as she finished cleaning the boy's wound. 'That will soon be better.' She smiled at him and received a solemn stare back. 'How did this happen?' she asked the equally impassive mother.

'They won't answer you.' Jacey turned and saw a plump young woman in a white overall standing behind her. 'I'm Paloma,' the woman said. 'Your helper.'

'You're a nurse?' Jacey enquired.

Paloma smiled sunnily. 'No, I'm not qualified at all. But I've picked up lots of knowledge since I've been working here.' She turned to the boy and his mother and said something in a guttural language Jacey did not recognise. The woman smiled, turned and walked away.

'What language was that?' Jacey asked.

'*Chachté*,' Paloma said. 'One of the old languages. You know, the ones the people spoke before the Spanish came.'

'And you speak it too?'

Paloma shrugged. 'I had to learn some of it. Lots of the Indians won't speak Spanish. They think it'll bring them bad luck. And when you read how the early settlers used to treat them, you can't blame them. I mean, I'm Spanish but some of the things my ancestors did make me ashamed.'

Jacey soon realised that Paloma was a non-stop talker. As she dealt with a succession of patients, some silent, others chattering volubly, she learnt more about public opinion in Techtátuan than any of Major Fairhaven's carefully worded briefing papers had taught her.

'That's it,' Paloma said, at last. She glanced at her watch. 'Time for a quick coffee.'

She led Jacey to the tiny staff restroom. A sluggish ceiling fan stirred the hot air. Travel posters were pinned to the walls in an effort to brighten up the rather dismal decor.

Paloma unlocked a cupboard. 'You mustn't leave any valuables here unless you lock them up,' she warned Jacey. 'That includes coffee and cups. The people are poor and they will steal things to use or sell.' She added aggressively: 'You can't blame them. You'd do the same, if you were poor.'

'I would,' Jacey agreed.

There was a small picture stuck on the inside of Paloma's cupboard door. It was a pencil portrait of a handsome young man with a neat beard wearing a military style fatigue cap. His large eyes had an expression of soulful fervour. A faint circle behind his head hinted at a halo.

'Who's that?' Jacey asked Paloma. She already knew the answer.

Paloma hesitated for a moment. 'Oh, no one really,' she said awkwardly. 'Someone gave it to me.' She smiled. 'He's good-looking, isn't he? That's why I kept it.'

Jacey took a gamble. 'He doesn't look so handsome on the reward posters.'

'So?' Paloma looked at her calculatingly. 'You've heard about Loháquin?'

'Not really,' Jacey said. 'Only rumours. I'd like to hear the truth.'

'Well, you won't hear it from a stupid girl like Paloma.' The sound of Dr Rodriguez's voice startled Jacey. He glared at the Spanish girl. 'I've told you before about pinning up those drawings. You're turning a terrorist into some kind of saint.'

'So you think Loháquin is a terrorist?' Jacey asked.

56

Rodriguez turned to face her. 'What would you call a man who is supposed to have an army hidden in the rainforest and who says he wants to take over the country?'

'I'd call him an optimist,' Jacey said. She hesitated. 'Or maybe even a hero.'

Rodriguez snorted. 'Then you're as stupid as Paloma. I hope you don't go around voicing opinions like that. They'll get you into a lot of trouble.' He scowled at Jacey. 'And if you think your precious British passport will save you, you don't understand men like Nicolás Schlemann.'

'I thought he was a financier,' Jacey said, 'not a policeman.'

'He's anything and everything,' Rodriguez said. 'He has far too much power and he's very dangerous.' For a moment, Jacey thought she saw concern in the Spanish doctor's eyes. 'Just remember that when you deal with him.'

'Any dealings I have with Nicolás Schlemann will be strictly professional,' Jacey said lightly.

'Bear that in mind when you meet him at the party tomorrow,' Rodriguez said. His voice was dry.

How did he know about her social life? She masked her surprise. 'I didn't know he'd be there.' She shrugged.

'Nicolás wouldn't miss one of the famous Márquez extravaganzas.' Rodriguez's voice was bitter. 'Do you know that the money spent on one of those parties would keep this hospital running for a month?' She was about to speak but he silenced her. 'Don't feel guilty. Go and enjoy yourself. It won't make any difference if you sit at home like a martyr. But remember that because people are smiling at you, they're not necessarily your friends. Particularly people like Nicolás Schlemann.'

* * *

'Very interesting,' Peter said. He had come into her room on her invitation. 'But indecent.'

Jacey turned to him and smiled. She was wearing only her stockings, a wispy suspender belt and a silky thong. 'Are you complaining or is that a compliment?'

'A bit of both,' he said. 'Complaining because I haven't time to take advantage of you.'

'You mean you get thrown in jail if you're late for one of the famous Márquez parties?' she teased.

'I don't mind being late,' he said. He moved towards her. 'But if I start on you now, I won't even want to go out.'

She shrugged and turned slowly in front of him, her hands shielding her breasts in mock modesty. 'So we stay in. I don't mind.'

She could tell that he was tempted. To entice him further, she turned again, and stretched her hands above her head, tensing her buttocks, knowing that as the black line of her thong disappeared in the cleft between them it emphasised their rounded appeal. The stretch-lace suspenders attached to the dark bangles of her stocking tops were also an invitation to let his fingers stray. Peter was a 'legs-and-bum' man; he had already made that clear.

She smoothed her palms over her bottom, then half turned towards him and bent one leg, stroking her inner thigh. 'I can undress,' she suggested. 'It won't take a minute. And I have an unopened bottle of wine in the fridge.'

He unselfconsciously adjusted his swelling erection. 'No,' he said thickly. 'Paulo will be here in five minutes.'

She walked towards him and saw his eyes move from her naked breasts to the tiny vee of her thong which barely concealed the red bush of pubic hair.

58

'So?' she shrugged. 'We can tell Paulo to go away again.'

'No. Get dressed. We're going out.'

She was startled at his vehemence, and a warning bell rang at the back of her mind. Peter had never refused her before, and she knew that he didn't really want to now. But he was edgy. His attitude reminded her of the first time they had made love in the operating theatre; he had acted as if he had something on his mind. She knew that he wasn't being completely honest with her now, and it annoyed her. What was so special about this party? She walked towards the wardrobe door, where her black dress was hanging, and lifted it down. As she slipped it over her head, she saw an expression of relief in his eyes. Fully covered, she glanced at him. 'Better?' she asked sweetly. 'Do you feel happier now?'

'I feel uncomfortable,' he grunted, 'and you know it.'

'Well, you had your chance to do something about it,' she said unsympathetically.

She wanted to ask him what was wrong. Instead she quickly checked her appearance in the mirror. Her loose hair fell to her shoulders like a smooth, red curtain. She glanced down and saw the hard peaks of her nipples pushing against the silky dress fabric. The mock seduction act had aroused her as well as Peter. Maybe I should wear a bra, she thought. Then she heard the sound of a car horn outside; it was too late to change now. She noticed Peter was looking at her with unusual intensity. She pirouetted playfully. 'Do I look suitably dressed for this party?'

'You look fine,' he said. 'Very sexy.'

'But not sexy enough to persuade you to stay home.'

He looked suddenly guilty. 'The hospital gets

money from Carlos Márquez. So we have to be sociable.'

The warning bells started ringing again. She said nothing but she did not believe him. Was he suggesting that the Márquez family would refuse to fund the fashionable La Primavera if one or two of the medical staff weren't at a party? There was something wrong about all this. Peter was keeping something from her, and it made her feel angry. Whatever it was, she was determined to get to the truth before the evening was over.

Chapter Three

The Márquez villa was on the outskirts of Techtátuan. After driving for about twenty minutes, Paulo stopped in front of a pair of massive gates. He blasted his horn, and the gates swung open, letting through two burly men. They both wore smart suits that looked slightly too small for them and they stopped when they reached the car, one on each side. Paulo wound down the window and the largest of the two men peered in. A pair of dark, snakey-cold eyes gave Jacey a swift, impersonal glance. She shivered unexpectedly. She recognised this type of man; he would kill without compunction, if his paymaster gave the order.

'You have an invitation, sir?' The question, aimed at Peter, sounded only barely polite.

Jacey felt suddenly irritated at being so pointedly ignored. 'We both have invitations,' she said crisply.

The blank killer's eyes looked at her again. The man said nothing but simply held out his hand and took the card that Peter offered him. A quick look, and it was handed back. 'Is this your woman, sir?'

'Yes,' Peter said.

The man nodded and stepped back. A different face suddenly appeared at Paulo's window. 'Don't loiter, Indian. Drop your passengers and come straight out. We'll be waiting.'

'Of course, Señor,' Paulo said obsequiously. As the car moved forward he muttered something that Jacey recognised as *Chachté*. It sounded far from polite.

She turned angrily to Peter. 'So I'm your woman, am I?'

Peter shrugged. 'What did you want me to say?'

'You could have told him to go away and find some manners, the fat sexist pig!'

'You don't say that sort of thing to Schlemann's heavies,' Peter said.

She stared at him. 'I thought this place belonged to Carlos Márquez?'

Peter shrugged. 'It does. But the goons are Schlemann's. He gives the orders and they obey. Why do you think everyone's so afraid of him?'

'Doesn't Hernandez object?'

'Of course not,' Peter said. He smiled without humour. 'The Generalissimo needs Schlemann. How else would he get the money to buy all those pretty uniforms?'

The car swung round a thick clump of trees. Jacey had been expecting the Márquez villa to be impressive, but even so, she was surprised at its overpowering opulence. Before them was a massive, columned portico and huge double doors, and the whole building was swept by coloured searchlights that bathed the white walls in alternating shades of blue, pink and green.

'I don't believe this,' Jacey exclaimed. 'Disneyland meets the Grand Hotel.'

'I believe Señora Márquez had a hand in the design,' Peter said dryly, as he got out of the car. 'She had rather flamboyant tastes.'

62

'Had?' Jacey repeated curiously. 'She's dead?'

Peter hesitated. 'Presumed dead. She disappeared about six months after old man Márquez died. She didn't leave a note and she didn't take anything with her. She was always loaded with expensive jewellery, but she didn't take any money or clothes. Just went out for a walk, and never came back.'

'Kidnapped?' Jacey guessed.

'No one ever made a ransom demand.'

'Suicide?'

'Overcome with grief at her husband's death, you mean?' Peter smiled briefly. 'Very doubtful.'

Jacey got out of the car and mouthed a 'thank you' to Paulo. Paulo grinned at her, then reversed the car and drove away. Jacey walked towards the villa with Peter. 'Murdered?' she persisted.

'There was no body,' Peter said. 'No one was arrested, even though the Márquez family tried very hard to get information. They offered a huge reward but there weren't any takers.'

'Mysterious,' Jacey murmured. She added, only half joking: 'Perhaps the boys bumped her off to get the family fortune?'

'Unnecessary,' Peter said. 'Juanita Márquez doted on her sons and spoiled them rotten, and they all have nice fat trust funds anyway.'

They reached the villa doors. Jacey could hear laughter and a band playing Latin American tunes. 'Do you think Nicolás Schlemann had anything to do with it?' she asked lightly.

Peter shrugged. 'I wouldn't think so. Schlemann and the Márquez family have always been as thick as thieves. Carlos and Nicolás dine with each other regularly, and their fathers were great pals, too.'

'I bet they were,' Jacey murmured. 'The ambitious young lawyer and the ex-Nazi with plenty of illegal cash. Sounds like they were made for each other.'

They went inside, and for a moment Jacey was dazzled by the central chandelier which blazed with the light from hundreds of flickering candles. Squinting up at them, she realised that they were all fakes, powered by electricity.

'Beautiful, isn't it?' Jacey turned to see a stately, elderly lady smiling at her. 'One of dear Juanita's little extravagances. She designed it herself, and it was made in Europe. Very expensive.'

'Señora Collados.' Peter took the proffered hand and kissed it lightly, surprising Jacey. 'How lovely to see you again. Allow me to introduce you to my new colleague at La Primavera, Dr Jacey Muldaire.'

'I know who she is, foolish boy,' the old lady said. 'Everyone's talking about the beautiful young doctor with the extraordinary hair.' She smiled at Jacey. 'Please, you must call me Ana.' She took Jacey's hand. 'You won't know anyone here, of course, so let me introduce you to all the best-looking men.'

'Are you going to steal my partner, Señora Collados?' Peter asked.

The question sounded light-hearted but there was a note of displeasure behind it. Ana Collados smiled at him, and Jacey realised that she must have been quite a beauty in her youth. She still had dark, luminous eyes and a wide, sensual mouth. 'You must let me gossip with her, Peter. I'll return her to you soon.' Turning her smile to Jacey, Ana edged her away from Peter Draven. Jacey felt sorry for Peter, standing alone in the glittering foyer. 'Peter is a dear boy,' Ana said. 'But English men can be so chilly, can't they?' She glanced up at Jacey. 'Are you sleeping with him?'

Startled, Jacey said coolly: 'I really think that's my business.'

Ana nodded. 'That means you are. Well, never mind. After tonight, maybe you'll have found someone whose temperament will match that fiery hair of yours, eh? But first, come and meet my nephews. Carlos is married, and very boring, but as he's our host perhaps we ought to speak to him first.'

'I didn't realise you were related to the Márquez family,' Jacey said.

'I'm Juanita's aunt.' Ana nodded.

For a moment Jacey was uncomfortable. 'Oh. I'm sorry. Peter told me –'

'That she was dead?' Ana laughed. 'Well, I suppose he would believe that story. Lots of people do. It's nonsense, of course.'

'You think she's alive?' Jacey was surprised.

'Of course she's alive.' Ana's eyes were bright and conspiratorial. A thin hand patted Jacey's arm. 'You must understand that dear Juanita was a woman of great passions. Making this house look beautiful, a love affair, a great cause; whatever claimed her attention, she gave herself utterly. And, of course, she didn't care a fig for convention. She thought it necessary to leave here, so off she went. She's pursuing one of her dreams. Believe me. I know.'

Jacey looked at the old lady and smiled. 'Well, I hope you're right.'

'You think I'm an old fool, don't you?' Ana said bluntly. 'But Juanita isn't dead. I'd know if she was.' Jacey realised she was being guided through a crowd that parted to move out of her way. Suddenly she was facing a thick-set man with glossy, slicked-back hair. He was wearing an immaculate evening suit. A slim woman, glittering with too much jewellery, stood next to him.

'Carlos,' Ana said, 'this is Dr Muldaire.'

Carlos smiled and held out his hand and Jacey noticed the heavy gold Rolex on his wrist. 'Delighted to meet you at last, Dr Muldaire. I'm glad you could come.'

They exchanged pleasantries. Carlos Márquez exuded the kind of professional charm that Jacey knew could be turned on and off at will and his bejewelled wife next to him gave Jacey a frigid smile and an unresponsive hand to shake.

'Carlos takes after his father,' Ana said, as she guided Jacey away. 'Alfonso Márquez was a very boring man. Rich, of course – that's why Juanita married him – but so dull. Raoul and Leonardo are quite different, thank God.'

'They take after their mother?' Jacey asked.

'Oh, no. They take after their fathers, too.' Ana smiled at Jacey. 'Raoul's father was a Frenchman. Charming, a beautiful man. Leonardo's was an Italian. Tall and thin, and rather shy. I didn't see the attraction but Juanita was besotted with him for at least a year.'

'She chose her children's names according to the nationality of her lovers?' Jacey was amazed. 'Didn't her husband mind? I thought Spanish men were very jealous.'

Ana shrugged. 'Alfonso was too busy making money to care, scheming with that disgusting Nazi, Heinrich Schlemann. And Juanita had done her duty by him, hadn't she? She gave him Carlos. That's what he wanted: a son. There's no doubt about Carlos's paternity. He looks just like Alfonso.' She pointed suddenly. 'There's dear Raoul. Come and meet him. You'll love him. All the women do.'

Jacey saw a young man in a crowd of laughing guests, and as Ana urged her forward she suddenly realised that he looked familiar. Much too familiar. She recognised the large, brown eyes, the perfect oval face, the dark, brown hair with a hint of gold. She felt her cheeks begin to flush with embarrassment.

'Raoul, my dear.' Ana pushed Jacey forward. 'I

want you to meet our new doctor. This is Jacey Muldaire.'

The young man turned with the same dancer's grace that Jacey had admired before, and smiled. Jacey remembered the smile, too.

'We've already met,' he said.

'Oh?' Ana looked slightly put out. 'You didn't tell me,' she challenged Jacey.

'Aunt Ana,' Raoul said, 'I doubt if you gave the poor lady a chance to get a word in edgeways.' He held out his hand to Jacey. 'I'm so glad you could come, Dr Muldaire.' Instead of relinquishing his grasp, he tightened it, and pulled her gently forward. 'Please, come and talk to me. I'd like to practise my English.'

The crowd parted for them and Raoul led Jacey towards an open French window and on to a wide balcony surrounded by a balustrade. There were several other couples already out there but they slipped discreetly back inside when Raoul appeared.

By now Jacey's embarrassment was turning to anger. 'You let me make a complete fool of myself at the hospital,' she said. 'Why on earth didn't you tell me who you were?'

He turned her to face him suddenly, and held her by both shoulders. Once again, she saw how handsome he was, but his perfectly proportioned body and flawlessly regular features made him seem vaguely androgynous. Looking at him gave her the same kind of pleasure she got from seeing a beautiful painting but it did not excite her sexually.

'Please,' he said, in English, 'you must forgive me.'

'Please,' she said, in the same language, 'explain why you lied to me.'

He laughed. 'Because it was so amusing to be mistaken for a gigolo. And one of Julia's gigolos at that. Julia thought it was hilarious. But she also thought I would be worth a thousand dollars for a night of love. I was very upset that you did not agree.'

'It was a ridiculous price,' she said. 'And fancy telling Señora Atriega. Whatever will she think of me now?'

He shrugged. 'Nothing bad. How could she? She has often told me that I am so desirable that I should sell myself and make a fortune.' He looked suddenly mournful. 'And then you tell me you wouldn't buy me. I'm desolated.'

'No, you're not,' Jacey said crisply. 'I'm sure this house is full of young women who would be only too happy to leap into bed with you.'

'You're absolutely right,' he agreed with disarming honesty. 'But I don't want them. I want you.' He moved closer to her. 'We could make sweet music together,' he said soulfully.

It was so corny that she almost laughed. She had to put him off. 'I'm already in a relationship,' she said.

'With Peter Draven? I can give you so much more than he can.' His brown eyes explored her face with such intensity that she felt as if they were stroking her skin. 'Much, much more,' he murmured. 'What do Englishmen know about making love? They're always in a hurry.' He fixed his gaze on the expanse between her neck and the top of her black dress, moving his eyes deliberately to where her nipples pressed against the silky cloth. He pursed his lips slightly and smiled, leaving her in no doubt as to what he was thinking. 'I could arouse you just with my mouth,' he said softly. 'Just my lips and my tongue. I would start by kissing you until you were breathless, and then I would move all over your body, very slowly. Can you imagine the tip of my tongue exploring you? Exploring every part of you?

68

Every secret part.' He leant closer and she felt the warmth of his breath brushing her cheek. 'Think about it. Imagine my lips on your skin, torturing you with pleasure.'

It was a ridiculously theatrical speech, she thought, like a seduction scene out of a bad movie. Yet it was also curiously stimulating. She longed to be aroused by the intimate movements of someone's mouth. She had always enjoyed the sensation, but several of her previous partners had no idea of the interesting ways in which they could use their tongues. Some of them didn't even know how to kiss properly. They had often left her disappointed and frustrated. She had a feeling that Raoul would be one of those rare men who actually enjoyed lengthy foreplay, and that he would take the trouble to discover exactly how his partner liked to be caressed.

'Maybe I would explore your beautiful neck?' His voice was a low, hypnotic monotone. 'Would you enjoy that? And then your shoulders. And your throat. And then down to your breasts. I think you would unfasten your dress for me. I think you would encourage me.'

He was closer still, his mouth approaching hers. Although his words were certainly making her feel sexy, she was acutely aware that in her mind's eye she was seeing a totally different kind of man. Taller, harder, and more masculine. Nothing like the beautiful Raoul; her composite man was not unlike Nicolás Schlemann. And the more she tried to banish the image, the stronger it became.

She remembered his dark, unreadable eyes, the firm grip of his hand, and the attractively irregular hair framing that dangerous-looking face. She remembered the way his taut muscles moved under his tanned skin when he stripped off his shirt. All right, she thought, Nicolás Schlemann is physically attractive. And he was deliberately being nice to me. Like a cat playing with a mouse? The image came to her unexpectedly. He had reminded me of a cat, a cat preening. That prompted another memory: the controlled power of his movements when he had partially undressed and then pulled his clothes back on. How would he make love, she wondered? She had a feeling that he would like to be in control. All the time. Would it exciting to be told what to do?

She suddenly remembered Faisel, and his brutal use of her body and emotions. She heard his voice, still clear in her mind after all those years, demanding: service me! But that was different, she thought. He wasn't acting out of love, or even sexual desire. He used me for his own selfish ends. I was an innocent, silly teenager. And he was a bastard who really hated women.

She remembered the first time she had seen Faisel with one of his boyfriends, seen them holding hands, then kissing. She had watched Faisel turn his head and stare at her as she gawped at him, her mouth half-open with shock. He had deliberately reached for his companion's crotch, fondled the bulge of his erection for a few moments, then unzipped the boy's jeans and pulled them slowly down to his knees.

The boy was not wearing any underwear. His penis looked huge as it strained upwards. Faisel knelt down and grasped the boy's buttocks, fingers digging and massaging, while his mouth sucked greedily at that swollen cock. She remembered the boy's noisy orgasm, his body shaking violently, and the way Faisel had turned to her and smiled triumphantly afterwards.

It was then that she had discovered why he had duped her into marriage. His family expected him to conform. She must have looked like a gift from heaven, too young, infatuated, and innocent to sus-

70

pect the truth. A foreigner, who would be a virtual prisoner once she arrived in his native country, trapped by her ignorance of the language and the law. He had married her with callous disregard to her future and her happiness because his family expected him to be a dutiful son, and a husband. She remembered sobbing with frustrated rage, determined to find a way of informing his parents about his deception, and wondering how to enlist their help to get back home. She did not realise that the true horror was yet to come, and that his family would be willing collaborators.

She dismissed her memories. She was well aware that Nicolás Schlemann was probably a womaniser, but if she had an affair with him, at least she would be in control. She could walk away from him any time she liked. Then her common sense took over. Don't even consider it, she told herself. You, of all people, should not be seduced by appearances. And Nicolás Schlemann is probably a selfish, hasty lover.

Raoul put his hands on her waist and began to slide them upwards. 'I think you would like to feel my tongue circle your nipples,' he whispered. 'I think maybe they are already erect, waiting for me to excite them even more.'

She abruptly stopped daydreaming, and tried to think of a polite way of discouraging him from going any further. She didn't want to hurt his feelings.

His voice changed tone, became more urgent, louder. 'Come upstairs with me. There is a beautiful room where we can be alone.'

She put her hands on his chest and pushed him back playfully but firmly. 'You're very sweet, Raoul, but I'm . . . too old for you.'

He laughed. 'You're not. I'm twenty-one and you're maybe six years older?' She did not correct him. 'That's no age at all,' he said. 'I wouldn't care if

71

you were forty. I have made love to many older women. I adore older women. They're adventurous and knowledgeable. I adore all women.' He closed in on her again. 'I adore you.'

She backed away again. 'I'm with Peter,' she said.

He caught her hand, and kissed it. His mouth felt light and warm on her skin. 'I see no ring on your finger.'

'We have an agreement,' she said.

Raoul looked at her with his melting brown eyes. She wondered suddenly if he gave that soulful look to all women to entice them. His voice dropped to a seductive whisper. 'Peter won't mind. He brought you here, didn't he?'

She stiffened. 'What is that supposed to mean?' Her voice was sharper than she intended.

Raoul was close again. 'We are very modern here.' His lips brushed her ear. 'Do you understand me? Peter knows that.' His hands went round her waist. 'I want you, Jacey. I wanted you as soon as I saw you in the hospital corridor. I wanted you more than anyone else in the whole world. Is it so bad of me to feel that way?'

'No,' she said. 'Foolish, maybe.'

But a suspicion was forming in her mind, and the more she thought about it, the more she felt certain it was the truth. Peter had been very anxious for her to come to this party. He had turned down her blatant offer of a nice, private sexy evening, something he had not done before. Why was he so keen for her to go along with him? So that Raoul Márquez could try and charm her into making love?

Raoul could have engineered any number of ways to meet her, but here at the villa everything was laid on. There was even a convenient bedroom upstairs. A bedroom with a two-way mirror? she wondered. With a hidden camera?

Was Raoul into exhibitionism? Maybe Peter had been testing the water by asking her if she would perform with Nicolás Schlemann? Maybe he was going to suggest instead some fun and games with Raoul Márquez. Perhaps I'm supposed to be a bribe, she thought. Raoul's family helps finance La Primavera. If they're happy, they'll be generous. Was that why Peter had objected weakly when Ana commandeered me? Did he know she would take me straight to Raoul?

Raoul was nibbling her ear but although the sensation was pleasurable, she jerked her head away from him. 'Did you ask Peter to bring me here?' she demanded.

He looked surprised. 'I suggested it. I thought you would like to come to a party.'

'This was all planned, wasn't it?' She couldn't disguise her annoyance any longer. 'Peter brought me here for you.' She pushed him hard away from her, and he staggered back. 'Well, I'm not having it.' She headed for the French window. 'Peter's a bastard, so are you, and I'm not interested in either of you.'

She did not notice the man standing beside the French window until she had almost cannoned into him.

'Lover's tiff?' His dark eyes showed sardonic amusement.

She stepped back. 'Do you normally listen in on private conversations, Señor Schlemann?'

'Often.' He leant against the doorpost, blocking her exit. 'But your conversation was far too noisy to be considered private, Dr Muldaire.' He shifted his position, with lazy elegance, and again she was reminded of a sleek jungle cat. 'Exactly who are you no longer interested in?' he asked, curiously. 'Our young cut-price Valentino, Raoul Márquez?'

'Don't try and be humorous, Nicci,' Raoul interrupted angrily. 'You're not very good at it.'

'I could say the same about your attempts to be romantic,' Nicolás said. 'Not having much success with Dr Muldaire, are you?' He smiled, moved towards her, and put a hand possessively on her shoulder. 'Maybe I'll have better luck.'

Raoul stepped forward, his face tight with anger, and for a moment Jacey thought there would be a fight. Nicolás Schlemann was outwardly relaxed, but she felt the tension in his body. Instinct told her that he was well able to take care of himself. She was not so certain about Raoul.

Anxious to diffuse the tension, she pulled away from Nicolás. 'Please, gentlemen, do stop behaving like silly children.' She smiled brightly at both of them. 'It's very flattering to be wanted, but I'm not on offer to either of you. I'm here with Peter Draven.'

She was relieved to see Raoul stop, and then shrug. Nicolás made no further attempt to touch her. Raoul turned to him and said, with a note of challenge in his voice, 'Dr Muldaire is quite right, Nicci. We shouldn't force our attentions on her, should we?'

Nicolás smiled mockingly but did not move. 'I've never forced myself on a woman in my life.' He paused, and his voice changed to a seductive murmur. 'Although the right kind of force can be exciting.' His hand reached for Jacey again. His fingers rested lightly on her neck, then tangled briefly with her hair. 'Don't you agree, Dr Muldaire?'

Jacey knew that the next move was hers. Common sense told her that she should snub Nicolás Schlemann, and go back to the main room to find Peter. But she still couldn't fathom why Peter had brought her to this particular party. Had he really been planning some voyeuristic fun and games with Raoul, it would serve them both right if she ended up with

Nicolás Schlemann instead. Just for the evening, she told herself. She certainly did not intend to get seriously involved with this conceited – and undoubtedly dangerous – political racketeer.

Nicolás was regarding her with amused confidence. 'The desirability of using force is always open to debate,' she said lightly.

'I enjoy a good debate,' he said smoothly. 'Let me get you a drink, and we'll talk.'

He moved round her and at the same time managed to put himself behind Raoul, so that as he walked towards the French window he edged Raoul forward. Before he left, Raoul turned to glance at Jacey, and she felt suddenly and unexpectedly sorry for him. He looked young, vulnerable, and disappointed. But at least this scenario would prove that she really wasn't interested in ending up in bed with him.

Do I really want Nicolás Schlemann? she asked herself. Although she had been determined to dislike him, she found it very hard to actually do so when he was close to her. Again, she had a strong feeling that she should walk out on him, there and then. But, for some reason, she waited until he returned, carrying two glasses. He had not asked her what she wanted, but had brought her champagne, and whisky for himself.

She took the glass from him. 'What are we celebrating?' she asked.

'The fact that I've saved you from being pestered into bed by Raoul Márquez,' he replied. 'Or is making love to an overgrown schoolboy your idea of an exciting evening?'

'I had no intention of going to bed with Raoul,' she said. 'I was about to go and find Peter.'

'You wouldn't have found him,' Nicolás said. 'Peter's gone home.'

She stared back at him incredulously. 'I don't believe you.'

Nicolás shrugged. 'Then go on. Find him.' He lounged back against the balustrade. 'I'll wait here. Come back when you get tired of looking.'

She paused. She felt certain that Nicolás was telling the truth. How dare Peter bring me here and dump me, she thought. Now she was certain that he had connived with Raoul. She glanced at Nicolás. He was watching her with a sardonic smile. To hell with Peter, she thought, and to hell with Raoul. I'll stay with Nicolás for the evening.

'It looks as if I've been abandoned,' she said, trying to sound flippant.

'Aren't you lucky,' he said. 'Instead of being bored to death by Dr Draven, or pawed by that idiot Raoul, you can enjoy a far more stimulating evening with me.'

'Peter is a good friend of mine,' she said. 'And I'm sure Raoul isn't an idiot. He was just getting a little emotionally over-enthusiastic, that's all.'

Nicolás laughed. 'What a neat way of putting it. Raoul is always getting over-enthusiastic about something. A woman, a new hobby, or a splendid good cause. He's an emotional dilettante. But what do you expect from the offspring of a Frenchman and a whore.'

'Just because Juanita Márquez had a couple of affairs after she was married, it doesn't make her a whore,' Jacey said.

'She was a whore before she married,' Nicolás said. 'A whore who thought marrying money would make her a lady. Which it didn't, of course. And she didn't just have a couple of affairs, as you so politely say. She fucked everyone she could lay her hands on, male or female. She even made a play for me. She liked to tease, to lead people on. In the end, someone obviously got frustrated with her games, and killed her.'

'You think she's really dead?' Jacey asked.

'Of course.' He gave her a quizzical look. 'Don't you?'

'Some people think she's still alive.' Jacey was hedging.

He grinned suddenly. 'You've been talking to that senile old fool Ana, haven't you? She believes all that reincarnation rubbish that the Indians teach. She probably thinks Juanita has come back as a parrot, or something equally ridiculous.'

'She thinks Juanita was bored with her life here and ran away with a lover,' Jacey said.

Nicolás laughed derisively. 'He would have to have been a very rich lover to persuade Juanita to leave Techtátuan. Alfonso Márquez treated her far too leniently when he was alive, and she inherited this villa and a sizeable portion of his money when he died. She would never have willingly left all this.' He smiled mockingly at Jacey. 'Like most women, she was far too fond of money and comfort.'

'Am I included in that sweeping condemnation?' Jacey asked.

'Why call it a condemnation?' His smile was meant to challenge her. 'Women have their place in the order of things. It's natural for them to want to live a life of luxury, and natural for them to expect a man to pay for it.' He was watching her closely. 'In return, of course, they have to be taught obedience. To behave themselves in the bedroom. To please their man, and act out his fantasies for him. That's far more natural than wanting to wear a white coat and be a doctor.' For a moment Jacey was speechless. Nicolás smiled, with genuine humour this time. 'However, as a patient I must say I preferred your professional touch to that of Dr Draven. I haven't

77

forgotten how delightful your hands felt when you examined me.' His put his empty whisky glass on the balustrade. 'But you enjoy being thought sexy and desirable too, don't you, Dr Muldaire? You enjoy men?'

'Some men,' she said carefully.

'Men like Peter Draven?' He shook his head in mockery. 'Whatever did you see in that colourless Englishman?'

Although she was feeling angry with Peter, Jacey could not be disloyal; she didn't intend to criticise him to Nicolás Schlemann. 'He's dedicated his entire life to helping people,' she said.

'Well, so have I.' Nicolás took a step forward but she stood her ground. She was close enough now to feel the masculine warmth of his body, and smell the very faint, sharp scent of cologne as he spoke. 'I'm responsible for most of the modernisation you see in Guachtàl.'

'And for turning it into a police state?'

He lounged back against the balustrade again. 'What an odd accusation. I'm just a simple business man. Generalissimo Hernandez controls the army.'

'And who controls the professional heavies who insulted me when I arrived here?'

'I provided the security men for this party,' Nicolás admitted. 'Which one insulted you?'

'The large one, on the gates.'

He thought for a moment. 'That sounds like Marco. What exactly did he say?'

'Nothing,' she said. 'That's my point. He ignored me. He asked Peter if I was his woman.'

'Oh dear.' Nicolás grinned lazily. 'How very politically incorrect of him.'

'Don't compound the insult by laughing at me,' she snapped crossly. 'If you're going to let your pet goons loose on the general public, at least teach them to be polite.'

'Marco is useful,' Nicolás said, 'but perhaps a little uncouth.' He straightened up and stretched, and she was reminded again of his prowling, feline strength. 'I can understand you not wanting to be Peter Draven's property.' One step brought him close to her. 'But what about me? Would you object to belonging to me?'

'I don't like the word "belong",' she said. 'I'm an independent, professional woman, remember? I believe in equality.'

'At work, maybe,' he agreed. 'I have no quarrel with that.' Another step forward. 'But that's not the kind of relationship I'm referring to.'

Although she knew she should back away, instead she wanted to reach out and touch him. Trace her finger round the line of his jaw. She found herself wondering what his mouth would feel like pressed over hers. Or travelling downwards, to excite her body.

'I really don't know what you're talking about,' she lied.

'Yes, you do,' he said. 'I'm talking about sex. And you're thinking about it.'

She felt herself blushing. Was she that transparent?

'Don't tell me I've embarrassed you, Dr Muldaire?' He grinned crookedly. 'An independent, professional woman like you? You knew we were going to end up together, didn't you? You knew it when I first met you at the hospital.'

No, she thought, I didn't. When you walked across to me with that charming smile, and your hand outstretched, it reminded me of the way I felt when I first saw Faisel. That sudden, dangerous, unmistakable physical thrill.

'Do you always assume that every woman you

79

meet is going to fall for you, Señor Schlemann?' Jacey
asked coolly.

'The ones I want usually do,' he said. He stepped
back, then reached out and placed his hands lightly
on her shoulders. He began to massage her flesh
gently. 'And I want you, Dr Jacey Muldaire.'

'Don't take me for granted,' she warned.

She felt his grip tighten. 'But you like being dominated, don't you?' His fingers dug into her flesh. 'You
like strong men, and power turns you on. Once the
bedroom door has closed you're quite happy to stop
giving orders, and start taking them. Master and
servant? Master and slave?' She was swaying as his
hands worked on the muscles of her shoulders. 'The
idea excites you, doesn't it?' His voice became softly
seductive. 'And luckily for you, that's just the way I
like to play it, too. We'll make an ideal couple. I'm
going to enjoy finding out exactly how far you're
willing to go. How far I can push you. Exactly what
you'll do to please me.'

'You can't assume anything,' she said unsteadily.
'You don't know a thing about me.'

'I know enough,' he said. 'You want me as much
as I want you. And what's more, I can prove it.' He
let her go and stepped back, smiling his charming,
crooked, and utterly self-confident smile. 'Walk away
from me, Dr Muldaire. Walk away, and I promise I'll
never bother you again.' He paused. 'Even if you
change your mind and beg me to. Walk away from
me. Now.'

She should take him at his word. You're just a
trophy to this man, she told herself. One more victory
on his score sheet. He knows you're attracted to him
and that gives him power. He'll use that power
ruthlessly to get what he wants. Just like Faisel, she
thought suddenly. But this is different; my eyes are
wide open now. This isn't a romance, and neither of

us need to pretend that it is. This is almost a business arrangement. Nicolás Schlemann wants what I want: a no-strings affair, like a courtesan with a client. The idea was beginning to excite her. And so was the possibility of finding out exactly what kind of games he liked to play.

'I don't beg,' she said.

He raised one eyebrow. 'That's a rash claim, Dr Muldaire.' His smile was dangerous now, the smile of a predator, sure of his prey. 'I'll have to put it to the test.' He held out his hand. 'Come with me.'

He linked her arm in his, and she walked beside him through the French window towards the chattering guests. She noticed how swiftly people stepped aside to let them pass, as if Nicolás was royalty. When he stopped to talk to anyone, he was greeted with effusive jollity. But the smiles looked forced, and Jacey had a strong feeling that anyone he talked to was heartily glad when he moved on.

And yet he seemed determined to linger. He put his arm possessively round her shoulders while he was talking, and although he included her in his conversations only once or twice, she received her share of smiles. But they looked wary, she realised, rather than sincere. Nicolás guided her through the crowd, and she knew his indulgent friendliness was as hypocritical as that of the guests. He reminded her of a leopard stalking at a waterhole, looking for the most succulent victim to devour.

When he finally made for the door she murmured ironically, 'You do seem to have a lot of friends.'

'I do, don't I,' he murmured back, equally ironic. 'Is there anyone in particular you'd like to meet?'

'The famous Generalissimo Hernandez?' she suggested.

He looked momentarily startled. 'Whatever makes you think he's here?'

81

She shrugged. 'Peter told me these parties get lively later on. Even dictators like to relax occasionally, don't they?'

Nicolás laughed. 'Hernandez wouldn't like to hear you call him a dictator. And he doesn't attend parties like this. His wife wouldn't let him.'

This time she joined in the laughter. 'You're joking?'

'I'm not,' Nicolás said. 'Pilar Hernandez is a very formidable woman. The Generalissimo is devoted to her and he respects her opinions.'

'The power behind the throne?' Jacey hinted.

'Not as often as she thinks,' Nicolás said smoothly. 'But as it happens, this is one of the few times that I agree with her. Attending this kind of party would be bad for the Generalissimo's public image.'

Jacey shrugged. 'Why should he care about his image? He has the guns to back up his position.'

'I'd rather he didn't need guns,' Nicolás said. 'Guns are expensive, but public affection is cheap. And you don't try to depose a leader that you love.'

'But the people don't exactly love him, do they?' She was determined to challenge him.

They had left the crowded room behind them and Nicolás was guiding her towards the wide stairs. 'What makes you think they don't?' he asked.

'A lot of them want a change of leadership,' she said.

He stopped abruptly and swung round to face her, trapping her against the ornate bannister post. 'Really?' His voice was cold. 'Who told you that?'

'No one,' she said. 'But I'm sure Loháquin would confirm it, if I asked him.'

Nicolás stared at her for a moment, and she saw fury in his eyes. Then he relaxed, and laughed, but there was no humour in his dark gaze. 'That play-acting clown. Who's been talking to you about him?'

'No one in particular.' She was fascinated by his sudden mood change. 'I saw the wanted posters in town.' Ingenuously, she added, 'But I did hear a rumour that you're offering a huge reward for Loháquin's capture. He must be very dangerous if you're so anxious to arrest him.'

'He's not dangerous,' Nicolás snapped. 'He's just a scruffy trouble-maker who's talked a few Indians into believing they can run this country better than we can. He skulks in the rainforest, and tells people that he's some kind of mysterious saviour. The Indian boys are the only ones he can dupe with his ridiculous ideas about changing Guachtàl.'

'So there's no reward money?' she asked.

Nicolás shrugged. 'We would show our gratitude if someone helped us catch him, I suppose.' He smiled a predatory, dangerous smile. 'Why? Are you planning to supplement your wages at La Primavera by trying to arrest Loháquin?'

'I wouldn't know where to start looking,' she said innocently.

'Keep it that way,' he advised. His tone was light, but she suspected that he meant her to take his warning seriously. 'Don't meddle in our politics, Dr Muldaire. Stick to the things you understand.' He smiled and it softened the hard lines of his face. Here was the man who had charmed her so unexpectedly at the hospital. 'Things like making people feel good.' His voice changed, too. 'Making men feel good. You're going to make me feel good soon, aren't you, doctor? You're something of an expert at that, I believe.'

'You make me sound like a whore,' she said reprovingly.

'All women are whores at heart,' he said. His hands slipped under her arms, and his thumbs touched the underside of her breasts, then slid upwards to brush

83

her nipples. She was not wearing a bra, and because his light touch was intensely arousing, her nipples contracted noticeably. She gasped.

'No underwear?' He grinned. 'How delightful.' He put both thumbs against her nipples and then, with erotic roughness, captured her breasts in his hands and pushed them upwards until they met the tight neckline of her dress. He bent down and kissed the cleft between them with an unexpected gentleness before the tip of his tongue traced a moist pattern on her bare skin. His arms slipped behind her and down to her bottom, and suddenly, as she felt his fingers tugging at the dress, trying to pull it up, she remembered exactly where they were. 'For heaven's sake.' She tried to pull away from him. 'Not here.'

'Not embarrassed, are you, Dr Muldaire?' he asked, laughing. 'I assure you, what we're doing is totally innocent compared to what will be going on here very soon.'

'Just as long as I don't have to participate,' she said.

'You're quite safe,' he said. 'No one would dare to touch my property.'

She realised at once why he had escorted her so publicly through the crowd of guests; he had been making a clear statement of ownership. She did not know whether to feel angry or amused.

'You'll have to tell Peter that I'm your property,' she said lightly, testing him.

He gave her a curious look. 'You can tell him yourself,' he said. 'The next time you see him.' He stepped back, abruptly. 'Wait for me here,' he said. 'I have to arrange something.'

Before she could say anything, he strode away. She stood at the bottom of the stairs. Guests walked past her in pairs or groups, and nodded and smiled. Several of them peered at her surreptitiously from the main room, then dodged back when they saw that she had spotted them.

'You really shouldn't, you know.' The familiar voice made Jacey turn round. Ana Collados came towards her. 'It's very foolish of you.'

Jacey smiled politely. 'Foolish to be friends with Nicolás Schlemann, you mean?'

Ana nodded. 'I daresay you find him attractive. Many women do. But the Indians have offered him to the *lohá*. It will destroy him. And you as well, if you're with him.'

'Destroy him?' Jacey repeated, intrigued. 'How?'

'The *lohá* will strike him when he least expects it,' Ana said. 'It's very powerful. Powerful and cruel. It will not spare you because you're innocent.' She looked at Jacey, obviously concerned. 'Let me introduce you to someone less dangerous.'

Jacey smiled politely. 'Don't worry,' she said. 'I can take care of myself.'

'You don't understand,' Ana said. 'There is no protection against the *lohá*.'

'What exactly is a *lohá*?' Jacey asked. 'Something like Loháquin?'

Ana nodded. 'It's like a part of the Loháquin. The *lohá* lives in the space between the worlds. That's what the Indians say.' She glanced over Jacey's shoulder, and suddenly her face changed. She smiled brightly and patted Jacey's hand. 'So just remember what I've told you,' she said and walked away.

Jacey turned to see Nicolás walking towards her. 'What did that old fool want this time?' he asked.

'She was telling me about a *lohá*,' Jacey said. 'Whatever that is.'

'It's an idiotic native superstition,' he said. 'Some kind of spirit.'

'Well, apparently it's waiting for you,' Jacey said brightly.

Nicolás sighed irritably. 'Ana and Juanita made a good pair. They were both fascinated by all that rubbish the Indians teach.'

'Apparently the *lohá* is going to destroy you,' said Jacey. 'It's powerful and cruel. Don't you think you should be just a little bit worried?'

'It'll take more than a few natives dancing about in the forest muttering incantations to destroy me,' Nicolás replied. He grabbed hold of her hand and pulled her towards the stairs. 'Come with me. I've arranged something for you. I think you'll enjoy it.'

He hustled her up the wide staircase and along a carpeted corridor. When he opened a door for her, she fully expected to find herself in a bedroom, or a room designed for some kind of amorous dalliance, maybe furnished with comfortable chairs or a *chaise longue*. Instead she was in a rather conventional study.

A large, old-fashioned desk stood by the window, with a padded swivel chair behind it. There were glass-fronted bookcases, and framed photographs of polo players on the walls. Nicolás went behind the desk, sat down and picked up the telephone. 'Come in now,' he ordered abruptly.

Almost immediately the door opened and Marco came in. His cold, snake's eyes glanced at Jacey without obvious recognition, and then at Nicolás. Even larger than Jacey remembered, he made Nicolás look lightweight.

'Marco,' Nicolás said. 'You've offended my friend Dr Muldaire.'

Marco's eyes switched to Jacey, then back to Nicolás again. 'I wasn't aware of it, sir.'

Nicolás smiled. 'Are you calling me a liar, Marco?'

'No, sir,' Marco said quickly. 'Certainly not, sir.'

'That's good.' Nicolás pushed the revolving chair far back enough to allow him to stretch his legs and

86

put his feet on the desk. 'Apologise to Dr Muldaire, Marco.'

Marco looked at Jacey, his eye dark and glacial. 'I am sorry if I have offended you, Dr Muldaire,' he said blankly.

'That's not good enough.' Nicolás lounged back. 'I want Dr Muldaire to be absolutely certain that you're sorry for your boorish behaviour.' His feet swung to the floor suddenly, and he leant forward. 'Kneel on the floor, Marco, and ask Dr Muldaire to forgive you.'

Jacey was about to protest that this kind of apology was unnecessary, but Marco obeyed instantly. He knelt down, and as he looked up, again she found herself gazing into his impassive eyes. Jacey was flustered and surprised.

'I am very sorry that I offended you, Dr Muldaire,' he said, his voice as blank as his expression. 'I apologise.'

'I humbly apologise,' Nicolás prompted.

'I humbly apologise,' Marco repeated.

'Now kiss her feet,' Nicolás instructed.

'No, really —' Jacey began.

Marco hesitated.

'Do it!' Nicolás ordered.

Marco bent forward, and she felt the brief tap of his mouth against her shoe.

'Stand up,' Nicolás said. Marco stood up. Nicolás smiled. 'You'll be polite to Dr Muldaire in future, won't you, Marco?' He paused for a brief moment. 'As long as she's a friend of mine, you'll be very polite.'

'Yes, sir,' Marco said.

When the door closed behind him, Jacey couldn't help saying: 'You really are a bastard, aren't you?'

Nicolás lazed back in his chair again. 'Is that all the thanks I get? You enjoyed it, didn't you?'

'No.' But she knew it was a lie. While it had not

given her any kind of sexual kick to see Marco humiliated, she did derive a certain satisfaction from receiving his unwilling apology. 'And you've made me an enemy,' she added.

Nicolás stood up, and came round to the front of the desk. Reaching out for her, he put his hands on either side of her neck. She felt his fingers grip gently, then one hand moved to the back of her head. The other stroked the line of her jaw, and ended under her chin. His grip tightened and he forced her head back slowly. 'As long as you're my woman, you're quite safe,' he said.

She felt herself being drawn towards him. She wanted him to kiss her, and yet, perversely, she wanted to resist, to make him force her. Almost imperceptibly, she pulled away from him and immediately felt his grip turn to iron. Although she knew it was a fantasy, she was filled with the sensation that if she resisted him too much, he would snap her head back and break her neck. Why did she find this situation so arousing? His lips touched hers. Firmly closed, they rested on her mouth lightly. She felt the warmth of his skin and the hard strength of his body moving against her. Then, slowly, his tongue began to force her lips apart.

And then the phone rang. Nicolás pulled away from her abruptly, and said, in German, something brief and vicious. His phone conversation was short and to the point. 'Yes. You did the right thing. I'll be with you in ten minutes.' Turning back to Jacey he smiled, and shrugged. 'The police have just caught two boys they think I'd like to question. I'm sorry, but I have to go.'

'An interrogation?' she asked.

'An interview,' he said. 'All very civilised. I hope you don't think I use knuckle-dusters and a cosh.'

She wondered exactly how much power she

needed to entice him to stay. 'Can't it wait?' she murmured seductively. 'A couple of boys can't be that important.'

'That depends on who they're working for,' he said. 'They're Indian kids. They could be stealing for themselves, or if they're really stupid, they'll be doing it for Loháquin.'

She snuggled closer to him. 'Surely you don't have to go right now?'

He put his hands round her waist and held her tightly. 'Prisoners tend to tell the truth when they're confused and frightened. Don't you have a saying in English about striking while the iron's hot?'

She was close enough to feel his erection pushing against her stomach. She slipped her hand down and captured it with gently probing fingers. 'What a pity that maxim only applies to your prisoners,' she murmured.

'It doesn't.'

He lifted her suddenly, dumping her roughly on the desk. Moving quickly, he lodged himself between her outstretched legs, preventing her from closing them.

She wriggled, pretending to protest, only to ruche her skirt even higher round her thighs. He pushed at the hem until it reached her waist, revealing her wispy, black, suspender belt and her matching silky thong.

As she lay there spread-eagled, he surveyed her body. 'Very nice,' he approved. 'Very sexy.' His fingers touched the taut, shiny triangle that barely covered her pubic hair. 'You must wear something like this for me again. I like to see women's bodies decorated with silk, or lace, or jewellery.' She felt his nails scrape tantalisingly over the cloth. Her clitoris was already swollen and sensitive and his light touch excited it even more. 'But for my immediate needs, you're overdressed.'

He reached into a pocket and she was briefly aware of something small, dark and shiny in his hand. Then a thin blade appeared, released by a spring from its ebony handle. A quick hooking move cut the ties that held the thong in place. He pulled the tiny piece of cloth away, and tossed it on to the floor. 'That's better.'

The knife disappeared back into its handle. He pulled her towards him, forcing her legs even wider apart. Before she realised fully what was happening, he had unzipped and thrust into her with brutal urgency.

Everything that had happened to her that evening had aroused her to some degree, including Nicolás Schlemann's unconventional seduction techniques, and now, as she felt him deep inside her, she was unable to disguise a groan of pleasure. His hands slipped under her bottom, lifting her slightly, pulling her close. After his initial haste, he seemed willing to slow down, but she discovered to her surprise that she had found his rough dominance exciting and erotic. To provoke him, she made a pretence of struggling. He caught her wrists and forced her arms back over her head, pressing them against the desk top.

'Trying to escape?' She felt his grip tighten. His hips thrust faster, and she writhed against him. 'You don't fool me, doctor. You like it quick and hard, don't you? And you like servicing a man you've only just met.' His breathing was ragged now. She could feel him losing control. 'You want me. Just as much as I – want – you.'

His climax came suddenly and she felt the shuddering spasms of pleasure roll through his body.

Although she did not manage to reach orgasm, she still felt a certain erotic glow.

'Well,' he said, zipping himself up, 'this isn't exactly the way I planned it. But it was very nice, all the same.' He held her hands and pulled her up to a sitting position. 'I have to go now. You can stay, of course. I'll have a car standing by for you, when you want to go home.'

'Will you be coming back here?' she asked.

'No.' He walked to the door, and added smoothly: 'I've accomplished my objective for this evening.'

She stood up and adjusted her dress. Smug bastard, she thought, without rancour. I saw, I conquered, I came! 'Don't bother about the car,' she said sweetly. 'I'll ask Raoul to drive me home.'

Nicolás turned. 'If you're trying to make me jealous that isn't the way to do it. Raoul isn't man enough to satisfy you, and you don't want him anyway. You have what you want now, and what you need.' He smiled his crooked smile. He paused, briefly. 'I'll phone you when I want you again. Good night, Dr Muldaire.'

He closed the door before Jacey had a chance to retaliate. She sat down on the edge of the desk. Is that true, she asked herself. Is he really what I want? Right now, he is, and I'm not ashamed to admit it. Why shouldn't I have an affair, without commitment, with this conceited, but undeniably attractive, man? I've been sent to Guachtàl to check out the political climate, and Nicolás Schlemann seems to be the country's ruler in everything else but name. She smiled to herself. He's everything I need, is he? Perhaps it's just as well he has no idea how accurate that is.

She had no qualms about ending her relationship with Peter Draven. Inadvertently Peter had helped her to do the job she was sent here to do. She was disappointed in him, though. And in Raoul Márquez. Peter had behaved like a pimp, and Raoul had condoned it. She gave her dress one final tug and glanced down at the remains of her silky thong lying on the floor. Well, she thought, that'll give the cleaners something to gossip about in the morning.

But when she went out into the corridor she realised that her discarded underwear would be small fry compared to some of the other items the staff would probably find littered about the next day. The party atmosphere was changing. There were new guests of a type Jacey was certain that Carlos and his wife would have nothing to do with. As she walked towards the stairs a statuesque blonde in a stunning, full-length silver dress swayed past her. The hip-hugging skirt was split from waist to ankle at the back, and as the woman moved, her naked bottom was tantalisingly revealed.

'Dr Muldaire?' The woman turned suddenly, and Jacey recognised Carmen, Señor Valienté's 'secretary'. 'Whatever are you doing here?'

'The same as you, I imagine,' Jacey said.

Carmen laughed. 'I hope not. I'm working.' Turning round she parted the long, silver skirt, revealing even more of her bottom, and wiggled provocatively. 'As you can see.'

Jacey smiled. She was beginning to like the earthy Carmen. 'I hope Señor Valienté approves?'

'Oh, he's not here,' Carmen said. 'He wouldn't dare come to a party like this. His wife might find out. Pity really, he's a lot easier to please than the bastards who'll be fucking me later on this evening. He pays me promptly, too.'

'And the people here don't?' Jacey asked.

'Carlos pays us,' Carmen said. 'Eventually. But it's like getting blood out of a stone. The girls are nice to people he owes favours to, or wants favours from, or whatever, and if we're lucky we get our money in about six months' time.' There was a touch of contempt in her voice. 'Good old respectable Carlos. We can hardly sue him, can we?' She gave Jacey a curious stare. 'But why are you here? Don't you know what goes on when Carlos and his stuck-up little wifey go home?'

'I heard things might get a little wild,' Jacey admitted.

'Wild?' Carmen laughed. 'This place turns into a whorehouse. Didn't anyone tell you that? And the wives of some of the guests are worse than we are. I'm not judging you, but it's not the kind of thing I think you'd enjoy.'

'I wouldn't,' Jacey agreed. 'But Peter asked me to come, and –'

'Peter Draven? Dr Draven?' Carmen sounded shocked. 'You're not serious? I mean, some of the young doctors at La Primavera, they've enjoyed themselves with us, you know, especially in that operating theatre. But not Dr Draven. He was always so decent. He actually asked you to this party? I'm amazed!'

'He did promise to take me home before things got out of hand,' Jacey explained.

'Why hasn't he?' Carmen demanded. 'Where is he, anyway?'

'He's gone,' Jacey said. She knew that Carmen would find out about her relationship with Nicolás before very long, and decided that she might as well forestall any gossip. 'Actually, I'm with Nicolás Schlemann now.'

Carmen stared at her with a look that Jacey realised was almost one of pity. 'Well,' she said, 'our Nicci didn't waste much time, did he?'

'I have to admit I didn't exactly discourage him,' Jacey said.

Carmen sighed. 'Why do so many decent women fall for that bastard? Men like Nicolás should simply pay for sex. He can't hurt whores like me; we don't matter. But you're an educated woman. Don't you know that Nicolás likes playing kinky games, and when he gets tired of you, he'll dump you? It usually takes him about four weeks. Six has been the longest so far.' She looked at Jacey with genuine concern. 'I think he gets a kick out of it, especially if he knows the woman still fancies him. I wouldn't want to see that happen to you.'

'It won't,' Jacey said. 'Believe me. I know all about men like Nicolás Schlemann.' Impulsively she caught hold of Carmen's hand. 'And don't put yourself down. Whores don't matter, indeed! There's not a lot of difference between you and me. We're both trying to make people feel better.'

Carmen smiled. 'Well, at least no one here will dare touch you.' She paused. 'Except maybe Raoul, and I'm sure you can handle him.'

'Raoul and Nicolás are two of a kind, aren't they?' Jacey said dismissively.

Carmen looked at her in surprise. 'No, they aren't. Haven't you met Raoul? He's a sweetie, a romantic. His only problem is that he's seen too many American movies. He thinks life is all about fighting the bad guys and getting the girl, you know?'

No, thought Jacey, I didn't know. That isn't how I picture Raoul Márquez. Certainly some of his romantic dialogue wouldn't have been out of place in a film. But I can't see him challenging Nicolás Schlemann, or daring to steal his woman, come to that. Getting someone else to bring a woman to him seems to be more his style.

The two women walked down the wide staircase together. The Latin American band had disappeared and noisy rock music was beating out from hidden speakers. But nobody was dancing. Jacey saw one woman being manhandled by two men. They were both trying to strip her, pulling down the straps of her dress, and fumbling with her breasts. Giggling, she pretended to fight them off. Finally they both hoisted her up off the ground, one of them holding her under her arms, and the other by her feet, and carried her up the stairs, while she shrieked with delight.

Carmen watched in disgust. 'Look at that. She's a stuck-up bitch who'd refuse to talk to someone like me. The wife of one of the Generalissimo's chief advisors.'

'Where's her husband?' Jacey asked.

'Probably fucking his latest boyfriend.' Carmen shrugged.

Jacey looked round at the guests. Everyone seemed to be shedding both their clothes and their inhibitions with equal speed. The music thumped even louder. Through the open door she could see couples, and groups, kissing and pawing each other.

'Aren't any of these people afraid of being black-mailed?' she asked.

Carmen laughed briefly. 'Who by? Nicolás? If he wants to destroy someone he doesn't have to bother with blackmail.'

A half-naked man ran past them, pursuing a young, totally naked, Indian boy. The boy had a smooth, brown body and straight, shoulder-length, black hair. His delicate limbs reminded Jacey of a young gazelle's. His pursuer caught up with him, pinned him against the wall, and began to kiss him roughly, starting with his face and then quickly descending lower. The boy leant back against the wall submissively, neither helping nor hindering, his face blank, as the man nuzzled between his thighs. As the boy gazed out into the room, for a brief moment his eyes caught hers but they were dark and expressionless.

A group of guests, men and women, appeared suddenly and when they saw what was going on, began to laugh and shout lewd encouragement. The boy's face remained impassive, as if they weren't there, but the man responded. He stopped his rough caresses and turned, joining in the laughter. 'You want him?' he invited. 'He's for sale. Come on, make me an offer. Highest bidder gets him!' Jacey was incredulous and what was more, felt embarrassed. She turned and walked away, and Carmen followed.

'Don't blame the Indian boys,' she said to Jacey. 'It's hard for them to find work in Techtátuan. They have to either whore, or steal.' She paused. 'They give most of their money to their families, you know? And the families are forced to spend it on the over-priced food that the government sends out to the reservations.'

'There are reservations for the Indians?' Jacey asked.

'Some,' Carmen nodded. 'There was a move towards resettlement, some time ago. But I don't think the Indians were given any choice. Their villages were flattened, and they had to move, because of a scheme to start logging, which came to nothing in the end.' She shrugged. 'I sometimes wonder what the Indians really think of us. It's hard to tell. But I'm not surprised that they want to change things.'

'By supporting Loháquin?' Jacey hinted.

'I wouldn't know,' Carmen said, quickly. 'I'm not political.' She gave Jacey a hard stare. 'And don't start talking about Loháquin to Nicolás. It won't make you very popular.'

'I can handle Nicolás,' Jacey said confidently.

'That's what all the other women have said,' Carmen warned her.

96

Maybe, Jacey thought. But I think I have an advantage over most of them. In their case, Nicolás Schlemann was using them. In my case, I'm using him. In more ways than one. I'll use his knowledge, and I'll use his body. I'm going to enjoy every minute of it!

Chapter Four

Jacey woke up, glanced at her clock, then turned over lazily in bed, and stretched. She wasn't on duty until eleven, and she intended to enjoy breakfast on her balcony before sending a message to Major Fairhaven. This time, she thought, she had something interesting to tell him. While Nicolás Schlemann might want to encourage Hernandez to exploit Guachtàl and all its resources, Lohàquin and his supporters clearly had other ideas. Whether they had the power to act as a serious opposition was another matter. Maybe this mysterious Lohàquin could depose Hernandez with some outside help, but she knew that such help would come with a price – and that would be the kind of price a political visionary might not want to pay.

Any government willing to support Lohàquin would have to be sure that he was a viable alternative to Hernandez and Nicolás Schlemann, not just an impractical dreamer, or the kind of man who could encourage a revolution, but not govern. More important still, they would have to be sure that he would keep the promises he made to them when he gained control of Guachtàl. I need to know much more about Loháquin, she thought. In fact, I need to meet him and make a first-hand assessment.

She knew that her main point of contact was someone like Paulo. He was a native Indian, and she was sure that his involvement with Loháquin went further than just giving verbal support. However, he was hardly likely to trust her once he knew that she was considered to be Nicolás Schlemann's new woman.

But she was already planning ahead. Nicolás had openly admitted to her that he was a power freak, and she remembered what Carmen had said: that he enjoyed discarding his women when he grew tired of them. It probably made him feel powerful. She had no doubt that their affair would be interesting, but short. How many weeks had Carmen given her? Four? Six at the outside? And when Nicolás dumps me, she thought, I'll make it clear I want revenge. After a public humiliation, no one will doubt me. Nicolás may have even given me a perfect excuse to win sympathy from at least a few of Loháquin's supporters. She smiled at her optimism. There would be a certain poetic justice in that, but in her heart of hearts she knew that it was unlikely; revolutionaries took a dim view of the mistresses of dictators and military men.

She went into the kitchen to make coffee, and toast some slices of the tasty, seeded bread that the hospital chef baked for the staff. Afterwards, as she showered and washed her hair, she thought about the message she had intended to send to Major Fairhaven. Perhaps I'll wait, she thought. I'll wait until I have something more than speculation. In my next report I may be able to tell him tell him I've met the mysterious Loháquin in person.

Jacey was dreading seeing Peter. She walked past

his office and noticed that the door was half open. Let's get this confrontation over with, she thought, and went in. But the office was empty, and looked unusually tidy. Surprised, she went to her own office, and prepared for her rounds. She finished them without seeing Peter, and met Dr Sanchez in the corridor.

'Ah, Dr Muldaire.' The elderly Spaniard gave her a charming smile. 'I was looking for you. Will you be able to cope on your own?'

Jacey stared at Sanchez in surprise. 'Isn't Dr Draven here?'

Sanchez was equally surprised. 'Didn't he contact you before he left? He had a call from England last night. A death in the family; a road accident, I believe. He had to catch an early plane.'

'He didn't say anything to me about it.' Jacey did not know whether to be relieved or angry.

Sanchez looked concerned. 'Perhaps he didn't want to worry you. And he did have to leave in a great hurry. He told me he felt sure you could carry on here without him.'

'Of course I can,' Jacey said.

Sanchez patted her arm. 'It won't be for long. I'm sure Dr Draven will be back soon.'

Jacey couldn't help feeling that Peter's return to England had come at a very convenient time. Perhaps he's ashamed of himself, she thought. And maybe he ought to be, if he really intended to pass me round to his friends like some kind of fancy treat.

After a few days she began to suspect that Peter had no intention of returning. Her suspicions were confirmed when she heard nothing as the time passed. He made no attempt to even send her an e-mail. She wondered if Dr Sanchez would ask her to take on Peter's patients on a permanent basis. She could cope easily, but longer hours at La Primavera would mean she had less time to spend at El Invierno, where she knew she was really needed.

The next morning, when she went into Peter's office before making her rounds, she was startled to see a tall, slim woman with sleek, blonde hair pulled back into a plaited knot sitting in front of Peter's computer.

'Dr Muldaire?' The woman's voice was seductively deep. 'I'm delighted to meet you.' She had a slight accent that Jacey couldn't quite place. 'Perhaps you can help me? Some of the patients listed here have OH next to them. What does that mean?'

Jacey hated being caught unawares. 'Where's Dr Draven?' she asked abruptly, not bothering to conceal her annoyance.

The woman looked surprised. 'He's gone to England. I thought you knew that.'

'I was expecting him back by now,' Jacey said untruthfully.

'But he's not coming back,' the woman said. 'He has resigned. Dr Sanchez was not pleased, I understand. I am his replacement, Ingrid Gustaffsen.' She looked suddenly concerned. 'They didn't tell you? Really, they are so inefficient. But typical of this country, don't you think? *Mañana*, always *mañana*. But tomorrow never comes.' She stood up and held out her hand. Jacey noted that she wore a very short skirt, and had long, slim legs. 'I hope we are going to be friends, Dr Muldaire.'

'I'm sure we will be,' Jacey said, coolly polite.

Ingrids's smile did not waver. 'If I'm to take over Dr Draven's rounds, perhaps you can give me some details about his patients? I can see that many of them are not seriously ill. But what is this OH?'

'None of the patients here are seriously ill,' Jacey said. 'And OH means On Holiday.'

101

Ingrid frowned. 'But they are still here. Are they planning to leave?'

'It was Peter's way of indicating that there was nothing wrong with them at all,' Jacey explained. 'They've come in to get away from their wives and enjoy the company of their girlfriends. Or boy-friends.' She smiled briefly. 'La Primavera is basically a hotel. If you're hoping to get a lot of clinical experience, I'm afraid you're going to be disappointed.'

Ingrid shook her head cheerfully. 'Oh, I'm not looking for clinical experience. I went from my train-ing hospital in Sweden to the States for five years. Good pay, but hard work. So I needed a rest.' She lowered her voice conspiratorially. 'I'm looking for a different kind of experience here. Do you understand me?'

'I'm afraid not,' Jacey said frostily.

'Oh, you English!' Ingrid walked round the desk to confront Jacey. 'Of course you know what I mean. You're fucking that horny guy, Schlemann, aren't you?' She leant forward and tapped a beautifully manicured finger against Jacey's chest. 'Don't deny it. I wouldn't mind doing it myself. Long legs and nice smile. I've heard he's a sexist pig and a fascist, but so what? I wouldn't want to marry him, and neither would you.'

'No,' Jacey said coolly. 'I wouldn't.'

But Ingrid was unabashed. 'So, tell me,' she asked gaily, 'what is he like? Lots of staying power? Person-ally, I am so bored with men who come too fast. I had several in America like that. A little bit of panting and groaning, and then it was "aaah, baby, that was great".' She laughed. 'Great for them, maybe. A fast orgasm is all some men want. But I like to feel a cock inside me for a long, long time. I can take it. I'm not made of Dresden china. And I'm fit. Very fit. I work

102

out. Pump iron. It was very popular with my friends in America.' She crooked her arm. 'Feel that. Feel the muscle.'

Despite herself Jacey reached out and felt Ingrid's biceps. They were rock hard.

'So?' Ingrid insisted. 'What do you think? Am I not strong?' She struck a typical body builder's pose. 'Do you think I should enter for Miss Universe?'

Jacey laughed. Ingrid's tall, slim body looked more suitable for the catwalk than a musclewoman's competition. 'I think you should start making your rounds,' she said.

'Do you like strong women?' Ingrid was suddenly serious. 'Would it excite you to make love to a woman with muscles like a man's?'

'No, it wouldn't,' Jacey said.

'You've never thought about making love to a woman?' Ingrid persisted. 'Many women have that fantasy, even if they don't do anything about it. You have never looked at a particular woman, and wondered what it would be like to have sex with her?'

'Never,' Jacey said truthfully.

'It can be very satisfying,' Ingrid said. 'Sure, men are interesting. I like their hard bodies, and there are times when I like to have a cock inside me. But for sensual pleasure, women are best. Women understand each other physically. Have you ever known a man who can give head properly? Men don't understand the clitoris. They don't know what to do with it. They try a few flicks of their tongue, or they suck at you so hard it's just ridiculous, and they call that foreplay. They think they are doing you a great favour, that they've aroused you.' She gave a dismissive snort of laughter. 'After a few minutes, they want to enter you, and then it's all over. Women are different. They understand each other, and they are not in a hurry.' She smiled invitingly at Jacey. 'To have a really good time, you need a woman to go down on you. Why don't you visit me tonight, and I'll show you what nice things you've been missing.'

'My God,' Jacey said, amused despite herself. 'Do you normally proposition complete strangers five minutes after you've met?'

'If I think they'll be interested,' Ingrid admitted cheerfully, 'yes, of course. Then it's up to them to take advantage. Many women do. You'd be surprised how many.'

'What made you think I would be interested?' Jacey asked.

Ingrid smiled. 'I can see it in your eyes. I think you're a very sensual woman, and curious. I think you'd like to experiment.'

'And I think you're indulging in wishful thinking,' Jacey said. She glanced at her watch. 'We ought to start our rounds. Even if our patients aren't exactly dying, they do expect to see us every morning.'

Later that day, relaxing in her room, Jacey found herself thinking about her conversation with Ingrid. Had she really looked interested in Ingrid's suggestions? Or was it simply that all the talk about oral sex had encouraged her to picture what she and Nicolás could both do to each other when they got together again?

The thought of an expert tongue exciting her to near orgasm was a pleasant one. But not Ingrid's tongue. I've had never had any lesbian fantasies, she realised. Even when Faisel turned out to be such a bastard, it didn't put me off men. It did put me off love and romance, all the stupid emotional baggage that makes women so vulnerable.

She leant back in her chair and wondered idly what Ingrid looked like without her clothes on. She was obviously fit, and her legs were enviably long, but she had no noticeable breasts, and her height and build would probably make her look like one of those lanky, androgynous fashion models. She imagined Ingrid striding naked with that typical model's walk, her ribs visible, and her pelvic bones jutting. It did not excite Jacey at all.

She closed her eyes and imagined Nicolás Schlemann. That's much better, she thought. She had not seen him totally naked yet, but she could easily assemble a composite picture from the parts she had already observed. The body, with its natural tan, hard with muscle. The lean thighs. The impressive cock and balls bulging from the glossy mat of dark pubic hair.

Then the phone rang. She picked it up, still daydreaming. 'Dr Muldaire?' The voice on the other end was lazily confident, slightly mocking. 'I hope you're not too busy to talk?'

'Well, you're the one who's obviously been busy,' she retaliated. 'I thought you were going to call me?'

'I'm calling you now,' Nicolás said. 'I want your company tomorrow night.'

'Not another party at the Márquez house?' she asked.

'Would that be so unpleasant? Didn't you enjoy the last one?' He sounded amused. 'I did. The last ten minutes of it, anyway.'

'You walked out on me,' she reminded him. 'After a quick fuck over a desk. And you haven't contacted me since. I expected something better from a man with your reputation, Señor Schlemann.'

'What did you expect? A dozen red roses and a thank you note?' He laughed. 'You've got the wrong man for that, Dr Muldaire. And I didn't walk out. I was called away on official business, remember?'

'Oh yes, you had to go and interview a suspect,'

she said, coolly and with a hint of sarcasm. 'That's your job, isn't it.'

'Part of it,' he agreed amiably. 'I'll send a car for you at eight.'

'I haven't accepted yet,' she said. 'Is this going to be another semi-official orgy?'

'It's a fully official formal dance,' he said. 'Politicos and military, and Hernandez and his wife. They'll all be there on their best behaviour. And looking forward to meeting you.'

'I'm flattered,' she said. 'I wasn't aware they even knew I existed.'

'Of course they do,' Nicolás said. 'The new, beautiful doctor with the flame-red hair, who actually doesn't mind getting her hands dirty at El Invierno? Everyone's talking about you.'

'Including the Generalissimo's wife?' she asked sweetly.

'Especially the Generalissimo's wife,' he said. 'She wants to meet you more than anyone. But I'm the one who'll be enjoying tender moments with you later, and they know that. Be ready when the car arrives. I hate being kept waiting.'

He rang off abruptly, and Jacey put the phone down. Well, she thought, what a charmer you are, Señor Schlemann. Then she smiled. And how useful you're proving to be. This will give me the chance to check out the Generalissimo, his formidable wife, and most of the other big names in Guachtàl as well. Yes, dear Nicci, this liaison is just what the doctor ordered – in more ways than one.

Knowing how her evening was going to end made it easy for Jacey to decide what to wear. She opened her wardrobe and let her hands wander briefly over the high-necked, low-backed silver beaded gown that hugged her figure so tightly it would show the tiny peaks of her nipples, and accentuate the cleft of her behind. That would give the party guests something to talk about. What a pity it was totally inappropriate. Instead she chose the designer gown, which also hugged her figure, but was nowhere near as revealing.

Made of heavy, very dark, green silk, it could be dressed up or down as the occasion demanded, and would always look right. This time she decided to dress it down. She felt certain the female partners of Guachtàl's military and political élite would be taking this opportunity to display their finery. She would be a contrast. Her red hair would stand out like a beacon above a body sheathed in plain, dark silk. If they expected Nicolás Schlemann's woman to glitter, they were in for a surprise. And if Nicolás doesn't like it, she thought, too bad.

She was aware that the dress would come off much later in the evening. She guessed that Nicolás would like frilly, feminine underwear. The tarty look – black or red probably – with suspenders, and stockings with seams. She remembered him saying something about liking his women to be 'decorated'. Like dolls, she reflected. That's undoubtedly how he sees us. Playthings. Objects of pleasure, to be used.

She saw nothing wrong in dressing up for sex. She had an erotic but uncomfortable bra, some impractical lacy underwear and some black-seamed stockings, a legacy from her affair with Anton. But with her underwear, like her gown, she decided to go for spartan formality. She did not need a bra with the ball-gown, which was beautifully cut and discreetly boned, and gave her a full, comfortable cleavage. She took out a pair of French knickers, tailored by hand from silk almost the same colour as her gown. She knew they fitted her perfectly, like a second skin, smoothing over her buttocks and pulling just tightly enough between her legs to emphasise her sex. Instead of a suspender belt she wore hold-ups, plain dark grey, with no seams. She chose black sandals, with medium heels and narrow, black straps.

To top all this, she was tempted to leave her hair loose. She knew it would look stunning; she would be the only natural redhead in the room. But again, she felt it was too obvious. Instead she made a semi-formal pleat, carefully pinned to look as if any strenuous activity would make it tumble to her shoulders.

She was ready when the car arrived for her. An official flag on the bonnet, and tinted glass windows that she suspected were bullet-proof, it was driven by one of Nicolás's cold-eyed thugs, who opened the door for her, but did not speak, and drove all the way in silence.

Because of the darkened glass she found it difficult to know where she was going, but when they arrived at the huge gates of the Generalissimo's official palace, she could see it clear enough, picked out by floodlights, and decorated with elaborate shields. The car stopped and a uniformed guard peered in. He looked at Jacey and, much to her surprise, jumped back and saluted. The car eased forward again until it reached the palace forecourt and stopped at the foot of a flight of white, balustraded steps that led to the palace doors. Impressively huge, they now stood open, and once she was out of the car Jacey could hear the sound of sedate music, voices and laughter.

The car cruised away, leaving her alone at the foot of the steps and she stood there for a full minute, feeling increasingly angry. Was she supposed to wait, or go inside and look for Nicolás? The night wind stirred her hair. Another car drew up and an elderly man with a plain-looking younger woman got out, passed her on the steps with an indifferent stare, and said nothing. Jacey's patience evaporated. She headed up the steps, rehearsing some cutting remarks with which to greet Nicolás when he finally appeared.

Inside, the couple who had just passed her were having their invitations checked by a large, plain-clothed, and slow security guard. The elderly man was clearly annoyed, but said nothing. Jacey waited in the marble-tiled entrance hall, under a huge chandelier, until the guard finally allowed the couple to proceed. When he did glance at her, she glared back, willing him to come and ask her for an invitation, or to challenge her in some way. At that moment she would have been delighted to take advantage of her association with Nicolás, and tell him exactly who she was waiting for.

'Good evening, Dr Muldaire.' She turned to see Nicolás coming towards her, tall and elegant in his black evening suit. The brilliant white of his shirt emphasised his tan. When he smiled she was irritated with herself; not only was she pleased to see him, but she felt a surge of sexual excitement as well. He offered her his arm. 'How very delightful you look. Not that I expected anything else. You're a classy lady, aren't you?'

She took his arm. 'For a man who doesn't like being kept waiting,' she said coolly, 'you're not very punctual, are you?'

'I didn't say I minded keeping other people waiting,' he said amiably. 'Particularly women.' He bent his head towards her and for a moment she felt his lips close to her ear. 'It makes them appreciate me just that little bit more. Don't tell me you weren't pleased to see me.'

'Only because I was getting tired of standing around,' she said.

He laughed. 'You'd only just arrived.' She opened her mouth to protest and felt his hand tighten on her arm. 'Don't deny it. I know exactly what time the car picked you up, and what time it arrived here.'

They moved further inside and past the couple she had seen on the steps. The elderly man's eyes flicked briefly from her to Nicolás, and back again. His expression changed from surprise to an ingratiating smile. His female companion also smiled, displaying her large teeth.

'Well,' Jacey said, 'that's not how those two greeted me earlier on. They looked right through me outside.'

'Now they know you're with me,' Nicolás said, 'they'll be polite to you. He's a local tradesman of some sort. Not important, but he served with the Generalissimo in the army years ago, so he gets invited here once in a while. The ugly girl is his daughter. Single, of course. Can you imagine anyone being stupid enough to marry her?'

'Beauty is more than skin deep,' Jacey said lightly.

'Not from a man's point of view,' Nicolás said.

They entered the ballroom and for a moment Jacey was overwhelmed by the combination of glittering light from the chandeliers, and the white of the marble floor. An orchestra played a slow, Spanish tune. Some of the guests wore decorative military uniforms, but the majority wore evening suits. The women were on the whole middle aged, and wearing heavily boned Spanish-style dresses, with boat neck-lines and long skirts lavishly decorated with frills. A few emphasised the Spanish theme of the evening with a lace mantilla and a large fan. All the guests turned as Nicolás strolled across the polished floor. The men acknowledged him with slight bows, or a deferential movement of their heads and the women smiled. Nicolás nodded back once or twice, with sardonic condescension.

Suddenly Jacey saw a face she recognised, one of her 'patients' from La Primavera. One, she remembered, who had been visited regularly during his stay by a series of good-looking young men. He inclined his head towards her, politely, as did the haughty-looking woman standing next to him. Jacey wondered how many more of her ex-patients were there tonight.

Nicolás seemed to be reading her thoughts. 'Seen anyone you recognise?'

'Yes.'

'Señor Controssna, with his wife?' Nicolás grinned. 'They're probably both thinking about their boyfriends. They used to share the same one. In fact they shared him with a lot of people. Until he started to get greedy and tried to blackmail the wrong client.'

'And what happened?' Jacey asked, finding it hard to imagine Señor Controssna and his frigid-looking wife in a *ménage à trois*.

Nicolás shrugged. 'He disappeared. And I doubt if anyone missed him, except maybe those clowns in the rainforest. It was rumoured he wanted the money to give to Loháquin.'

'You had him killed?' She was ready to challenge him.

'It was politically expedient to have him removed,' Nicolás corrected. 'That's what happens to anyone who supports the so-called rebels.' His fingers tightened round her arm. 'Don't ever forget that.'

'I'm sure you won't let me,' she said.

'It's for your own good.' He guided her forward. 'You women are so easily fooled by romantic ideas about freedom fighters and revolutions. The truth is, this Loháquin is a scruffy illiterate, and so are his followers. He couldn't govern Guachtàl, even if he was given the chance.'

That's exactly what I want to find out for myself, Jacey thought. Nicolás was guiding her towards a uniformed group standing apart from the others, and surrounded by plain-clothes security men.

She recognised Generalissimo Hernandez, but at close quarters this rotund little man in his braided, bemedalled uniform looked even less like a dictator than he had in the photograph Major Fairhaven had shown her. She was far more impressed by the imperious woman who stood a head and shoulders taller behind him. She guessed that this was the formidable Pilar. Unlike her husband, she looked perfectly capable of governing and perfectly capable of challenging anyone who opposed her, Jacey decided. No wonder Nicolás didn't like her.

'Generalissimo,' Nicolás said, 'may I present Dr Jacey Muldaire.'

Jacey felt a warm hand enclose hers. 'Dr Muldaire.' At least Hernandez sounded pleased to see her, Jacey thought. 'Dear lady, welcome to my home. Welcome to my country. We've heard so much about you.' He guided her forward and turned to his wife. 'Haven't we, my dear?'

Pilar gave Jacey a frosty smile. 'Your work at La Primavera has been commented on, Dr Muldaire.'

'Beautiful hospital, isn't it?' Hernandez enthused, patting Jacey's hand. 'Do you have anything like it in England?'

'Well, not quite,' Jacey admitted truthfully.

'Nicolás helped raise most of the money,' Hernandez said. 'Private subscriptions. People were very generous.'

'I believe you also do some work at El Invierno, Dr Muldaire?' Pilar Hernandez said unexpectedly.

'Well, yes.' Jacey nodded.

'El Invierno was funded from the treasury,' Pilar said, 'which explains the differences in the amenities.' Her dark eyes fixed on Jacey. 'My husband does try and fulfil the needs of the people.' Her eyes moved briefly but obviously over Jacey's shoulder to Nicolás, and back to Jacey again. 'When he is able.'

There was a moment's uncomfortable silence, then Hernandez gave a forced laugh, let go of Jacey's hand, and turned to his wife. 'Now, my dear, no politics tonight. No politics.'

And that, Jacey thought, probably says it all. The Generalissimo likes the parades, the social functions, and the roar of the crowd. And Nicolás gives him all that, in exchange for a free hand with the economy. A very nice arrangement. For Señor Schlemann.

She was aware that Nicolás was edging her away from the Generalissimo's group, and back towards the dancefloor. The band were playing a slow waltz and Nicolás swung her round to face him. Without asking her if she wanted to dance, Nicolás guided her in time to the music.

'Señora Hernandez seems rather frosty toward you,' she said. 'Did you oppose the building of El Invierno?'

'No,' he said shortly. 'I opposed the amount of money spent on it. Let's discuss something more interesting, please. Tell me what you're wearing under this expensive dress?'

'Certainly not,' she said. 'That's for you to find out.'

His hand moved against her back. 'No bra,' he said. An elderly couple waltzed by. Nicolás treated them to a charming smile. Jacey saw their eyes follow his hand, as it slipped down to her buttocks. They quickly looked away. 'No knickers?' he guessed.

'Wrong,' she said.

His hand moved up to the small of her back again. 'We'll spend precisely one more hour here, and then I'm taking you back to my apartment.'

'Won't the Generalissimo think that's rather impolite?' she asked. 'We've only just arrived.'

'I've fulfilled my part of the bargain,' Nicolás said. 'Hernandez wanted to see you. Now he has.'

'And everyone that matters knows that you've added the beautiful English doctor to your list of conquests,' she added. 'Congratulations.'

'I've done you a favour,' he said. 'You'll find doors will open for you now. You'll be invited to the best dinners, and the best parties. You'll have a good time.'

Until you drop me, Jacey thought. Then all the creepy little social climbers, and the people who have been nice to me because they're afraid of you, or want something from you, will ignore me, and start smiling at your next trophy. Who will it be, she wondered. Someone else from the hospital, perhaps? What about Ingrid Gustaffsen? Jacey found it difficult to believe that the Swedish doctor would appeal to Nicolás. She was too obviously strong-willed and too masculine.

The hour passed quickly. After the first dance Nicolás seemed content to let Jacey circulate on her own. It was as if he had put his mark on her, and felt quite confident that no one else would usurp his property. While he spent most of the time talking to some of the other male guests, she waltzed sedately with two of Hernandez's military aides (who kept their conversation carefully neutral and their hands immobile), and exchanged pleasantries with several old men, tactfully ignoring the way their eyes strayed along the curved edge of her neckline to the swell of her cleavage. She noticed Carlos Márquez and his wife on the edge of the dancefloor and they acknowledged her with polite nods and cool smiles. There was no sign of Raoul.

After almost precisely one hour, Nicolás strolled over to her and said, 'Time to go.'

As he escorted her across the dancefloor, she felt

114

the guests' eyes on them both. She suspected that he had waited until she was at the farthest edge of the ballroom before coming for her, to make a show of the fact that she was his. He's like a schoolboy, she thought, displaying his possessions. Look, but don't touch!

Despite the fact that he had mentioned taking her to his apartment, she half expected to end up at a palatial estate on the outskirts of town. Instead the car-ride was surprisingly short, and she quickly found herself outside a forbidding-looking official building with a façade of blank windows, and a large, national flag flapping on a jutting pole. The car eased round a corner and stopped. Nicolás got out and opened the door for Jacey.

From the pavement, the side of the building looked as grim as the front. She turned to Nicolás. 'You live here? It looks like a prison.'

'It is,' he said. 'And Police Headquarters.' He guided her to a blank, iron-reinforced door. 'I stay here when I'm in Techtátuan.' He smiled briefly. 'I never get burgled.'

He slotted a card into the external security lock and waited. When, after a few moments, the door swung open, Jacey smelt polish, and the faint tang of disinfectant, the smell of official buildings. Her footsteps sounded loud on the bare, stone flags as Nicolás ushered her down harshly lit corridors and up steps to another door.

Once through it, she was in another world. The floor was deeply carpeted, the lighting subdued and the walls papered in warm, burnt-orange silk. The door shut behind her with an ominously loud click. Startled, she glanced back at it.

Nicolás watched her. 'Yes, it's locked. But even if you tried to leave without me, you wouldn't get far.

My security card activated an internal alarm system, so we've been on camera all the way here.'

He opened another door and she preceded him into a room furnished with richly upholstered chairs and dark, carved furniture, much of it antique, she guessed. The walls, panelled with polished wood, were hung with a variety of pictures, several of them modern portraits. Nicolás lounged against a tall cabinet as she surveyed the scene. Over a huge marble fireplace – it looked rather out of place and was clearly never used – was a large oil painting of a slim man in a black suit and black shirt. He was clearly European, with slicked-back, pale hair, and an arrogant expression. Jacey thought the dark outfit looked far too much like an SS uniform. She suspected she knew exactly who this man was.

Nicolás confirmed her suspicions. 'My father. Heinrich Schlemann.'

'I can see a resemblance,' she said. 'And what about your mother?'

He pointed to a smaller portrait on the other side of the room. A slender Spanish girl in traditional costume stared solemnly down at Jacey. Señora Schlemann had clearly been much younger than her husband.

'She's beautiful,' Jacey said truthfully.

'She was one of the most beautiful women in Techtátuan, so I'm told,' Nicolás said. 'Apparently she was planning to marry a penniless Spaniard. My father persuaded her parents that he would make a much better son-in-law.'

Jacey gazed at the Spanish girl. How had she felt, forced into marriage with a cold and arrogant foreigner? Had she pined for her chosen lover? Had she ever been happy?

'What was your mother like?' she asked.

Nicolás shrugged. 'I've no idea. She died giving

116

birth to me. I was told my father had a choice, and he chose to save me.'

Jacey glanced at Heinrich Schlemann again. And I bet you didn't even agonise over the decision, she thought. You'd got what you wanted. A son to carry on the family name.

Nicolás turned and opened the tall cabinet. He took out a bottle and two glasses. 'Wine, Dr Muldaire?'

'It's about time you started calling me Jacey,' she said. 'And yes to the wine.' He filled a glass and handed it to her. 'Do you feel Spanish rather than German?' she asked. 'I mean, you were born here. Do you feel close to your mother's roots?'

He stared at her for a moment, and then startled her with a quick burst of laughter. 'Roots?' He shook his head in disbelief. 'I learnt my creed from my father: look after yourself. He knew Germany was going to lose the war and he deserted the sinking ship, before it was too late. If he'd believed in that "Fatherland" rubbish he'd have stayed home, and died young.'

'And if Guachtàl starts sinking?' she asked. 'Will you desert the ship, too?'

His laughter was more patronising this time. 'Guachtàl won't sink,' he said. 'Not while I'm in control of the treasury.' He went over to one of the large, padded armchairs and sat down. 'That's another thing my father taught me. A healthy respect for money. Because money ensures that other people have a healthy respect for you.' He lifted his glass to her in a mock toast. 'And he taught me how to treat women, of course. A very valuable lesson.'

She lifted her glass to him in return, and smiled. 'Your father was a compulsive womaniser too?'

'I've been told he never lacked for female companionship,' Nicolás said. 'Either before my mother died,

117

or afterwards. But compulsive? That implies lack of control. My father was always in control. And so am I.' He leant back in his chair. 'My father chose his women with care. He was a connoisseur. He used to bring them here, to this room. These walls have seen more sexual conquests than a brothel.'

Had all the women come willingly, she wondered. Were they seduced, or were they paid? Were any of them threatened or blackmailed? And if they were, did the element of coercion sometimes make it more exciting for both parties? Heinrich Schlemann was probably a sexist bastard, but judging from his portrait, he was not unattractive. Sometimes it was exciting to be coerced into sex by someone you were already attracted to. It took the responsibility out of your surrender, or the sin out of your adultery. She also knew that she was not immune to this type of excitement. She could tell herself that it was in her professional interest to let Nicolás think he had seduced her, but she could not deny that she was physically attracted to him, and she was finding it stimulating to mix business with pleasure.

'I had my first woman here, too,' Nicolás said.

'And how old were you?'

'Nearly sixteen.' He relaxed back in his chair and stretched out his legs, slightly apart. 'I was educated by private tutors. I had a desk by the window over there, and I had to be at the desk at eight o'clock sharp. It was just like being in a real school.'

'It couldn't have been much fun,' Jacey said. 'All on your own.'

He grinned lazily. 'It had its compensations. One of my tutors was a woman. She was young, probably in her early twenties. She wore very expensive perfume; it used to smell beautiful. I suppose if I'd had any sense, I might have wondered how she could afford it. At first she dressed very conventionally, in

118

a jacket and rather long skirt, but after a few days she started to wear those peasant-style blouses. You know the kind of thing? With a drawstring round the neck?

'She used to bend forward over me when she was correcting my work, and I could see the cleft between her breasts. I knew she wasn't wearing anything under the blouse. The string was getting looser, and the neckline was getting lower, and she used to smooth the cloth over her body, and pull it tight, so that I could see that her nipples were erect. I knew enough to realise that she was arousing herself by teasing me.

'I got a hard-on just thinking about her. Imagining her stripped to the waist, her hands tied behind her back, so that I could touch her anywhere I wanted, do anything to her that I wanted. I imagined her protesting, but really enjoying it. I imagined her naked, with her legs spread apart. While she was teaching me arithmetic, I was daydreaming about fucking her, and trying to prevent her from seeing the bulge in my trousers.'

'Poor boy,' Jacey teased, smiling. 'It must have been very uncomfortable for you.'

He grinned back, and shifted in the chair. 'It was. But not for long. I decided that if the game was cat-and-mouse, I'd prefer to be the cat. The next time she leaned over me to correct some mistake I'd made, I grabbed that blouse with both hands, and ripped it.' He paused. 'That was one of the most erotically satisfying moments of my life. She gave this startled yelp, and the cloth split, and I saw everything. The full round breasts, the hard, little nipples, and her shocked expression as she tried to cover herself.

'It was great. I felt powerful – and damned uncomfortable. Now I'd seen it all, I wanted to have it all. We ended up on the carpet, rolling around together.' He laughed softly. 'Right up to the end, I honestly thought she was trying to fight me off. I thought she was afraid because things had gone too far, got out of hand. Because I was in control now, and she knew she'd have to play the kind of games I chose.

'I managed to get one of her nipples in my mouth, and my hand up between her legs. I pulled her panties down to her knees, and then to her ankles. And then there she was, just like I'd always imagined, lying there naked, and making futile little protest noises, with her legs wide apart. And I was on top of her, with the best hard-on I'd ever had in my life.'

'You didn't feel sorry for her?' Jacey asked.

He laughed. 'I was fifteen. I just wanted it, and at that time I only knew one way of getting it.' He shrugged. 'And it was good. Probably one of the best orgasms I've had. Certainly the one I remember most clearly.'

'You raped her,' Jacey said. 'And I suppose you got away with it?'

He looked at her for a moment, then burst out laughing. 'I didn't rape her. I told you, she was asking for it.'

'She was teasing you. It was pretty irresponsible of her. But that didn't give you the right to force yourself on her.'

Nicolás stopped laughing. 'You just don't understand, do you? Perhaps I should have said, she was getting paid for it.' He leant back comfortably in his chair. 'She was a whore. My father paid her to make a man out of me. Or to see whether I was capable of behaving like one. After I'd proved myself, he let me go to all the whorehouses in town. He wanted me to learn what women were like.'

'And did you?'

120

'I learnt that women will give you what you want if you pay them,' he said. 'And they always have their own agenda.'

'Is that supposed to include me?'

'Of course.' His voice was suddenly cold. 'Very much so. Why else did you break with Peter Draven, and give yourself to me?'

For one horrible moment Jacey thought that Nicolás knew exactly why she had come to Guachtàl. And exactly how she was planning to use him during their relationship. But her apprehension did not show in her face.

'I wanted to find out if you were as good a stud as everyone said you were,' she said coolly.

'You knew I would be,' he said. 'Powerful men turn you on. For all your intelligence, and your smart job, you like to behave like a whore. You like to be treated like a whore.' He smiled coldly. 'Peter Draven would have bored you in a week. So you willingly dropped him for me. I'm exactly the right kind of man for you. Tell me I'm wrong, Dr Muldaire.'

'Would you believe me if I did?' she asked.

'No,' he said. 'I wouldn't. I know you better than you know yourself. Now, take off that dress.'

She smiled. 'You've been longing to say that all evening, haven't you?'

'I've been looking forward to seeing you do it all evening,' he agreed. 'I didn't get a chance to inspect you properly when we had our little tête à tête at the party. Now there's no hurry. Take the dress off.'

Jacey put her wine glass down, reached behind her back and tugged at her zip. She did it slowly, turning until her back was to Nicolás. The dress slipped off her shoulders, over her breasts to her waist. She turned again, slid her hands under the heavy, green silk of the skirt, and tugged it downwards, bending forward so that her breasts swung tantalisingly. The

121

skirt rustled as it reached her knees, and then her ankles. Pleased that the hold-ups were still in position, she stepped out of the dress, lifted it and placed it over the back of a chair.

'No suspenders?' He sounded regretful. 'How do those things stay up?'

'Elastic,' she said. She walked forward, stopped in front of him, and straddled his outstretched legs. Slowly and deliberately she lifted one foot and put it on the seat of the armchair. She ran a finger round the top of her hold-up, delicately easing the grey garter band away from her thigh. 'See?'

'Ingenious,' he said. But he was not looking at the stocking top. His eyes were on the cleft between her legs, where the damp, green silk clung to her inner lips as mute evidence of her own arousal. He put his fingertips on her stomach and pushed her backwards. 'Get them off,' he ordered, abruptly.

'The stockings?' she asked, deliberately misunderstanding.

He stood up and grasped her silky French knickers in both hands. 'Not the stockings.' One violent tug and the knickers were round her ankles. 'You can keep them on.' He stepped back and sat down again. 'They won't get in the way.'

'In the way of what, exactly?' she asked sweetly.

'They won't get in the way when I tongue you,' he said. 'Which is exactly what you're asking for right now, isn't it?'

He put his hands on her waist and pulled her towards him, so that she was forced to straddle his legs again. Then his hands slipped round to cup her bottom and pull her closer still. His lips touched her stomach, and she felt his tongue circling her navel, slowly, before descending to the red bush between her thighs.

'Open your legs wider,' he demanded. She felt the

122

warmth of his breath, and tried to obey him, but her feet began to slip.

'I can't,' she said. 'I'm sliding . . . falling –'

He pushed her back suddenly, and swiftly slid down to lie on the floor. 'Kneel over me,' he instructed.

She obeyed, her knees on either side of his shoulders. 'Your nice suit will get dirty.'

'To hell with my suit.' He grinned. 'Let's see how well you dance, Dr Muldaire.' His hands reached for her waist again, and he pulled her down until she faced him, her thighs spread above his face. 'Lower,' he said. 'I want to taste you.'

She leant forward over his head, and bent her legs until he could reach her, until she felt the insistent probing of his tongue. He lifted his arms and reached for her breasts, finding her semi-erect nipples, inciting them into harder peaks with rough fingers.

'Move,' he ordered. 'All the best whores know this dance.'

She expected him to just lie there and let her do all the work, but his tongue encouraged her, circling the tip of her clitoris, then tantalised her by sliding away and forcing her to gyrate her hips in erotic, choreographed movements, in order to bring him back to the spot that gave her the most pleasure. As she lifted her hips above him, briefly, she heard him say something, but she was barely conscious of anything except her need for release.

She felt him grasp her wrists and flip her suddenly over on to her back. He unzipped his trousers with one hand, and then she felt his knees between her legs, forcing them apart. His mouth nuzzled her neck and breasts, now with a lack of control. An animal noise came from the back of his throat; it was clear that his mind was on his own needs rather than hers. But she was so wet and aroused that his first thrust pushed into her deeply, filling her, exciting her with new sensations. Her own ragged breathing began to match his rhythm, but he seemed selfishly determined to postpone his own climax for as long as possible, without any thought for her. And then, suddenly, he withdrew. She moaned in frustration, her body limp. He turned her over, on to her hands and knees, his erection as strong as ever, and spread the cheeks of her bottom. One hand slid under her, finding a nipple, while the other sought her clitoris. She felt the sensations that had been slowly dissipating gather together in strength once more, building up to new peaks of pleasure. When he entered her, pushing between her buttocks, she heard herself gasping in tandem to each of his thrusts.

'Do you like it, Jacey?' His mouth nuzzled the back of her neck, his voice muffled by her tangled hair. 'Do you like it this way?'

She groaned in affirmation, surprised at how turned on this man made her feel. Again he withdrew, and again she was turned over. By now her body was sheened with sweat, and she felt as exhausted as if she had run a marathon. He slid his hands roughly under her buttocks, his fingers kneading her flesh, as he pulled her towards him. Through half-closed eyes she could see his face. He was smiling, and his black hair was dishevelled.

'Can Draven keep it up this long?' His voice was savagely triumphant. 'Do you want to come, Jacey?' His mouth was close to her ear. 'Ask me nicely. Beg me. You're exhausted, aren't you? I'll make you come, but you've got to beg.' He entered her once more, with a strong thrust. 'Otherwise I can keep going – for a very – long time.'

'I told you once,' she panted. 'I don't beg.'

She heard him laugh, and tried to contract her muscles and pull him deeper, forcing him into an orgasm against his will. He frustrated her by shortening his thrusts, making them shallow and fast. They battled for supremacy for a little longer, until Jacey suddenly felt an overwhelming desire for relief, even if it meant admitting defeat.

'Yes,' she groaned. 'Yes, please, now.'

His rhythm changed to accommodate hers rather than fight it, and she felt him search between her legs again with his long, expert fingers. Then the sudden intensity of her own orgasm blinded her to everything else.

As her sensations subsided she realised that he had climaxed with her. She had a strong suspicion that he had probably been nearer to reaching the end of his undoubtedly impressive staying power than he wanted her to believe. But after all, she felt so happily exhausted and fulfilled that she did not care which of them had won.

He helped her to a chair, and tidied himself up. She lay back and closed her eyes. She heard him open the wine cabinet, heard the clink of bottles and then felt him put a glass in her hand. She sipped the wine with her eyes still closed and sighed. This really was the best kind of exhaustion, she thought. How lovely it would be to be lifted into a wide bed, with fresh, white sheets, and fall asleep.

'The car will be round for you in five minutes,' Nicolás said. 'Put your dress back on.'

The abrupt order brought her sharply back to the present. She opened her eyes. 'So that's it?' she said.

He smiled at her cynically. 'What else is there, Jacey? I told you not to expect any romantics. This isn't that kind of relationship. You wanted sex, and so did I. Didn't you enjoy it?'

'Yes.'

He poured himself a glass of wine while she

struggled into her dress, the silk clinging to her damp skin.

'My women always do,' he said.

'Not another exciting invitation?' Ingrid perched on Jacey's desk as she opened her morning mail.

'Another boring invitation,' Jacey corrected her.

'It's amazing what having sex with the right man will do for your social life,' Ingrid observed. 'Please hurry up and finish with Nicolás Schlemann, and give him to me.'

Jacey laughed. 'I don't think Nicolás would approve of being handed over as a present,' she said lightly. To her surprise she found it impossible not to like Ingrid Gustaffsen. The Swede had already had brief flings with some of the patients in La Primavera, both male and female. She was also a very good doctor, and Jacey was trying to persuade her to spend some time at El Invierno.

'If I gave him good sex, Nicolás would approve. And I always give good sex.' Ingrid crossed her long legs. 'What does he like? Tell me, please. If it's something I have never done before, I'll go away and learn about it.'

'From what you've been telling me,' Jacey said, 'there isn't anything you haven't done before.'

'Oh, you're so flattering.' Ingrid laughed. 'But I know it's only because you want me to go with you to that funny little native hospital. It's guilt, you know? You slap on a few dressings to sublimate your guilt about the money you're earning here.' She stretched, and exhaled contentedly. 'Certainly, this is a sinecure. So many opportunities to fill up the piggy bank. Do you know how much Señora Ittápaz gave me to go down on her? I won't tell you, because you'll be envious, and wish you'd got there first.'

'I wouldn't,' Jacey said, opening another envelope.

'Poor woman,' Ingrid sighed. 'She is so bored, so frustrated. Her husband wanted her to walk around the house wearing only high-heeled shoes and stockings, and she refused. So now he doesn't touch her, and pays whores to do it instead. Personally, I would have obliged him. This is a warm country, after all, and I like to walk around naked anyway, so what the hell? The Señora wants me to visit her when she goes home, and maybe I will. Señor Ittápaz is hardly ever there. He has a plantation or something, somewhere or other, and he spends most of his time there.' She giggled suddenly. 'Perhaps he gets all his staff to walk about naked? Or maybe only the pretty ones?'

'A plantation worked by underpaid Indians,' Jacey said.

Ingrid shrugged. 'It's an unfair world. You can't change it overnight. It's too big, too complicated.'

'If everyone thought like that, there wouldn't be any changes at all,' Jacey said.

'But you're not a politician,' Ingrid said. 'Your job is to make people well.' She watched Jacey toss another invitation card into the wastepaper bin. 'And maybe enjoy yourself a little,' she added. 'Surely you can accept just one party invitation?' She paused. 'And invite me to come with you?'

Jacey laughed. 'OK,' she said. She waved an embossed card at Ingrid. 'This one. A polo match. A nice, healthy afternoon in the open air.'

'Well, that sounds great.' Ingrid obviously approved. 'Lots of rich, young men in very tight, white trousers. Will Nicolás be there?'

'In tight white trousers?' Jacey grinned. 'Maybe.'

'So you'll introduce me?' Ingrid hinted.

'Maybe,' Jacey said.

Jacey didn't even know where the polo ground was, but Ingrid had found out all the necessary details, and had arranged a car. She was slightly miffed when Jacey insisted on using Paulo as chauffeur.

'His car is an old wreck,' she said.

'It isn't,' Jacey said. 'It's clean, and Paulo needs the money.'

'You are a one-woman charity,' Ingrid grumbled. 'No doubt he will expect a large tip as well.'

Paulo seemed politely pleased to see Jacey again, but she sensed this was simply a business façade. Clearly he had heard about her association with Nicolás and, as she expected, it had altered their original relationship. Paulo was wary now. Despite working at El Invierno, she had placed herself in the enemy camp. But not for long, she thought; in a few weeks' time, everything will change. I won't be Nicolás Schlemann's woman. I'll be his nemesis. And I'll be looking to you, dear Paulo, to help me get revenge!

When they reached the polo club Jacey was amused to see Ingrid hang back and slip Paulo a handful of money.

'I doubt if Paulo expected quite that big a tip,' she murmured, when Ingrid caught up with her again.

'I was just ensuring that he will be here to take you home,' Ingrid said.

'To take us home, you mean?' Jacey said.

'I intend to go home with someone exciting,' Ingrid proclaimed. 'I hope to get off with a nice polo player.'

Given that ambition Jacey wondered why Ingrid had not dressed in a more feminine fashion. She was wearing a pale linen suit, tailored in a rather severe style, and a matching, wide-brimmed trilby hat. Combined with her long-legged, angular frame, it looked decidedly masculine. Jacey had chosen a summer dress in a subtly printed, silky material, with a fitted bodice and a flowing skirt that clung to her hips and legs when the wind stirred. Her hair was loose, and she wore a simple, brimmed straw hat to protect her head from the sun.

She had been rather worried that her outfit would look too casual, but when she entered the club she realised that she had made a wise choice. Most of the other women were in smartly casual clothes. Only a few of the older ones looked as if they were planning to attend a formal dinner party.

'Dr Muldaire.' A smiling, middle-aged man came towards her. 'I'm Enrico d'Osolo. We met at the Generalissimo's party. Do you remember? You were gracious enough to dance with me.'

'Of course I remember,' Jacey said. 'It was kind of you to invite me here today.' She saw Señor d'Osolo's eyes move to Ingrid. 'This is Dr Ingrid Gustaffsen,' she said. 'She works with me at La Primavera. She's very interested in polo.'

'Really?' Señor d'Osolo looked distinctly sceptical. 'Do you play, Dr Gustaffsen?'

'No,' Ingrid said cheerfully. 'I just find it exciting to watch all those men in boots. And with lovely whips too. Such fun.'

Thrown by this comment, Señor d'Osolo turned back to Jacey. 'Señor Schlemann will be playing, of course. His team is expected to win.'

'If Señor Schlemann is playing, I'm sure they will,' Jacey said. After d'Osolo had handed them drinks, and left them alone, Jacey turned to Ingrid, half angry, half amused. 'Shame on you, you embarrassed the poor man.'

'Nonsense,' Ingrid said. 'It got him hard. Didn't you see how he was walking when he left us? Now when he sees the polo players, he'll remember what I said, and he'll have a lovely fantasy of me being whipped by a sexy guy in boots.' She thought about it for a moment. 'Or maybe he'll imagine me in boots, whipping him.'

'It's more likely to remind him to ban you from coming here again,' Jacey said. She glanced round and saw a couple of large men near the door of the club room. She recognised them as Nicolás's heavies. 'See those two over there,' she murmured to Ingrid. 'If you don't behave, I'll get them to throw you out.'

'Really?' Ingrid looked over Jacey's head and surveyed the men. 'You mean those apes in suits? Who are they, anyway?'

'Security,' Jacey said. 'They work for Nicolás.'

'They have a sort of primitive charm,' Ingrid said. 'I wonder what they're like in bed?'

'Dr Muldaire,' a familiar voice said, in English. 'Please tell me you've forgiven me?'

Jacey turned, and found herself face to face with Raoul Márquez. He was kitted out for polo, and she had to admit that he looked extremely attractive. She could tell from Ingrid's smile that the Swedish doctor thought so too.

'Why should Jacey have to forgive you?' Ingrid asked curiously.

Raoul treated her to his most charming smile. 'I offended the doctor. I was overcome by her. I forced myself on her.'

'And that offended her?' Ingrid marvelled. 'How bizarre.'

Raoul smiled, but before Ingrid could ask any more questions Jacey interrupted firmly: 'I've forgiven you, Raoul. It was all a misunderstanding, anyway.' She smiled brightly. 'This is my colleague, Dr Ingrid Gustaffsen. She works at La Primavera with me.'

Raoul held out his hand. 'I have heard of you,' he said. 'The beautiful doctor with hair like spun gold.' He held on to her hand, and gazed at her soulfully. 'If I am injured today, will you take care of me?'

'Even if you are not injured,' Ingrid offered. 'I'm a very good nurse. A very good surgical nurse.'

It seemed an odd remark to make, but Jacey sensed that Raoul somehow understood what it meant.

'You are a liberated lady,' he said. 'But I am a romantic. I like to make love in a large, four-poster bed, with the windows open and the moonlight streaming in.'

'Well, I could enjoy that too,' Ingrid said. 'In fact, it would be quite a novelty.'

Jacey pushed her empty glass determinedly into Ingrid's hand. 'Ingrid, be a dear and get me another drink.'

Ingrid took the hint, and wandered away. Jacey turned back to Raoul.

'Listen,' she said, 'it's true I was angry with you at the party, but that's all in the past. Did you know that Peter's gone back to England, and I'm with Nicolás now?'

'Everyone knows you're with Nicolás,' Raoul said dolefully. 'I can't imagine why. You could have had me. Why were you so angry with me?'

'I don't like being manipulated,' Jacey said.

He looked at her in surprise. 'I wanted to make love to you. Is that manipulation?'

'Peter was very anxious for me to be at that party,' Jacey said. 'He wanted to push me into bed with you. And you probably put him up to it. That's manipulation.'

'I know nothing of Peter's motives,' Raoul said. 'I only know my own.' He gazed at her again. 'I would not insult you by treating you as if you were a commodity to be exchanged between two men. I am deeply hurt that you should think this of me.'

Jacey stared at him. She had a feeling that he was being honest with her. She remembered Carmen praising Raoul. What was it she had called him? A sweetie? A romantic? A man whose only problem was that he had seen too many movies, and thought life was black and white, a battle between the good guys and the bad guys? She remembered how she had rejected this description of Raoul at the time. Now she wondered if it was much nearer the truth than she wanted to believe.

'Perhaps I've been unfair to you,' she conceded.

'You have,' he agreed, 'if that's what you thought of me. But misunderstandings can be forgiven. Now, maybe, we can be friends?'

'Just good friends?' she teased gently.

'Of course,' he said. 'I am capable of friendship with women. I would ask you to dine with me, but I am certain Nicolás would not approve.'

'I'm sure he wouldn't,' Jacey said. 'You two aren't exactly friends, are you?'

'We are mortal enemies,' Raoul said dramatically. 'Today we will battle it out on the polo field. In the future – who knows? Governments are not indestructible.'

'You're not thinking of opposing Hernandez?' Jacey asked.

'Hernandez is a fool,' Raoul said. 'A weak fool. But he is not evil. Nicolás Schlemann is another matter altogether.'

'Nicolás has a lot of power.'

'The Márquez family have been in Guachtàl much longer than he has.' Raoul's voice was suddenly cold. 'And they will be here long after he has gone. Believe me.'

'Aren't you taking a risk, telling me all this?' Jacey asked. 'I might report you.'

Raoul laughed, and the mood between them lightened. 'You wouldn't do that. You are too beautiful to be treacherous.' He shrugged. 'And you wouldn't be telling Nicolás anything he doesn't already know.'

'So you would support Loháquin?' Jacey asked. 'You'd support a revolution?'

Raoul laughed again. 'I support my country. I am a patriot.' He glanced up at the clock. 'And I am also the captain of my team. I must go.' He took her hand and kissed her fingers theatrically. 'Will you forgive me when my team defeats your lover's?'

'I've been told Nicolás is going to win,' Jacey said.

Raoul shrugged. 'If the best man wins, as you say in England, it will obviously be me. We shall see.'

Ingrid wandered back to Jacey. 'What a cute guy,' she said. 'It's a pity he talks like a bad romantic novel. Was that nice bulge all genuine cock and balls?'

'I've no idea,' Jacey said.

'Surely you've fucked?' Ingrid sounded surprised. 'Didn't he say he forced himself on you?'

'He tried,' Jacey said. 'But I said no.'

'Are you crazy?' Ingrid shook her head in disbelief. 'He's beautiful. Think of the fun you could have, dressing him up as a woman.'

Jacey stared at her in disbelief. 'That would be fun?'

'Oh, yes.' Ingrid nodded. 'It's very sexy. Have you never played that game? Men love it. You know those very conventional men, in their suits and ties and their polished shoes? They love to be put into stockings and suspenders, and lots of frilly things. Make-up, too. I had a guy in the States who got a hard-on just talking about it, and really it was very difficult getting the silk panties on him. I had to scold him. Make him behave.' She grinned wickedly. 'A nice paddle across his bottom. It works wonders. I can whack very hard. Maybe I should have been a dominatrix instead of a doctor.'

'I don't find men in drag very sexy at all,' Jacey said. 'If I was expected to make love to a man in a dress, I'd probably start laughing.'

'What's wrong with laughing?' Ingrid shrugged.

133

'Who says you have to be serious when you fuck? And believe me, you would fuck. It's an amazing turn-on to see a guy in women's underwear, doing whatever you tell him. It's like having a slave. They're so anxious to please. And your friend would look perfect; he's far too pretty to be a man. I'm sure he would like to play kinky games with me.'

They heard clapping, and moved over to the large window. The two polo teams were already on the field. It was difficult to make out faces at that distance, but Jacey thought she recognised Nicolás.

'Let's sit outside,' she said.

They found themselves a table under the shade of an awning. A waiter appeared with a tray of drinks and bowed deferentially. 'With the compliments of Señor d'Osolo, refreshment for Dr Muldaire and Dr Gustaffsen.'

'Well,' Ingrid said, arranging her lanky frame comfortably. 'This is the life, don't you think?' The polo ponies thundered past. Ingrid glanced at them. 'Do you understand what this funny game is about?'

'Not really,' Jacey admitted. 'They play so many chukkas, and score goals.'

'Like football, but on a horse?' Ingrid shrugged dismissively. 'Very exciting, I'm sure. Let's talk about something more interesting. Like your pretty friend. Your pretty, rich friend.' There was a sudden polite cheer and burst of clapping from the crowd. 'Maybe someone has scored a goal,' Ingrid guessed. 'Bravo. Your friend is rich, isn't he?'

'I believe so,' Jacey said. 'But I'm not sure I'd call Raoul my friend.'

Not yet, anyway, she thought. But he soon will be. If Loháquin has supporters among the upper classes, and Raoul knows something about him, I shall certainly have to cultivate his friendship.

Ingrid said: 'The ponies have stopped galloping

about. I wonder why? Do you think someone has been hurt?'

'It's the end of the first chukka, Señorita.' The waiter passing behind them had overheard Ingrid's remark. 'The players will rest for three minutes, and then play again for seven.'

'So you don't have to run over and administer your skills as a doctor,' Jacey murmured, after the waiter had gone. 'And while we're on the subject, what did that comment about surgical nursing mean?'

'Doctors and nurses,' Ingrid said. Jacey looked blank, and Ingrid prompted: 'At La Primavera.' She stared at Jacey. 'Are you going to tell me you have never played those games?'

'I don't know what you're talking about,' Jacey said. But she suddenly recalled something else that Carmen had said to her. Something about the young doctors at La Primavera enjoying themselves in an operating theatre, but Peter being too 'decent' to be involved. 'Unless it's got something to do with an operating theatre?' she hinted.

'Of course.' Ingrid nodded. 'That special operating theatre with the viewing gallery.'

A nasty suspicion was beginning to form in Jacey's mind. 'I didn't know that operating theatre had a viewing gallery,' she said.

Ingrid looked at Jacey curiously. 'Do you mean to say you've never watched the girls playing nurses with those frustrated old men? I have to admit, it isn't always interesting; sometimes they just fuck. But often they are asked to use the rubber tubes and the dildoes, and the electric clamps. And sometimes the old men want to play at being doctor instead of being nursed. They can be most inventive. And if you know the right people, you can get an invitation to watch.'

'I don't think I'd want to,' Jacey said rather primly. But she had a sudden clear picture of herself in the sparkling clean operating theatre. A picture of herself submitting to Peter Draven's exploring hands. With her trained memory, she distinctly recalled a snippet of their conversation. She had jokingly protested that it was hardly the time or place for a medical examination, and Peter had said something about it being 'exactly right'.

Now that comment made sense! The bastard, she thought. She remembered lying back on the operating table, thinking how bright the lights were, and fantasising that a group of medical students were looking down at her. But that was my personal fantasy, she thought furiously. I was in control of it. The idea that she probably had been watched, without her permission, made her angry.

She also remembered that Peter's technique had lacked control, in contrast to his performance on later occasions. Was that because he found the idea of a hidden audience almost too stimulating? Or should she give him the benefit of the doubt? Maybe he was embarrassed. But in that case, why agree to perform? Who put him up to it? And who was watching?

Until that afternoon she would have suspected it was Raoul. But she no longer thought that likely. Raoul's romanticism was clearly genuine, if unusual. She did not believe he would indulge in underhand, voyeuristic tricks. But Nicolás Schlemann would.

For the next hour, Jacey found it difficult to concentrate either on the polo, or Ingrid's conversation. The more she thought about it, the more convinced she became that she had been used as a sexual puppet, to amuse a hidden viewer. When the game finished her anger had reached boiling point. She hardly noticed Señor d'Osolo when he came up behind her.

Tapping her on the shoulder, he handed her a note. 'From Señor Schlemann, Dr Muldaire.' He smiled obsequiously. 'I believe he wishes to give you an opportunity to congratulate him.'

'His team won, did it?' Ingrid asked.

'Of course,' d'Osolo said.

'Do you think that pretty little friend of yours let him win?' Ingrid asked Jacey, after Señor d'Osolo had left them.

'Raoul wouldn't do that,' Jacey said. 'Definitely not.'

'Your sexy Nicolás does seem to get his own way around here,' Ingrid commented. 'Jacey, do you want me to wait for you?'

'Of course,' Jacey said shortly. She glanced at the note. 'Nicolás is in the members' bar. I'll just tell him how marvellous he is, and I'll be back.'

'Now, now,' Ingrid chided, grinning. 'That's no way to talk about your lord and master.'

'Considering he didn't even bother to invite me to see him play,' Jacey said tartly, 'he's got a nerve to expect me to rush over and compliment him.'

The members' bar was noisy and crowded when she reached it. Some of the players, with their girl-friends and wives, were grouped round a buffet table, good-naturedly discussing the game. The conversation stopped, rather disconcertingly, as Jacey pushed through the swing doors. The crowd parted to let her through.

'I'm looking for Nicolás,' she said.

'Of course you are.' One of the polo players smiled condescendingly at her, and she took an instant dislike to him. He pointed to a door. 'Through there, Dr Muldaire.'

Jacey found herself in a corridor, panelled in dark wood. There was another door directly in front of her. She opened it into a changing room, as darkly-panelled as the corridor, the walls crowded with framed photographs of polo matches.

Nicolás was lounging against one of the polished wooden lockers. His polo shirt was damp with sweat, and his knee-high boots were spattered with mud. Despite his dishevelled appearance, the sight of him gave her a sexual thrill. His tight, white breeches clung to his body like a second skin, emphasising his lean thighs and the very noticeable bulge of his penis.

Jacey deliberately kept her eyes on his face. 'I've been told I'm supposed to congratulate you,' she said tartly.

'Congratulations are in order,' he agreed. 'We won. But that's not why I asked you here.' He leant back against the locker and slowly unzipped his breeches. As she watched, he disengaged himself from the support pouch he was wearing, and stood in front of her, cupping his balls. He was semi-erect. 'Come here,' he said.

Despite herself, she took a step forward. 'For God's sake,' she said. 'The door isn't locked. Someone might come in.'

He smiled briefly. 'No one will come in. They know I'm here, and they know you're here. And they know why.' He ran his fingers up and down his cock. 'Get on with it, doctor. Use your mouth.'

Jacey moved closer. She told herself that it was part of her plan to humour him, but she knew very well that she was going to enjoy it. She could smell leather, and the musky, masculine scent of his sweat. His overpowering maleness was an extremely potent aphrodisiac.

She knelt down in front of him and took him in her mouth. She felt his body shudder as he parted his legs and leant back. She moved her lips, caressing him with her tongue.

'That's right,' he muttered. 'Nice and slow. Make it last for me, Jacey.'

She tried to oblige him, but his excitement built up

much more quickly than she expected. Suddenly his hands were on her head, holding her close, while his hips pushed forward, almost against her face. He filled her mouth, and her throat, and for a moment she felt suffocated. Then his orgasm rocked him, and she heard his groan of relief.

It took him a moment to recover. Unselfconsciously, he tidied himself up, and then grinned at her. 'To the victor the spoils,' he said. 'That was just what I needed.'

'Just as long as you don't expect me to do the same for all the other victors,' she said.

He put his hands on her shoulders and she felt the strength of his fingers biting into her flesh. 'Would you object?' She saw a gleam of excitement in his eyes. 'You like behaving like a whore, don't you?'

'I like to choose who I share my body with.'

'You'll do it with a man you've only just met,' he persisted. 'That's what a whore does.'

'A whore does it for money,' Jacey said. 'It's work. If I do it with a man I've just met, it's for pleasure. Because I fancy him. It's my choice.' She stepped back out of his grasp. 'My body. My choice.' Suddenly her well-trained memory kicked into gear again. 'You accused me of that before,' she remembered. 'Of not minding if I serviced a man I'd just met. Why?'

'You fucked Peter Draven quickly enough,' he said. 'In the operating theatre at La Primavera.'

'You were watching us?' She felt her anger rising once more. 'What a disgusting trick.'

He shrugged, and laughed. 'I'm a busy man. I can't afford to waste time on someone who isn't going to be worth it. I like to see my women in action, before I try them out myself.'

She slapped him without thinking, across his face. The blow was harder than she intended; it snapped his head back, and sounded like a pistol shot. She immediately regretted her impulsiveness. What if he retaliated? She knew he was quite capable of doing so; he would not have any chivalrous notions about not hitting women.

In that case, should she use her training to try and defend herself? Perhaps resistance would infuriate him. And she wasn't even sure if she could handle him if he attacked her. She had been taught to take a victim by surprise, and kill him, not to stand up to a fully grown man in a raging temper.

In that brief moment, as she stood in front of him, and saw him lift his hand to his face and shake his head slightly as if to clear it, she realised how vulnerable she was. Here in Guachtàl, Nicolás Schlemann was the law. He could probably have her murdered, and get away with it. He could block any investigations. A few diplomats might make angry noises. A file would be opened. There would be an insincere promise of an investigation. Weeks would drag into months, and the file containing details of her case would gradually find its way to the back of a shelf, where all the other unsolved cases mouldered.

Then Nicolás smiled with a sinister expression in his eyes. 'I really don't deserve that. Peter Draven was quite happy to oblige me by putting on that little performance. And he didn't mind obliging me by bringing you to the Márquez party either.'

'Suppose I'd chosen Raoul instead of you?' Jacey challenged.

The smile returned. 'I wasn't afraid of that, Dr Muldaire. Raoul would bore you. I've told you before, you need a man like me. And you know it. You come running when I call you, because you enjoy it.' He opened the nearest locker. 'And now I must get changed. I have a meeting with Hernandez in an hour.'

140

'And how about a meeting with me? From my point of view, this one hasn't been very satisfying.'

He smiled at her condescendingly. 'I'll call you. When I have some time to spare.' He slung a towel over his shoulder. 'Make sure you're available. I don't like being kept waiting, particularly by women. And especially when I want sex.'

Chapter Five

Jacey's anger simmered for the next few days. It hurt to have her suspicions about Peter Draven confirmed. Whatever his reasons, he had used her. She would have broken off their relationship herself, if it had become necessary to do so. But she would have had a legitimate excuse: she was not a free agent. She needed information, and she had to take any opportunity she was offered in order to get it. And I would have made it a gentle break, she thought. Peter had no excuses. He had left without an explanation. I trusted him, and he used me. Like Faisel, she realised.

She did not want to remember Faisel, but she could not banish the memory now her mind had dredged it up. At their last meeting, Faisel was sitting between his glacially beautiful mother, and his Savile Row suited father. Faisel listening mutely as his parents spelled out her fate. He let them calmly tell me how they intended to ruin my life, she thought. She had hated him, then. Wondered why she ever found him attractive. Wondered how she could have believed she was in love.

She remembered the cold, hard knot of anger in her stomach, when she realised that she was powerless. Faisel's family could do what they liked. She was in a foreign country, and alone. She had felt naked and helpless. It was horrible, frustrating, and infuriating. She made a vow never to be put in that position again. In the future she would always be in control of her own life.

She had also been determined never to fall in love again, either. It had been an easy resolution to keep in the early years. The pressure of work kept her from thinking about the past. She took up her studies again, qualified, and became an overworked junior hospital doctor. There wasn't much time for romance during that period, even if she had wanted it. Most of her leisure time was spent sleeping. She had a few one-night stands with fellow doctors, but they meant nothing. Anton had been her first steady relationship, and she had been honest with him about not wanting a long-term commitment.

She leant back in her chair, and sighed. Not that he had taken any notice. He could not accept the idea of a woman who did not want to get married. He would probably have made a good husband, she thought. She tried to imagine waking up and seeing him every morning. Chatting about work, discussing what they were going to do that evening. Anton would probably take his lead from her, accept what she wanted. And perhaps that was the problem, she thought. He was far too nice. If I had to live with him, I'd be bored to tears in a couple of months. Perhaps Nicolás is right; I need someone unpredictable, I need excitement. I need a dominant man for sex, and I need freedom in my everyday life. And I don't want to be used by men whenever they feel like it.

To relieve her feelings, she slammed down a medical chart on her desk. Ingrid came through the door.

'Oh dear,' Ingrid said. 'A touch of PMT?'

'I don't suffer from PMT.'

'Then it's frustration.' Ingrid perched on the edge of Jacey's desk. 'You miss your sexy boyfriend. You want to give him another blow job, maybe?'

'No, I don't,' Jacey said, 'and I wish I hadn't told you about that.'

'You think no one knew? All those people in the members' bar knew. And I've been hearing things about your Señor Nicolás. Treating women like whores gives him a kick.' She leaned towards Jacey. 'You are tense. You need to relax. Come on, forget about Nicolás. Come out with me this evening. I know a very nice little club. We can have a few drinks and a dance.'

'I'll think about it,' Jacey said.

'About eight o'clock.' Ingrid stood up. 'And we'll use your little Paulo as a chauffeur, to ease your social conscience. OK?'

Jacey did not think any more about Ingrid's offer until later that afternoon. She had to admit that she did feel edgy. She had been remembering far too much about her past, and about Faisel. It can still hurt me, she thought, even after all these years. I thought I'd come to terms with it, but it's like a wound just waiting to be reopened when I least expect it. Will it haunt me for the rest of my life? Will I ever be able to forget?

Perhaps an evening out would be a good thing? she wondered. Although knowing Ingrid's liberal sexual orientation, she would probably end up in a lesbian hideaway, or a bisexual's S&M dungeon.

In fact later that evening, she realised her worries were unfounded. Ingrid took her to a discreet club, where a local band played sixties and seventies ballads. The couples moving gently round the small dancefloor were young, and smartly dressed. This

144

was Techtátuan's professional middle class, Jacey guessed. The food, a selection of local dishes, was delicious.

'What do you think?' Ingrid tucked into a bowl of mixed vegetables, spiced with an aromatic sauce. 'Wonderful, isn't it? The best vegetarian food in town.'

'It's very good.' Jacey had chosen an omelette, cooked to perfection.

'You like this club?' Ingrid munched contently. 'I love the music. It reminds of when I was at school.'

'It's very nice,' Jacey said. 'Not what I expected.'

'What did you expect?' Ingrid poured herself another glass of wine.

'Something a little more – unorthodox,' Jacey said tactfully.

'Oh? Lesbians with strapped-on dildoes?' Ingrid grinned. 'Do you think I'm only interested in sex?'

'You do give that impression,' Jacey admitted.

'To be honest,' Ingrid said, 'I wouldn't know where to find a lesbian club in this town. And I don't think I'd want to. I get enough sex at La Primavera. Here, have some more wine.'

By the end of the evening Jacey felt pleasantly light-headed. Several couples, recognising Ingrid, had come over to talk. They greeted Jacey politely enough, but she sensed a certain reserve in their attitude. Later, when Paulo had dropped them both off at La Primavera, she mentioned it to Ingrid.

Ingrid shrugged. 'It's because you're Nicolás Schlemann's woman. They're afraid of you.'

'He's the one with the power,' Jacey said, more sharply than she intended. 'I'm just his current entertainment.'

Ingrid looked at her, and then smiled. 'You can't blame them for being cautious. You know Señor Schlemann's reputation.' She put her hand lightly on

Jacey's shoulder. 'Come into my room for a nightcap. I'll mix you something special.'

Without really thinking about it, Jacey let herself be guided into Ingrid's apartment. She sat on the settee while Ingrid went to a cupboard, took out some bottles, and mixed two drinks.

'Do you know who told me about that club?' Ingrid handed a glass to Jacey, but did not sit down. 'Your pretty friend, Raoul Márquez.'

'Really?' Jacey was surprised. 'You're not going to tell me you've added Raoul to your list of conquests?'

Ingrid shook her head. 'No. He is a nice young man, but quite wrong for me. I would be very bored with all that romantic nonsense. If I want to fuck a man, I do it, and that's that. I don't want to receive red roses and poetry.' She moved behind the settee, and put her hands lightly on Jacey's shoulders. 'But maybe that's what you would like? Someone to make you feel special? You know, you won't get it from Nicolás Schlemann. Why don't you exchange him for Raoul? He would make you much happier.'

'That's not what I would like,' Jacey said shortly. 'The last thing I want in my life is a romance. Nicolás is absolutely right for my purposes at the moment. Good sex, and no strings.'

She felt Ingrid's fingers kneading her flesh. 'So your life is fine? Then why are you tense?'

'I'm not,' Jacey said abruptly.

Ingrid said: 'Did I tell you I once worked as a masseuse? When I was a medical student, I needed the money. I was a real masseuse. I did not give quick hand jobs.' She laughed suddenly. 'Not very often, anyway.'

Despite herself Jacey felt her body relax. Ingrid's fingers were strong, but soothing. The wine, and Ingrid's nightcap, had made her drowsy. She closed her eyes, and her body rocked slightly as Ingrid worked on her neck and shoulder muscles. She was not really aware of exactly when Ingrid changed position, moving to sit next to her. She simply felt Ingrid's hands, palms flat, massaging her chest, making circular movements.

'No –' Jacey protested, without much conviction.

'Yes,' Ingrid insisted softly. 'It will make you feel good.'

Jacey realised that Ingrid was right. She did feel good. Relaxed, and strangely sexy. Ingrid's hands smoothed over her breasts, gently now. It was quite unlike any sensation she had ever had before.

'Now,' Ingrid said, 'if you want me to stop, you must tell me. Then we will say good night, and that will be that. I will not be offended.' Her fingers lingered near the buttons of Jacey's blouse. 'I find you attractive. I want to make love to you. But you have to want it, too.'

'I . . . don't know,' Jacey murmured.

Ingrid opened her blouse. She touched Jacey's nipples, massaging them softly through her cotton bra. 'Tell me to stop, and I will.'

Part of Jacey's mind prompted her to leave, but her body told her something different. She did not want the massage to stop. Ingrid's caresses were both soothing and pleasurable. She felt Ingrid tug at the thin straps of her bra, loosen them, and then unfasten the clasp at the back. Then Ingrid was kissing her, first on the neck and shoulders, and moving down to her nipples. Moving slowly, as if she was enjoying the taste of Jacey's skin. Her hands felt quite unlike a man's. They lingered, exploring. Her mouth closed over one nipple, and her tongue circled it gently. Her other hand cupped Jacey's breast and massaged it. Jacey closed her eyes and sighed, curiously divorced from reality. Sleepy and warm. So sleepy, in fact, that she wondered vaguely if Ingrid had put more than alcohol in her 'nightcap'.

She felt Ingrid's hands become rough and more demanding. It broke the mood, and when she opened her eyes, she was startled to see that Ingrid had removed her linen jacket and cotton shirt, and was naked to the waist. Her body was angular and muscular, and her breasts small. With her blonde hair tied back, she looked distinctly masculine. Her hands reached for the waistband of Jacey's skirt, and at the same time she leant forward and kissed Jacey on the lips. The kiss, and the sight of Ingrid's androgynous body, dispelled Jacey's lethargy. She sat up quickly and her action caused Ingrid to jerk back.

'No,' Jacey said. 'I'm sorry – but no.'

Ingrid looked hurt rather than angry. 'I thought you were enjoying it.'

Jacey felt confused, and a little guilty. She had been enjoying Ingrid's caresses, without actually connecting them to the thought of any kind of follow-up sex. The massage had been pleasant: even the touch of Ingrid's lips on her nipples had not repulsed her. Perhaps, she thought, that was because I had not really been picturing Ingrid there. I was just enjoying the sensations. But the sight of Ingrid's body had brought her back to reality. She felt no desire to touch Ingrid, or indeed to have Ingrid touch her, in any more intimate way.

And if she let Ingrid continue, she knew very well what would follow, knowing Ingrid's predilection for oral sex.

'I'm sorry.' Jacey reached for her blouse. 'I'm sorry, but I can't –'

She was surprised to see Ingrid smile. 'That's all right. I'm sorry too. But we are both adults. If this is not for you, then we will never mention it again.'

'You must think I'm the worst kind of tease,' Jacey said.

'No.' Ingrid shrugged. 'Sometimes you don't know what you want until you try it. I have always liked women, but I wasn't sure about men. Then I fucked a few, and decided that I could like that, too. It was different, but still good.' She stood up unselfconsciously and reached for her shirt. 'The important thing is not to be ashamed. And to be honest. You have been honest, and we will still be friends.'

Despite Ingrid's apparently graceful acceptance, Jacey found it difficult to believe that her rejection would not put a strain on their relationship. But the next morning Ingrid greeted her as cheerfully as ever, and later that week handed her a heavy vellum envelope which turned out to contain an invitation from Carlos Márquez.

'A garden party?' Jacey read the invitation and looked up at Ingrid in amazement. 'Why is Carlos inviting me to a garden party? I didn't think he even liked me.'

'He probably doesn't,' Ingrid said. 'But Raoul does, and the invitation comes from him. He has invited both of us.' She smiled. 'You should feel complimented. Normally such an invitation would cost you several weeks' wages. It's a fundraising party, to send food parcels to the forest Indians.'

'Carlos is involved in that?' Jacey asked in surprise.

'It's a tradition,' Ingrid said. 'Started by his mother. She must have been an interesting person. It's a pity she died. I would have liked to meet her.'

'I met her aunt,' Jacey remembered. 'She said Juanita was still alive.'

'Well, perhaps she is,' Ingrid said. 'She was never found, was she?'

'It's easy enough to lose a body in the rainforest,' Jacey said.

'Yes.' Ingrid nodded. 'Nicolás Schlemann could certainly arrange it.'

'Why would he want to?' Jacey asked.

'He doesn't like opposition,' Ingrid said. 'And especially not from women. I was told that after her husband died, Juanita made no secret about giving money to Loháquin's followers. That was brave of her, don't you think?'

Jacey was immediately interested. 'Very brave, if it's true. It could be a rumour.'

'Well, the fundraising for the food parcels is true,' Ingrid said. 'Clearly this lady wanted to help the Indians.'

Jacey tapped the invitation card against her palm as she thought. If Juanita Márquez really was involved with Loháquin, Raoul might know more about the elusive rainforest rebel than he was willing to admit. He's clearly forgiven me for snubbing him. Perhaps I should start to cultivate his friendship. And when Nicolás gets tired of me, I'll have a willing shoulder to cry on, and maybe a lead to Loháquin, too.

Having only seen the Márquez villa at night, Jacey realised she had totally misjudged the extent of the grounds. They were far larger than she expected. A huge marquee, liberally decorated with flowers, housed a buffet and bar. A band played under an elegant, striped canopy. A wooden dancefloor, surrounded by poles festooned with fairy lights, had been laid over the grass. Several couples were already dancing to gentle, traditional tunes.

Jacey had tried to sound Paulo out about the food parcels, and found him unimpressed.

'Yes, it is a kind idea,' he admitted. 'Señora Márquez was a kind lady. But these Indians only go hungry because they are forced to live in reser-

150

vations. They are people of the rainforest. If they were left in the rainforest, they would not need help to eat.'

'So why were they moved?' Ingrid asked.

'Because they were in the way,' Paulo said. 'There were many rumours that the trees would be cut down.'

'But it didn't happen,' Jacey said. 'There hasn't been any logging in Guachtàl. Why haven't the Indians been allowed to go back?'

She saw Paulo's hands tighten on the wheel. There was brief silence before he replied. 'Because it will happen. It is only a matter of time. Those who want to make money out of the trees will make it happen. When the roads are built, the trees will be destroyed, and more Indians will be moved. Perhaps my village, too. And then there will be no rainforest left.'

'And Loháquin opposes this?' Ingrid asked.

'Many people oppose it,' Paulo said. 'Not only Loháquin. Not only the Indians. Many people.'

'But it will make your county prosperous,' Ingrid said.

'It will make certain people prosperous,' Paulo answered.

'Like Nicolás Schlemann?' Ingrid suggested.

'Certain people,' Paulo repeated. 'But not the poor people. And not the Indians.' Despite some gentle probing, he refused to discuss the matter any further. Jacey saw his eyes in the rear view mirror glancing towards her now and again, and knew her presence was making him uncomfortable. That's what you get for being Nicolás Schlemann's woman, she thought.

Later, as they mingled with the party guests, Ingrid said: 'Do you really think the Indians will benefit from any of this?'

'If Raoul has anything to do with it, they'll get their

151

food parcels,' Jacey said. 'If you can call that a benefit.'

'I'm sure they'll adjust to their new life,' Ingrid said, 'in time.'

'They shouldn't have to adjust,' Jacey responded angrily. 'They should never have been forced to leave their villages in the first place.'

'Your good friend Nicolás would probably argue that this is progress,' Ingrid said tartly.

'I'd call it vandalism,' Jacey answered. 'There must be a better way to boost the economy than by destroying something irreplaceable.'

'Don't let Nicolás hear you say that,' Ingrid said lightly. 'I'm sure he'll get a lovely handout from the men who build the roads, and from those who do the logging.'

Jacey knew that this was probably true. And the chattering guests, who had bought the expensive tickets to attend this charitable party, would also probably benefit from new roads and a timber industry. What a lot of hypocrites, she thought angrily.

Another thought occurred to her. What about the British government? Why did Major Fairhaven really want information about the political situation in Guachtàl? Because he would have to advise the government on whether or not the country was an economically sound proposition for investment. We're all as bad as one another, she thought, feeling suddenly depressed. Now I know how Loháquin must feel.

'So you both managed to find time to visit our little jamboree?'

Jacey turned, and faced Raoul Márquez. He was dressed in an elegant, pale linen suit, with an open-necked shirt, as if he was about to pose for a glossy fashion magazine. He kissed Jacey's hand, and then

152

turned to Ingrid. 'Are you going to make me a happy man? Are you going to stay with me tonight?'

'You don't want a wicked woman like me,' Ingrid laughed. 'I would corrupt you.'

'But I would enjoy that,' Raoul said earnestly.

Jacey glanced over Raoul's shoulder and saw a tall, slim young man walking towards them. His body looked loose and coltish under his pale suit, but unlike the self-assured Raoul, he gave the impression that he had dressed hurriedly, and felt slightly uncomfortable in his smart clothes. His hair was thick, straight and black and his face had a vulnerable look that Jacey found surprisingly appealing.

Raoul turned round to follow Jacey's gaze. 'What kept you so long?' he asked the young man in Spanish. 'Carlos has been asking for you.'

'Well, now I'm here,' the boy said sullenly.

'Let me introduce you to my little virgin brother,' Raoul said, continuing in Spanish. 'Ladies, this is Leonardo, who hates being sociable, and is still young enough not to care who knows it.'

'I don't mind being sociable,' Leonardo said. He stared hard at Jacey. 'I just care who I'm sociable with.'

'Shake hands with Dr Muldaire,' Raoul said, 'or you'll have me to answer to.'

Leonardo held out a slim hand to Jacey.

'I'm delighted to meet you, Dr Muldaire.'

'You're a very bad liar,' she said, sweetly. 'What have I done to annoy you?'

She wondered why she found his unsmiling mouth so desirable. She had never been attracted to anyone younger than herself before, but his finely drawn, slanting eyebrows, his smooth natural tan, and his narrow, almost feminine hands, were all surprisingly seductive. He looked untouched, unspoiled and petulant. She felt she wanted to shake him. Or, she thought, surprising herself, strip off his clothes and spank him.

'He's an idealist,' Raoul said. 'You know what it's like when you're young?'

Jacey smiled at Raoul. 'I thought you were an idealist, too?'

Raoul looked suddenly serious. 'I am.' He held her gaze. 'But I'm sensible enough to know who my real enemies are. Leonardo hasn't yet learned how to make that distinction.'

Leonardo had already shaken hands with Ingrid, and treated her to a brief smile. He turned back to Raoul. 'Must you always make me sound like an idiot?'

'If you dislike Dr Muldaire simply because you don't approve of some of her friends,' Raoul said, 'you are an idiot.' He smiled suddenly and patted his brother on the shoulder. 'Go and find Carlos, and then go and be nice to Aunt Ana. And stop looking so miserable.' After Leonardo had walked away, he added, in English: 'Don't you have an expression "a pain in the neck"? That's how I sometimes feel about my dear little brother.'

'He's not so little,' Ingrid said. 'And he's rather sweet. Is he really a virgin? Maybe I should educate him?'

'Dear Dr Gustaffsen,' Raoul said, 'it would be much nicer if you would educate me.'

'You don't need educating.' Ingrid laughed.

'Does Leonardo approve of Loháquin?' Jacey asked. 'Like your mother?'

Raoul shrugged. 'Leonardo approves of anything he thinks is unconventional. And anything he thinks will annoy Carlos and Schlemann. In that respect, he is certainly like my late mother.'

And maybe he could furnish me with the lead I'm looking for, Jacey thought. Either a direct lead to

Loháquin, or someone who can provide me with one. I need him to trust me, and unfortunately he won't do that as long as I'm with Nicolás.

After Raoul had left them to chat to other guests, and Ingrid was commandeered by a vivacious-looking woman, Jacey wandered off on her own, hoping to see Leonardo. She caught sight of him several times, but always at a distance. Then, when she least expected it, she turned to see him standing close by, staring across at her. He quickly looked away, but for an instant their eyes met. His expression was angry but also had a hint of curiosity. He doesn't dislike me as much as he pretends, she thought.

She decided to shadow him until she was able to corner him. She smiled to herself. Then she could accuse him of following her. That would annoy him, and maybe make him defensive but at least it would start a conversation. Given an opening, she could charm him.

She told herself she was doing this purely to gain information, but she knew very well that she was also going to enjoy it. No doubt Leonardo's brothers, and his Aunt Ana (and his mother, when she was alive) had spoiled him silly. Now someone would have to teach him how to act like an adult. She would enjoy proving to him that he shouldn't judge people too hastily. She would enjoy getting him to eat out of her hand.

As Leonardo moved away, and she prepared to follow, her mobile phone rang. For a moment she could not place the gentle trilling sound. It was the first time anyone had contacted her on the mobile since she started work at La Primavera. Her mind immediately switched from the pleasure of Leonardo to work. Convinced that it must be an emergency, she mentally listed her current patients. None of them had any life-threatening illness. She held the phone to her ear.

A familiar voice said: 'Good evening, Dr Muldaire.'

'Nicolás?' She was startled, then angry. 'This number is for emergencies only. What exactly do you want?'

'You,' he said, 'of course.'

'I'm at a garden party,' she said.

'I know where you are,' he drawled. 'I always know where you are. And I also know where you'll be in about twenty minutes.'

'Still here,' she said.

'In my apartment,' he corrected. 'I have something for you. A car will collect you in about five minutes.'

As she started to protest, the phone went dead. She wondered briefly what would happen if she refused to go with Nicolás's driver when he appeared. He could hardly pick her up and carry her. She did not believe that even Nicolás would dare to give that kind of order.

She glanced round. Leonardo had disappeared. There'll be plenty of time to pursue that lead later on, she thought. Nicolás had aroused her curiosity. What did he have for her? A present? She rather doubted it. Not after what he had already told her about the kind of relationship he wanted. She managed to catch sight of Ingrid and wave to her, and was looking round for a last glimpse of Leonardo when she saw the large, dark-suited security man walking towards her.

'You're leaving us, Dr Muldaire?' Carlos Márquez stopped her as she reached the edge of the crowd.

'I have another engagement,' Jacey said.

She saw Carlos look first at the security man, then back at her. A chilly smile touched his mouth. 'Of course.' He paused for a moment. 'You met my brother Leonardo, I believe?'

156

'Very briefly,' Jacey said. She smiled. 'I don't think he approved of me.'

'He's young,' Carlos said. 'The young sometimes have foolish ideas.'

So that's why you've condescended to speak to me, Jacey thought. You're worried that your little brother has been indiscreet. She kept smiling. 'We didn't discuss any of his ideas,' she said, 'foolish or otherwise.'

'Good,' Carlos said. He stepped back. 'Good evening, Dr Muldaire.' He paused. 'I hope your next engagement is an enjoyable one.'

'Oh, I'm sure it will be,' Jacey said, sweetly.

At Police Headquarters, the driver used his own card to open the iron door, and preceded her down the stone-flagged corridors until they reached the entrance to Nicolás's apartment, where he left her. She walked down the carpeted, silk-walled corridor to the panelled living room. Nicolás was lounging in a leather armchair. He was wearing a dark, formal suit, and a tie, and looked as if he was about to go to a board meeting. He glanced at his watch.

'Congratulations,' he said. 'You must have come straight here.'

'Did I have a choice?' she asked.

'Of course,' he said. 'You came because you wanted to.'

'I came because you said you had something for me,' she said.

He smiled. There was a box on the table next to him. He tapped it with one finger. 'Take this into the next room. When you open it, you'll know what to do. Then come back to me.' He shifted in the chair. 'And don't be too long.'

She took the box without a word, and went out into the corridor. One door stood half open. She went through it and found herself in an old-fashioned bathroom, with a huge bath standing on clawed feet, and brass pipes running round the walls. The floor tiles were black and white squares, and there was a full-length mirror fixed on the wall.

She opened the box. The first thing she took out was a bright, red blouse, made of a shiny material. It had a deep scoop neckline, and was liberally decorated with frills. She held it against her body, not sure whether to laugh or be angry. The next item was a very short skirt made of imitation leather, with a buttoned front. Then she found a pair of silky black stockings with fancy seams, a leather-look suspender belt, and some black patent shoes with absurdly high stiletto heels and narrow ankle straps.

She did not need an explanatory note to know that he wanted her to put these clothes on. She looked round the room, wondering if there were any hidden spyholes. Was he watching her? She thought not. There would be no point. He was going to see all he wanted of her very soon.

She removed her dress, and hesitated about her bra. Another look at the red blouse confirmed that it was not designed to be worn with any kind of underwear. She picked up the suspender belt, and then looked in the mirror. Her plain, stretch cotton briefs looked absurdly prim. After a moment, she slipped them off. Clearly this outfit did not go with functional Calvin Klein underwear. She rolled on the stockings, spent some time straightening the seams, then stepped into the tight, button-fronted skirt. Finally she strapped on the high-heeled shoes. They were an excellent fit.

She practised walking in the shoes – they were much higher than she had ever worn before, and then stopped in front of the mirror. Her hair was still folded into a neat French pleat. She loosened it and let it fall to her shoulders. Almost without thinking, she adjusted the blouse so that the neckline exposed most of her breasts, then posed with one hand on her hip, her legs apart, forcing the lower buttons on the fake leather skirt to pop open.

You look like a tart, she thought, amused at her unfamiliar image. She knew this was exactly what Nicolás intended. It was another way of exerting control. He had turned her into the kind of woman he felt comfortable with. A woman who offered herself for money. A woman who would do what she was told. Sex with no ties. And isn't that exactly what I want, too? Jacey thought. The fun, without the emotions? She turned, inspecting herself from all angles. I'll play the whore for Nicolás, if that's what turns him on. Let's see if he likes the woman he's created.

She walked back into the dark-walled room, even darker now that the light outside was failing, and saw Nicolás still lounging in the armchair. Now he had a bottle and a whisky glass on the table next to him. She posed in front of him, the same pose that she had tried out in the mirror.

'Is this outfit supposed to be a present for me?' she asked sweetly. 'Or for you?'

He took his time inspecting her. Finally he said: 'For both of us. Come here.'

She walked towards him, the stilettos making her both shorten her stride and swing her hips. He stood up, and caught hold of the waistband of her skirt. 'You've got this on the wrong way,' he said. 'Turn around.'

She turned, and he tugged the skirt round her, so that the buttons ended up at the back. She felt him opening them, and the cleft between her buttocks was exposed.

'Part your legs,' he ordered.

159

She obeyed. He traced the division between her cheeks, following it down from the base of her spine until it curved between her thighs. 'Do you like dressing up?' he asked softly. 'Most women do.' He pulled her closer until she was astride his lap. 'It's a kind of freedom, isn't it?' He leant forward and reached up to cup a breast, searching for the nipple beneath the silky, red blouse. 'Freedom to be someone else.'

She felt both nipples tighten as he played with her, lightly at first, and then harder, pinching her flesh. His other hand explored between her legs, up towards her clitoris, and she gasped sharply as his fingers slid over her moist and sensitive flesh. He rubbed her gently, and then with increasing pressure, and she felt the familiar sensations stirring in her body, the delightful tension, the ache for release. His breathing quickened as he felt her react. 'It doesn't take much to turn you on, does it?' he murmured.

'Not when you do that,' she replied.

He laughed and stood up. Somehow he managed to manoeuvre her towards the nearest armchair, while keeping his hand between her legs. She expected him to swing her round, and maybe encourage her to use her mouth on him, or perhaps to straddle him so that he could use his tongue on her. Instead he bent her over the arm of the chair, then gripped her waist and hoisted her roughly upwards into the position he wanted, her face pressed against the chair's leather seat, her bottom jutting into the air.

His fingers returned to the moist warmth between her legs. He played with her soft flesh for a few more minutes, before he unzipped himself and entered her, easily and quickly. She was so relaxed and wet. His weight pinned her against the chair and she felt captive and helpless. She was surprised to realise

160

how much she enjoyed this sensation; she could surrender to his strength and have his total physical attention. He half withdrew, and then thrust again, using her selfishly now, intent on his own climax, and she heard her own gasps matching the rhythm of his harsh breathing.

His fingers dug into her waist, holding her. As his excitement mounted she tightened her internal muscles, squeezing him each time he pulled back. At the same time she reached between her legs with one hand and worked herself, rubbing her clit furiously, determined to indulge her sensual self for both their pleasures. She heard him groan once, then his body began to shudder. At the same time, her own climax gripped her, and she writhed beneath him. For a brief moment his full weight crushed her, and the air rushed from her lungs in a cry of relief and consummation.

She hardly felt him lifting her up and turning her round so that she slumped in the chair. She realised that she was panting as if she had been running, and her hair was damp with sweat. She closed her eyes and took several deep breaths. Her body relaxed. Then a glass was pushed into her hand. Without thinking she took a mouthful and choked as the fiery liquid stung her throat. She heard Nicolás laugh. 'What a way to treat good Scotch whisky.'

She looked up at him. His face was sheened with sweat, and his hair was dishevelled. 'I thought it was wine,' she said.

He sat down opposite her, and smiled. 'That was very satisfying.' He swallowed a mouthful of whisky. 'As good as any whore I've ever had. You look that part, and you act the part. Very satisfying indeed.'

'So why not just get the real thing?' she asked.

'Why pay, when I can get it free?' His eyes assessed her again. 'And where would I find a whore as good-

161

looking as you?' Then he glanced at his watch. 'You'd better get changed. The car will be here for you in about five minutes.'

'You arranged it in advance?' She could not keep the anger out of her voice.

He looked surprised. 'Of course. I knew how long I was going to be.'

She stood up. 'That's a little cold-blooded, isn't it?'

He looked at her for a moment, and then shrugged. 'Did you expect us to sit and hold hands?'

'I expected something more than wham-bang-thank-you-ma'am,' she said.

He smiled lazily. 'I seem to remember warning you not to expect a romance.'

'Ten minutes or so spent talking to me would hardly constitute a romance,' she said.

He gave her a mocking smile. 'What would we talk about, Dr Muldaire? Do you think we have anything in common?'

'Maybe,' she suggested, 'we could try and find out?'

He laughed indulgently. 'Why do you women always want the illusion of a relationship?' His smile turned suddenly cruel. 'Make the most of what you have. You can never be sure of how long it will last.'

'Why do you put up with it?' Ingrid asked. 'I don't understand you.'

Jacey shrugged. 'He's a very attractive man. You said so yourself. And he gives me a great orgasm.'

'His body is attractive,' Ingrid agreed. 'But to be called, and fucked, and sent home? That is degrading. You are letting him control you. Is this what you really want?'

'He isn't controlling me,' Jacey said lightly. 'It's just a fantasy thing. We're playing games.'

'Nicolás Schlemann does not play games,' Ingrid

162

said. 'Dump him. Give him a taste of his own medicine. There are plenty of men out there. If they're not good at sex, you can teach them.'

'I like Nicolás,' Jacey said. 'I don't want anyone else.'

But it was only partly true, although Jacey didn't want to admit that to Ingrid. She enjoyed sex with Nicolás, and she intended to stay with him until he dumped her, and gave her the chance to play the woman scorned. But when she had an idle moment, and was able to let her thoughts wander, she found them centring more and more on Leonardo Márquez. Why? she asked herself. Ever since the nightmare with Faisel, she had never been attracted to younger men, and Leonardo was at least ten years her junior. Furthermore, there had been something innocent about him that made her sure he was a virgin and she had never liked inexperienced men. So why Leonardo Márquez?

After Ingrid had left the office, Jacey leant back in her chair and recalled the time she had noticed Leonardo watching her. He was sure he wouldn't like me, she thought, but he found me interesting. That must have confused him. And maybe excited him? She remembered the way his hair had fallen forward, a heavy, uneven fringe that almost reached his eyebrows. She remembered the delicate slant of those brows, and the slightly petulant mouth. Then she remembered Ana Collados describing Juanita Márquez's Italian lover as tall and thin, and rather shy, commenting that her niece was besotted with him for at least a year. If he looked like his son, Jacey thought, I can understand exactly what she saw in him.

She tried to imagine Leonardo without his clothes. Not completely nude, but in an interestingly brief bathing slip. He would lack Nicolás's taut strength. His body would be more angular, but his tan would

163

probably be darker, and, if he had any body-hair, that would be dark too. She imagined the ridges of his ribs would be visible. His stomach would be flat, but not yet hard with muscle. His legs would be long and lean, and his bottom small. And his cock and balls? She smiled.

They protruded attractively from between his thighs in the bathing slip she had mentally dressed him in and their weight strained the narrow holding thongs. She imagined cutting them, snapping them, letting all that enticing flesh bulge free.

Leonardo would probably try to cover himself. She would grasp his wrists and force his hands apart. He would have to stand there, naked, while she inspected him. Despite his embarrassment, being forced into that position would excite him. His cock would swell and rise, and he would blush and apologise. And, she thought, smiling to herself, she would thoroughly enjoy his humiliation. That would teach him to judge her arbitrarily. Maybe she would even pretend to be angry with him. She had a tantalising vision of him bending over, his neat bottom exposed and ready, perhaps quivering a little in anticipation, and then her own hand landing flat on it, in a satisfying flurry of slaps.

She realised, in surprise, that it was arousing her. She had never really been interested in sexy spanking games before, apart from the one occasion with Anton. But now the scene was in her mind she found it difficult to dislodge. Wriggling in her chair, she felt herself growing moist and warm at the idea of disciplining Leonardo, and her imagination began to invent other scenarios, mostly ones which involved her ordering him to take his clothes off, or where she stripped him herself.

The telephone suddenly interrupted her reverie.

'Dr Muldaire? Jacey?' For a moment she did not

recognise the voice. 'I hope I haven't caught you at an inconvenient time?'

'Raoul?' She dismissed all thoughts of Leonardo from her mind. 'I'm just about to start my rounds. Is this important?'

'To me,' he said. 'I'm coming to La Primavera to visit a friend. I have a personal favour to ask of you.' As if sensing her rejection, he added quickly, 'Not for myself. It's for Leonardo.'

Later, when Raoul was sitting in front of her in her office, as beautiful as ever in a dazzling, white open-necked shirt, and immaculate sand-coloured chinos, Jacey could hardly believe what she was hearing.

'But your brother doesn't even like me,' she protested. 'He won't want to come and take English lessons from me.'

'He will,' Raoul said. 'Actually, he reads quite well already, but he hasn't had much chance to practise his conversation. All you would need to do is talk to him.' He smiled. 'It might improve his manners as well.'

'Your English is excellent,' Jacey pointed out. 'Surely you could coach him?'

'I don't have time,' Raoul said. He leant forward. 'Jacey, my little brother will kill me if he discovers I've told you this, but he actually asked me to approach you. I think he's fascinated by you.'

Jacey masked her surprise. 'Oh, I see,' she teased. 'You're acting as a matchmaker.'

Raoul smiled. 'I'm sure Leonardo would be shocked at such a suggestion. He's an innocent. I don't think he'd know what to do with a real woman.'

But I know what I'd like to do with him, Jacey thought, after Raoul had arranged a date for her first meeting with Leonardo. Rather than visiting the Már-quez villa, Jacey preferred that Leonardo came to La

165

Primavera. 'It'll save time,' she said. 'And stop any tongues wagging. Leonardo could always say he was visiting friends.'

'If you're worried about Nicci finding out what you're doing,' Raoul said, 'he will anyway.'

Jacey shrugged. 'Nicolás won't be jealous of Leonardo.'

He'll be sure that I couldn't possibly find a younger man like Leonardo sexually attractive, she thought. And up until now he would probably have been right.

Although she found Leonardo physically appealing, the thought of holding him at arm's length was surprisingly seductive. She liked the idea of being obvious about what she had to offer, but withholding an invitation for him to take advantage of it. She knew very well that he would not force himself on her; he would sit there and suffer. She could tease him, and enjoy watching him getting uncomfortable. She had never had sexual control of that kind before. She began to look forward to giving Leonardo his first lesson, and wondered whether he was anticipating it with as much pleasure.

In fact, when he arrived at her room, he looked cross rather than eager. He was dressed in a lightweight suit, and a shirt and tie, and carrying a zipped leather folder. He asked, in Spanish, if he could take off his jacket, and when she nodded, he removed it slowly. Once again she admired his loose-limbed body. His waist was so narrow, she thought she could span it with her hands. He looked like a healthy young colt. His trousers were smartly casual, and not tight enough for her to see through fabric what she hoped to see in the flesh later.

Having taken rather too long to arrange his coat over the back of the chair she had positioned for him, he sat down, hugged the zipped folder close to his body like a shield, and fixed her with a reproving gaze. 'This was my brother's idea,' he said in Spanish.

'Speak English,' she said abruptly. 'And put that folder on the floor.'

'I have brought paper,' he said in English. 'I might like to take notes.'

'You don't need to take notes,' she said. 'Put it on the floor.'

He hesitated, and then put the folder down. Without it he suddenly looked vulnerable.

'Now talk,' she ordered.

She saw his lips tighten, and wondered again why she found his mouth so sexy.

'What do you want me to talk about?' It sounded like a challenge.

'Good heavens,' she said crisply. 'Talk about anything you find interesting. Films, books, food. Anything.' She very nearly said politics but checked herself. That would come later, when he trusted her. 'Talk about women, if you like. Tell me about your girlfriend.'

He wriggled on his chair. 'I don't have a girlfriend.'

She smiled, and then deliberately pulled her chair closer to his so that their knees were almost touching. For a moment their eyes met. 'Do you mean your brother was telling the truth?' she asked softly. 'You really are a virgin?'

She saw his body stiffen. He looked away from her. 'My brother talks a lot of nonsense,' he said.

'So you're not a virgin?' she persisted.

'I do not think this is a fit subject for conversation,' he said frostily.

'Dear me.' She mocked him gently. 'Have I embarrassed you?'

'No,' he said.

She leant back and stretched out her legs. She saw his eyes flick quickly to her knees, and then suddenly

167

shift to a neutral spot, over her shoulder. 'So you choose a subject,' she suggested. 'But talk.'

After a little more fidgeting he began, hesitantly at first, to discuss films he had enjoyed. Slowly he relaxed, and then became positively animated. Jacey prompted him with questions, and occasionally corrected his grammar. After half an hour, he was smiling at her.

'Well,' she said, after he had explained at length why he admired Clint Eastwood, 'that wasn't so difficult, was it?'

His smile disappeared. He looked wary. 'What wasn't difficult?'

'Talking to Nicolás Schlemann's lover,' she said.

'I really don't concern myself with other people's private lives,' he said.

'Then why were you so rude to me at the charity party?'

He twisted his long fingers together. 'I was not aware that I was rude.'

'You know very well you were,' she said. She paused. 'Nicolás Schlemann's politics really aren't anything to do with me.'

He stood up. 'Of course they aren't,' he said, and she noted the suppressed anger in his voice. 'You are a foreigner. A visitor to our country. You have come here to do a job, and to get very well paid. Why should you concern yourself with politics?' Jacey knew that the rapport they had built up while they were talking about films had now disintegrated. He picked up his leather folder. 'Thank you for your help, Dr Muldaire.' He turned towards the door.

'Maybe next time we can discuss some of the books you enjoy?' she said.

He stopped by the door, and hesitated. She knew that this was a crucial moment. If he was really interested in her sexually, he would agree to come back again. If not, any chance of starting a relationship – and any chance of learning anything about Loháquin from him – would be lost.

'Perhaps tomorrow evening?' she suggested.

It seemed like a very long pause, and then he said: 'That would be very agreeable, Dr Muldaire.'

Jacey was drafting out a report to send to Major Fairhaven. It sounded more optimistic than she actually felt. She was certain that Leonardo could provide her with a lead to the elusive Loháquin, but winning his trust was going to be difficult as long as she was with Nicolás.

And Nicolás showed no signs of wanting to end their relationship yet. If anything, he was becoming more possessive. His car had arrived three times that week, with the minimum of warning, to drive her to Police Headquarters. Each time he had offered her a drink, and then had abruptly unzipped and ordered her to get to work. He had delayed his orgasm as long as possible, forcing her to experiment with as many techniques as she could, until her mouth was sore with the effort of trying to satisfy him. Afterwards he had used his hands on her, rubbing her off with practised expertise. She had tried to withhold her own orgasm in order to prove that she could equal his iron self-discipline. But the closeness of his body turned her on as much as his sexual manipulation, and each time she lost control far more quickly than she intended.

When he had once triumphantly claimed: 'You can't resist me for long, can you?', even the touch of his lips on her ear had sent a shudder of need through her body. Sexually, he looked, and behaved, in a way that was guaranteed to arouse her. And she had to admit, the knowledge that he was both powerful and dangerous added spice to their meetings. But

God help anyone who actually fell in love with him, she thought. She could just imagine him taking full advantage of such a weakness. He'd probably arrange a fantastic wedding, invite the élite of Guachtàl, then leave the poor woman stranded at the altar.

He certainly had a sadistic streak. Once that week he had kept her waiting for an hour, and then arrived and taken her roughly and without any preliminaries, stripping her clothes off as he manhandled her towards the door that led to his bedroom. And his behaviour had given me a great orgasm, she remembered, contentedly. Afterwards, when she lay on the bed, exhausted but satisfied, she had made a token protest about him being late, and he had looked down at her, with his familiar crooked smile, and said: 'But it was worth it, wasn't it?' Yes, she realised, it was.

She stared at the computer screen, and her report. When Nicolás decided that he was no longer interested in her, hopefully she would be able to write something more positive to Major Fairhaven. Some information about Loháquin, and the extent of his strength, perhaps even details obtained first-hand from a personal meeting with the elusive rainforest rebel.

But what if Loháquin turned out to be just a scruffy troublemaker, as Nicolás had once claimed, with no back-up support, a man playing a game he could not possibly win? The thought depressed her. She was not against economic progress, but without protection the rainforest of Guachtàl would be destroyed by the road-builders and the loggers. Loháquin seemed to be the country's only hope against political entrepreneurs like Nicolás Schlemann.

She typed in the necessary codes, sent her report, and pushed her swivel chair back from her desk. Jacey Muldaire, she told herself, you're getting too involved in all this. Leonardo would have been surprised to find out exactly what type of job she had come to do as a foreigner in Guachtàl. When you've got enough information, you can go home, she thought, and before long Guachtàl and all its problems will be just another memory. Be sensible. Be professional. You can't set the world to rights all on your own.

Jacey's next meeting with Leonardo was almost as formal as the first. He came in his usual light-coloured suit, with his thick, black hair neatly combed, sat primly in front of her, and started a dry, academic discussion of books that he read, sounding as if he was reciting prepared notes. When he had finished dissecting his third book on political theory, she said, 'Don't you ever read anything light and entertaining, Leonardo?'

His dark eyes surveyed her reprovingly. 'I read to educate myself, Dr Muldaire.'

'That's fine,' she nodded. 'So have you read the Kama Sutra?'

She was gratified to see him wriggle uncomfortably. 'Certainly not,' he said.

'It's educational,' she teased.

'I am not a profligate like my brother Raoul,' he said pompously.

'Oh, really, Leonardo,' she scoffed. 'Stop talking like a dictionary. It doesn't impress me at all. Your brother's just a normal man. He's interested in women. And sex.' She leant towards him. There was a sheen of sweat on his upper lip. She had deliberately chosen to wear a buttoned blouse with a deep vee-neck, and her cleavage was clearly visible. 'A normal man,' she repeated softly. 'Like you.'

'I am nothing like my brother,' he said stiffly.

171

'But you'd like to be, wouldn't you?' she suggested. 'Not many women say no to Raoul.'

'You did,' he said. 'You preferred Nicolás Schlemann.' The name sounded like an insult.

She smiled, and relaxed back in her chair. 'Well, he is very sexy,' she said. 'And very powerful. That's a potent mixture, Leonardo.'

'He's a bastard,' Leonardo said angrily. 'He exploits our country. He has grown rich on the poverty of others. We would be better off without him.' He stared at her defiantly. 'And you can tell him that, if you wish.'

Jacey thought how attractive he looked when he was angry. She almost smiled. 'Nicolás and I don't talk politics,' she said. She paused, and added casually, 'If you deposed Nicolás, who would replace him?' Another pause. 'Loháquin?'

Leonardo had his emotions under control now. 'Loháquin has the interests of Guachtàl at heart,' he said. 'And you can tell Señor Schlemann that I said that, too.'

'Stop insulting me, Leonardo,' she ordered, sharply.

He looked startled. 'I am not insulting you, Dr Muldaire.'

'You are,' she said. 'You're implying that I'm some kind of informer. Nothing you say will go further than this room.' She managed to hold his gaze. 'I enjoy Nicolás Schlemann's body,' she said. 'But that doesn't mean he owns my mind.'

Leonardo looked embarrassed. 'You must have some feelings for him,' he said awkwardly. 'You are not a street woman. And women are not like men; men can approach sex in a purely physical manner, but women need love and romance, and so forth.'

He sounded so serious that Jacey laughed. 'Did Raoul tell you that?' she asked. He nodded. She

172

moved towards him again. 'Well, it may come as a surprise to you, Leonardo, but women can fuck and forget, just the same as men.' She had intended to shock him, and she knew she had succeeded. He was actually blushing. 'Oh dear,' she said. 'Did your brother also tell you that women never swear? You do have a lot to learn.'

'He did not tell me anything of the kind,' Leonardo said. He shifted uncomfortably on his chair. 'I am aware that I don't understand women. But I would like to learn.' He looked up at her and she thought there was a gleam of excitement in his eyes. 'I admire women. Particularly intelligent women. Strong women, with independent minds.' He lowered his eyes briefly, then glanced up at her. 'Women like this are usually older than me, but I find that kind of woman very attractive indeed.'

Jacey was certain that was an invitation for her to make the obvious suggestion. She thought how deliciously vulnerable he looked, sitting straight-backed, his long fingers clenched together. I could get him to do anything I liked, she realised. And he'd enjoy it.

'I'm sure there are plenty of women who would love to teach you,' she said. And added sweetly, 'Perhaps you could get Raoul to introduce you to some of his girlfriends?'

He looked away. 'They do not interest me. They are mostly young and stupid.'

'You're very particular, aren't you?' she chided. 'What makes you think an intelligent woman would be attracted to you?'

He gazed at her. 'I don't know.' Then he bowed his head submissively. 'I simply hope I will find someone, one day.'

She stood up briskly. 'Well, I'm sure you will,' she said patronisingly. 'If you wait long enough.'

She was gratified to see the disappointment on his

173

face. If you thought it was going to be that easy to get your own way, young man, she thought rather smugly, you were mistaken. You want something from me, but I want something from you, too. Having sex with you would probably be a delightful experience. But would it mean you'd trust me? Trust me enough to take me to Loháquin? I'm afraid we're both going to keep our clothes on until I've discovered the answer to that.

'I'll see you in two days' time,' she said. 'And we'll discuss art.'

The sound of her mobile phone no longer startled Jacey. She knew before she answered that it was very unlikely to be an emergency call. Medically, none of her patients at La Primavera were likely to need her immediate attention. When the phone trilled now, she expected to hear Nicolás's coolly authoritative voice telling her what time a car would be coming to collect her. He always seemed to know exactly where she was, and the calls always came when she was on duty at La Primavera, spending some leisure time in her apartment, or relaxing by the hospital pool. Although she was certain Nicolás knew she still worked regularly at El Invierno, he had never commented on it, and never summoned her while she was there.

Despite her involvement with Nicolás, her relationship with the staff at El Invierno remained friendly. She knew it would be pointless to try and discuss politics or Loháquin with them, and deliberately kept her conversation light and general. Dr Rodriguez was the only one who ever mentioned Nicolás. He criticised Nicolás repeatedly, and asked Jacey what she saw in him, but this proved to her that he trusted her and was confident she would not inform on him.

'He's sexy,' she said, defending herself yet again as she assisted Rodriguez during a minor operation.

'He's a crook,' Rodriguez grunted. 'A thief. I wouldn't mind, but the money he's stealing comes from my taxes.'

Paloma tut-tutted from behind her surgical mask as a warning for him to stop.

'It's no good you making those noises, my girl,' Rodriguez added. 'You know you really agree with me.'

Once or twice when they were alone, Jacey had attempted to draw Rodriguez out on the subject of Loháquin. In a rare moment of confidence he had admitted to Jacey that not only did he believe Loháquin would never gain control of Guachtàl, but that he did not deserve to.

'He should have made his move before now,' Rodriguez had said. 'But what has he ever done, except skulk in the forest while your boyfriend tightens his hold on Guachtàl?' He fixed her with an angry glare. 'Don't fall into the trap of hero-worshipping Loháquin. Leave that to silly girls like Paloma. Loháquin is a fraud and a failure, whoever he is.'

'Nicolás thinks he's important enough to offer a large reward for his capture,' Jacey said.

Rodriguez smiled briefly. 'He probably knows he'll never have to pay it. Loháquin takes care not to make himself visible. I've never met anyone who claims to have seen him. Even liars!'

Operating or assisting during an operation was one of the duties that Jacey really enjoyed. The patients at El Invierno frequently needed surgery, and to help save lives was particularly satisfying for Jacey. Once he trusted her, the over-burdened Dr Rodriguez passed more and more of his cases over to her. One day she was in the middle of a tricky suture when

175

her mobile rang. Paloma was acting as her theatre nurse.

'Answer that for me,' Jacey requested, without looking up. 'It might be someone at La Primavera.'

When Paloma started waving the phone at her and making cryptic gestures, she knew it wasn't.

'Nicolás?' she guessed.

Paloma nodded vigorously. For a moment, Jacey was tempted to ask Paloma to switch the phone off, or at least tell Nicolás to ring back later, but she knew this would not deter him from calling again. She indicated with her head for Paloma to bring the phone close to her ear, and heard Nicolás's voice giving her the familiar instructions.

She interrupted him more abruptly than she'd intended. 'I can't come now, I'm operating.'

There was a brief pause. 'Then hand over to someone else,' he said.

'I can't.'

'Are you the only doctor at El Invierno?'

There was an undertone of anger in his voice that she had not heard before. She realised this was the first time she had refused his orders.

'I'm in the middle of a delicate surgical procedure,' she said. 'I have a patient to consider. I can't come, I'm sorry. Ring me later.'

She indicated to Paloma to switch the phone off. Paloma's eyes were nervous. 'Maybe I should get Dr Ramez? I think he is still on duty.'

'You stay here,' Jacey said sharply. 'Nicolás will have to learn that I'm a doctor first, and his woman second.'

'I don't think he is going to be very happy about that,' Paloma mumbled.

'Too bad,' Jacey said brusquely, and turned back to her patient.

She was still busy when a frightened nurse

appeared at the operating theatre door and beckoned wildly to Paloma. An animated conversation ensued, and then Paloma came over to Jacey. 'There's a car outside,' she said. 'It's come for you.'

Jacey felt a wave of anger wash over her. 'Tell it to damn well go away,' she said. 'I haven't finished here, and even if I had, I just don't feel like indulging Nicolás right now.'

Paloma looked horrified. 'No one will say that,' she stammered. 'It's one of Señor Schlemann's men.'

'Then let him wait,' Jacey said, 'and I'll tell him myself. After I've finished here.'

She deliberately took her time completing the suture and cleaning up afterwards, and when she finally went outside she fully expected to find that the car had gone. But it was still standing there, its dark suited driver inside.

'Tell Señor Schlemann I'm not coming,' she said. 'I'm still working.'

The man stared at her for a full minute, and Jacey stared back. Then he turned, opened the car door and indicated that she should get in. The fact that he had ignored her comment, and assumed that she would obey him anyway, infuriated her. She had not imagined her showdown with Nicolás would come quite so soon, but she felt that this might be a good time to precipitate it. She was sure that Nicolás would break off their relationship if she openly opposed him. She could then claim that he was unreasonable, play the woman scorned – and get to work on Leonardo.

'You appear to be deaf as well as stupid,' she snapped at the driver. 'Not coming means just that. I'm staying here. And you're leaving. Now.' She paused, and added for good measure, 'Without me.'

When Jacey arrived back at La Primavera she wondered if she would find the car, and the security

177

driver, waiting for her. Then she smiled to herself. Nicolás would not stoop to following her around like a lovesick suitor. It simply wasn't his style.

She went to her apartment and ran herself a hot bath. After liberally sprinkling the water with scented oil, she spent half an hour lazing contentedly in its perfumed warmth. Feeling much more relaxed, and in a much better temper, she pulled on a silky kimono and poured herself a glass of wine.

As she dozed in her chair she heard the sound of a car pulling up noisily outside, then doors banging, and some shouting. It was only when the sounds came nearer, accompanied by the pounding of booted feet, that she began to take notice. There was an impatient thumping on her door.

Clutching her kimono round herself, she opened the door to find three uniformed men. Although they looked like soldiers, she knew they were actually police. Their faces were shadowed under the peaks of their military-style caps, and they were armed with light machine-guns.

'You are Dr Muldaire?' The tallest of them moved forward. He had three horizontal stripes on his sleeve. The barrel of his gun was pointing directly at her.

'I'm Dr Muldaire,' she confirmed. She noticed Dr Sanchez behind the policemen. He looked terrified. She added in her most authoritative voice, 'I hope you have a very good reason for this behaviour, sergeant?'

The sergeant smiled wolfishly. 'You are to come with me,' he said. His smile disappeared. 'You are under arrest.'

'Arrest?' Jacey repeated. It took a few moments for the word to make sense. 'What for?'

'No questions.' He jerked the gun barrel up at her. 'You may put on some clothes. But hurry.'

'They don't need a reason to arrest anyone.' Dr Sanchez held out his hands to her pleadingly. 'Do as they say. I'm sure it's all a mistake. After all, you do have important friends.'

A suspicion was forming in Jacey's mind. 'Yes,' she said grimly. 'I do, don't I?'

She went into her bedroom and pulled on a loose pair of drawstring pants and a cropped sweat top. When she came out, two of the police took up a position on either side of her. She smiled encouragingly at Dr Sanchez as she walked past him. 'Don't worry,' she said. 'I'll be back quite soon.'

Outside she was bundled into a windowless police van. The policemen did not speak to her. It was an uncomfortable ride, and she was glad when the van slewed to a halt. When she stepped outside she saw not the iron door to Nicolas's apartment but the pillared entrance to the main Police Headquarters building. Inside she was unceremoniously bustled down a stone-floored corridor, harshly lit by unshaded lights, until she found herself in front of a closed door. The sergeant pushed it open. 'Inside,' he said. He did not follow her.

Jacey stepped into a room that was dominated by a huge, old-fashioned office desk. Nicolás was seated behind the desk, wearing a dark suit and a black polo-necked shirt. She was reminded fleetingly of the portrait she had seen of his father. She walked towards him, but ignored the chair in front of the desk.

'Well,' she said with a brief, cool smile. 'That's one question answered. Now I know what all this is about.'

Nicolás returned her smile, equally briefly. 'I knew I'd get you here eventually, Dr Muldaire. The other question you should be asking yourself is, am I going to let you leave?'

Chapter Six

'If this is your idea of a practical joke,' Jacey said coldly, 'it's a very poor one.'

Nicolás pushed his chair back and stretched his long legs under the desk. 'I don't play practical jokes,' he said. 'Did you think I was joking when I sent for you today?'

'You know I was with a patient,' she said.

'You could have handed over to someone else.'

'I was in the middle of an operation. My patient could have died.'

He shrugged. 'I'm not unreasonable, Jacey,' he said. 'I wouldn't drag you from the operating theatre, even if you were only sewing up some Indian.' He paused. 'But my driver waited. You sent him away.'

'I needed rest,' she explained. 'Surely you understand that? I'd had a long day at the hospital.' She smiled. 'I wouldn't have been much fun.'

His expression changed. Ice touched his voice. 'That's for me to decide. You come when I call for you. As long as we're together, those are the rules. My rules. And you obey them.' She opened her mouth to protest, and he lifted one hand to silence her. 'Do you know why, Jacey?' His voice was silky now. 'Shall I explain some facts to you? Inside this building I can play all the games I like. Inside this building you don't have any rights at all. And you've already seen how easy it is for me to bring you here.'

'So I'm your prisoner, am I?' she said. 'Are you going to chain me up in a dungeon?'

'That's an interesting suggestion.' His eyes moved over her body slowly. 'But maybe you'd enjoy that.' Suddenly he sat upright, and leant forward. 'Here's another scenario. I call Marco, and tell him to fuck you, right now, on the floor. You do remember Marco, don't you? He certainly remembers you. And not with any great affection, either. Maybe you wouldn't enjoy that quite so much.' He smiled cruelly. 'Don't think I wouldn't do it, Jacey. If I wanted to, I could even arrange for you to, shall we say, disappear.'

'Why don't you just say you could have me killed?' she challenged.

'I could have you killed,' he agreed. 'Do you doubt me?'

'No,' she said.

She knew that was the answer he wanted. She also knew that it would be easy to dispose of her body in the rainforest, where ants could reduce her to a skeleton in less than a day. Another thought struck her. Who would investigate her disappearance? She had no close relatives. Major Fairhaven would be suspicious, but he wouldn't have proof. Questions might be asked, and letters exchanged, but Guachtàl was a long way from England. Was she important enough to warrant an international enquiry? Major Fairhaven might well prefer to play the whole incident down. She suddenly realised just how vulnerable she was.

But would Nicolás really murder her? And would

181

he really allow Marco to do whatever he wanted with her? She didn't think so. She might have believed it of him when she first came to Guachtàl, but now she wasn't so sure. She guessed it gave Nicolás some kind of pleasure to threaten her, but she felt that he was more feared for what people thought he could do than what he had actually done. He was obviously a crook in a smart suit, but whether he was liable to change into a thug with a knuckle-duster was another matter.

She decided to challenge him. 'You'd consider having me killed, just for not coming when you called for me?' she asked lightly. 'Isn't that rather extreme?'

'I enjoy sex with you, Jacey,' he said. 'But don't think that will save you if you oppose me. I'm not going to be made to look a fool. As long as we're together, you do as I tell you. I like it that way.' He smiled. 'And so do you, don't you?'

'I don't like being dragged out of my bed by your police goons,' she said.

He laughed, and lounged back in his chair. They stared at each other for a moment, and she found herself aroused, despite his threats. She hated herself for knowing that she still found him devastatingly sexy. 'Come here,' he said. She walked round the desk, and he pushed his chair back so that his legs were stretched out in front of him. 'Take off those unflattering trousers.'

She undid the drawstring and the trousers fell to the ground. She hadn't had time to put on any underwear. She stood there, wearing only the sweat top. He surveyed her for a few moments and then reached out to the red bush of her pubic hair.

'You haven't really hated all this at all, have you?' he asked, softly. His fingers probed her expertly, discovering in a second that she was moist and aroused.

182

'Nobody likes the police banging on their door,' she said.

He played with her gently. 'A little fear,' he said, 'can be an aphrodisiac.'

Pulling her towards him, he forced her to straddle his lap. He ran his finger over her clitoris, with just the kind of pressure she enjoyed. Her body began to shudder with delight and she could see his erection bulging attractively – and probably uncomfortably, she thought – against his fly. She reached down and unzipped him to free his cock, and felt it throbbing in her hand. She grasped him tightly, in revenge for the way he had treated her, but he merely groaned encouragement, and moved his own hand faster, pleasuring her roughly, sliding first one finger, and then two, into her warm depths.

She reached down to his balls and massaged them, but it was hard to concentrate when her own body was responding so strongly to his delightfully forceful handling. She rocked back and forth, locked in the rhythm of desire, hardly aware that she was still gripping him and exciting him, too. She closed her eyes, and when her orgasm came she heard a harsh cry, and only a few seconds later recognised her own voice. Her body thrashed wildly for several elated moments, and then she collapsed into his lap, falling forward against his chest. She lay there, disorientated by the physical waves of sexual euphoria that had just shaken her.

'You can let go of me now,' Nicolás said softly.

Jacey was still holding him. She loosened her hand gently. Even in its relaxed state, his penis was still an impressive size. Lulled by the drowsiness that often followed good sex, she felt blissfully calm and sleepy, and for a moment forgot exactly where she was, and how she had come to be there. Nicolás's body felt warm and comfortable under her. She could hear the beating of his heart. For a brief moment they could have been two lovers, recovering together after a session of shared passion.

But only for a brief moment. Her heartbeat slowed and her mind returned to the present. The cold, bare walls of the room jolted her back to reality, and reminded her that her partnership with Nicolás was far from romantic. He treated her like a possession. And, she knew, he could do it again, at any time. She untangled herself from him, and stood up. He zipped himself up, and she bent down to pick up the drawstring pants.

'No,' he said. 'Not yet.' He lounged back in his chair. 'Go over to the wall.' Surprised, she did so. 'Now turn,' he instructed, 'and come back.' She could feel his eyes on her crotch as she walked towards him. 'Stop,' he said, 'and lift up that unflattering sweater.'

She pulled up the sweat top until it was level with the underside of her breasts. Then, slowly, she lifted it higher. Her previous sexual excitement had contracted her nipples into hard, little buds, and the cool air in the office was tightening them again. Nicolás stared at her for what seemed like a very long time. She expected him to beckon her forward, but he simply said, 'Very nice. You can get dressed now.'

He watched her pull on her drawstring pants. 'Do you sleep in that outfit?' he asked.

'I sleep in my skin,' she said. 'I keep this outfit for when I'm dragged out of bed by the police.'

He laughed. 'They won't do that again, unless you keep disobeying me. And that's not going to happen, is it?'

'That's up to you,' she said. 'Remember, I have a job to do. I'm a doctor, and my patients always come first.'

'I appreciate that,' he said. 'But I come a close second. A very close second. Don't ever forget that, Dr Muldaire.'

'I can't believe that he could do that to you,' Ingrid said angrily, after Jacey had confirmed the previous night's story. 'Poor Dr Sanchez was convinced we would never see you again.' She leaned over Jacey's desk, her face serious. 'You must be very careful not to antagonise Nicolás. Dr Sanchez believes he murdered Juanita Márquez. He is a psycho! And are you sure it's safe to continue giving English lessons to your little virgin Leonardo? Won't it make Nicolás jealous?'

Jacey laughed. 'Nicolás wouldn't see Leonardo as a threat. Anyway, Leonardo doesn't even like me. You saw the way he behaved at the charity party.'

'You don't take private lessons from someone you don't like,' Ingrid said.

'You do if your big brother tells you to,' Jacey answered. And added untruthfully, 'The lessons were Raoul's idea, not Leonardo's.'

'Please.' Ingrid caught Jacey's hand impulsively, and gripped it. 'Promise me you will only teach the boy the English language.'

'There isn't anything else he wants to learn from me,' Jacey said.

But she knew that was a lie as well. She was playing a strange kind of game with Leonardo now. During each lesson he made at least one comment that she could take as an invitation to steer the conversation towards sex. He clearly hoped that things would go further than just banter, but was too nervous – or too inexperienced – to make the suggestion himself. Jacey found it enjoyable to tease him, sometimes by being deliberately obtuse, and sometimes by reprimanding him for being too forward.

She had decided to keep the game strictly at a flirtation level as long as she was with Nicolás and when he dumped her, as she had fully expected him to do, she would have an excuse both to encourage Leonardo, and to act the woman scorned.

But now she was not so sure of her plan. Nicolás seemed to be getting a perverse kind of enjoyment at having a different kind of woman than usual under his control. Most of his previous partners had probably been besotted with him, or paid by him, but she was a professional woman, with a mind of her own. He was enjoying the challenge, and like many people hooked on power-play, he would keep pushing to see how far he could go.

But she did not want to be the subject of his sexual experiments. She had a suspicion they would get more and more extreme. She had a vision of herself at Police Headquarters, forced to play prisoner to Nicolás's gaoler. She didn't mind a little sexual dominance in the bedroom, but didn't fancy exploring the more extreme forms of restraint. Major Fairhaven's mission was important, and now she wanted to complete it before her relationship with Nicolás escalated into risky games. She needed information on Loháquin and she needed it soon. Her best lead was Leonardo Márquez, and she wanted to make use of him as quickly as possible.

The next time they met, Jacey allowed Leonardo to talk about music almost until the end of their hour together. He sat in front of her, in loose-cut chinos and an open-necked shirt, his sleeves rolled up to his elbows. As he finally came to the end of his discourse – having revealed an unexpected liking for thirties and forties dance bands – she began to look at him intently, keeping her eyes on his face with an unwavering stare. It disconcerted him, just as she intended. He blushed and began to stumble over his words.

'And I enjoy Ellington's *Mood Indigo*. But also musicians like Gene Krupa and, er, *Blues in the Night*, from a film with the same title in 1941, I believe –' He tailed off, and then said abruptly, 'Please stop looking at me like that. It's making me feel uncomfortable.'

She did not shift her gaze. 'Why don't you tell the truth, Leonardo?' she said. And then without changing her tone, she said, 'You mean it's making you feel sexy, don't you?'

He looked startled and then his blush deepened. 'No,' he said.

'It's making you hard, isn't it?' she persisted.

'No.' His voice sounded strangled.

'Stand up,' she said.

For a moment he hesitated, and then slowly, he stood up, and she knew she had won. She stood up too, and moved close to him.

'If it isn't making you hard,' she said, 'I shall be extremely angry.'

'Why?' he whispered.

His face was only inches away from hers. She admired the smoothness of his tanned skin, and the delicate slant of his fine eyebrows. There was sweat on his upper lip.

'Because it's an insult to me,' she said. 'Every time we meet, you hint that you like intelligent women, strong women, older women. I think I fit that description. And now you're saying that you don't fancy me at all? That's an insult, Leonardo.'

'I can't –' he mumbled. 'I mean, you're Nicolás Schlemann's woman –'

'So why have you been coming on to me?' she demanded.

'I haven't.'

'You have.' She glanced down at him, but the loose

187

cut of his trousers disguised the physical reaction she was certain he was experiencing. 'It's a pity those trousers aren't tighter,' she said. 'If they were, I could see exactly how you're feeling. I'm determined to see if you really fancy me, Leonardo.' She moved away from him. 'So take them off.'

'Off?' he repeated. He took a step backwards. 'No. Certainly not.'

She was convinced that she detected a note of excitement in his voice now. 'You're not embarrassed, are you?' She smiled. 'I'm a doctor. I've seen hundreds of cocks.' She added, 'Maybe I'll strip you myself, and check out just how much of a man you are. Would you prefer that?'

She saw his mouth twitch nervously, but his eyes were bright with anticipation. 'No,' he protested.

She caught his wrist and twisted his arm, turning him so that his back was turned towards her. It would have been easy even if he had tried to resist. She felt the warmth of his body against her breasts and deliberately held him close, so that he could feel her nipples touching him through his white cotton shirt.

'All right then,' she said. 'You do it. Right now.'

'Please, let me go,' he said. It did not sound convincing.

She put her mouth close to his ear, and resisted the temptation to run her tongue round it. 'Take your trousers off, Leonardo,' she said. 'I want to see if your cock is paying me the right kind of compliment.' She tightened her grip on his arm. 'I shall be very angry if you haven't got a good erection.'

She watched over his shoulder as he reached down to his fly and fumbled with the buttons. His hands were shaking and she could feel his body beginning to tremble. If he didn't have a hard-on before, she thought, I bet he's got one now.

'Hurry up,' she ordered. 'You're not trying to delay things, are you?' She felt his body jerk as if an electric shock had touched it. 'Come on now.' She shook him crossly. 'Show me what kind of a man you are, Leonardo.'

She found it quite delightful to feel his body wriggling as he finally unbuttoned his trousers and they slid to the ground. She pushed him forward so that he stepped out of them, the tails of his shirt flapping gently against his thighs. His legs were long, slim and brown, with very little hair. She felt him react with another violent tremor as she reached under the shirt and cupped his buttocks. They were small and tight, arousing her with a sudden surge, but she resisted the temptation to explore between his legs. Instead she ran a finger round the top band of his tight briefs.

'These come off next,' she ordered.

He tried to push the briefs down, but had trouble getting them over his erection. His slim body writhed against her in an awkward, unintentionally sexy dance. She wanted to peep over his shoulder and see exactly what was hampering him but after he managed to get the briefs down to his knees – balancing on one leg to free them – she let him go and walked round to look at him. He looked beautiful: slim, young and desirable.

'Lift the shirt up,' she said.

He fumbled for a moment, catching the cloth and screwing it up in his hands. Very slowly, he raised the shirt tails, revealing an erection that was impressively upright, and surprisingly large. His balls were also bigger than she expected, full and heavy. The size was enhanced by his small waist and his narrow hips and coupled with his lean thighs, it was a seductively enticing sight. He stood there, looking at her with a mixture of anxiety and anticipation.

'Tie the shirt tails up,' she said, and when he had knotted them at waist level, she added, 'Now go into the bedroom.'

She enjoyed the way his cock moved as he walked past her, and then admired the movement of his taut buttocks. When he reached the bed, he turned. His slim, brown body, and thick, black hair, suddenly reminded her of Faisel. He was taller than Faisel, and his body was leaner and more angular, but there was enough of a similarity to make her angry. She knew that was not Leonardo's fault, but when she noticed a slight smile touching his mouth, and saw a gleam of triumph in his eyes, she realised that he knew exactly what he wanted, and exactly how he was affecting her.

She felt a combination of lust and anger grip her. She moved forward and grabbed him by the wrist, spinning him round and pitching him, face down, on the bed. He gave a grunt of surprise, and struggled, but she tightened the armlock, and held him down. The flat of her hand landed on his bottom with a sound like a pistol shot. Leonardo's yelp of surprise was almost smothered by the pillow. He turned his head sideways, and she slapped him again, several blows in quick succession. She knew she was being far from gentle with him, and during the first flurry of slaps it was as if she really was beating Faisel, in fury, not playing a sexual game with Leonardo.

For a moment she felt guilty. Then she looked at Leonardo's face. His black hair was spread out over the pillow, and his expression was as contorted as a man in the throes of an orgasm. Clearly he was loving every minute of this painful humiliation.

'Don't you dare come before I'm ready,' she said, matching each word with a slap, but lighter ones this time.

'Then hurry,' he muttered, between clenched teeth, 'because I can't hold out much longer.'

She let him go and turned him over. It took her a few seconds to strip off her skirt and panties. This was not how she had planned it, but suddenly she and Leonardo were rolling together on the bed. Then he was under her, and she straddled him. She grasped his cock and guided it in. She was wet and ready for him, and as she lowered herself on to him she heard him groan, a mixture of desire and relief. Using her weight to pin him down, she controlled him with thrusting hips. But she could tell from his shaking body, and the rising crescendo of his frenzied cries of delight, that he would not be able to hold back for long.

And she was right. His orgasm rocked him, and his body bucked and trembled. Although she had not experienced any release, she didn't feel any urgency. She made no further demands on him, allowing him to enjoy both the explosive sensations of pleasure, and the slow return to normality.

She lay on her back next to him. 'Well,' she said. 'That wasn't a bad performance, for a first time.'

'Is it always as good as that?' he murmured sleepily.

'Sometimes it'll be better,' she said. 'And sometimes maybe not so good. But that's all part of the fun.'

He turned his head towards her, and grinned mischievously. 'You really enjoyed spanking me, didn't you?'

'Every bit as much as you enjoyed it,' she agreed.

'Have you ever done it before?'

'As a matter of fact,' she admitted, 'I haven't.'

'Has a man ever spanked you?'

She gave him a mock frown. 'Don't ask impertinent

191

questions, young man. And don't start getting any ideas.'

'Oh,' he said, his voice suddenly low and seductive, 'I've got plenty of ideas. There are plenty of things I'd like to try with you.'

'The first one you can try,' she said, 'is learning how to give me an orgasm.'

'You mean, I didn't –? You didn't –?' He seemed genuinely surprised.

'No, you didn't. And I didn't,' she said. 'But don't worry. I'll forgive you – this time.'

'So I'll get another chance?'

He sounded so anxious that she laughed, and put her arm out to stroke his damp hair. 'You know you will. Lots of chances. But Leonardo,' she turned towards him, seriously, 'this has to be kept secret. Nicolás can be very jealous. And very dangerous. I didn't realise until recently how dangerous he can be. Don't even tell Raoul.'

'I wouldn't,' Leonardo said. 'He might guess, but he would never put you in any danger. And neither would I. But I know that Nicolás Schlemann is a very dangerous man. I am well aware of that.' He propped himself up on his elbow, and stared gravely at her. 'In fact, I'm already feeling some guilt. I should not have let this happen.'

'You didn't let it happen,' Jacey said. 'We both let it happen.' She turned towards him. Now, she thought, it's time to make him feel even more like a man. A protector. 'To be truthful,' she said, 'I'd like to end my relationship with Nicolás, but I'm afraid of what he might do. The decision will have to come from him, not me. Did you hear that he dragged me to Police Headquarters because I upset him?'

'Yes.' Leonardo nodded. 'I thought maybe it was an exaggeration.'

'No,' she said. 'It was true. He actually threatened

me. He told me how he could have me killed.' She paused, wondering just how frightened she should appear to be. 'I believed him, Leonardo. I'm certain he's quite capable of murder.' She paused again. 'I heard a rumour that he was responsible for your mother's death?'

Leonardo avoided her eyes. 'Well, no, I don't think so. Although I'm sure he was happy when my mother disappeared.'

'Your Aunt Ana doesn't think your mother is dead, either,' Jacey hinted.

'I didn't say she was alive,' Leonardo said quickly. 'But as you know, her body was never found.'

'Do you think she joined Loháquin?' She had caught Leonardo off guard, and she noticed the nervous twitch of his mouth.

'Of course not,' he said rather hurriedly.

'But people do go into the rainforest and join the rebels, don't they?'

He squirmed on the bed. 'I don't know. I think so.'

'Have you ever met Loháquin, Leonardo?' she asked bluntly.

'No.'

She believed him. 'Do you know anyone who has?'

He squirmed a little more. 'No.'

'You don't trust me, do you, Leonardo?'

'Yes,' he said. 'I believe now that you have a good heart. You care about people. You work at El Invierno. Dr Rodriguez likes you. I didn't understand why you became Nicolás Schlemann's woman, but now I understand a little better. You can't be blamed for finding him attractive. Many women do. Until they discover exactly what kind of man he is.' He looked at her seriously. 'Nicolás Schlemann has too much power. But maybe things will change. Many people hope so.'

'I hope so, too,' Jacey said.

Later that evening Jacey reflected that she had made a good start with Leonardo. She had made him want her, and feel protective towards her. It was a potent combination for a young and inexperienced boy to deal with. I have a feeling that Leonardo Márquez is going to be just the man I need, she thought contentedly. In more ways than one.

'You mean that Mr Aren't-I-Wonderful Curtis Telford hasn't asked you to fuck him yet?' Ingrid perched on Jacey's desk. 'I'm amazed. He's asked everyone else. Perhaps Nicolás has warned him off.'

Jacey shrugged. 'All I know is that he's an American friend of Nicolás's. We hardly had two minutes together. He wanted something for jetlag.'

'He wants his finger amputated,' Ingrid said. 'Not all the nurses here like having their bottoms pinched.'

Curtis Telford had arrived at the hospital with Nicolás, and in one of Nicolás's own cars. He was a large, golden man, built like a Chippendale, but not quite so pretty. He had cropped, blond hair, and a deep, Californian tan. Jacey put him around forty, maybe older. He had smiled at her, displaying perfect teeth, and his eyes had stayed on her face for less than a second before they lowered to her breasts. When they came back to her face, she returned his smile, professionally.

He turned to Nicolás. 'You didn't tell me your little lady was this pretty?'

Nicolás shrugged and said, 'All my women are beautiful.'

As he left, Telford had turned to Jacey and winked. She kept her smile firmly in place, but wondered whether he would have looked so smugly pleased with himself if he had really known what she was thinking. She wondered who he was, and why he was in Guachtàl. Unlike Ingrid, her questions about him were prompted by something more than simple curiosity.

But whoever Curtis Telford was, it was clear that Nicolás was anxious to impress and indulge him. He had the use of a car, and a blank-faced security man as a driver. He arrived unannounced at the hospital, and wandered about, making assignations with Carmen and the other girls. Carmen also grumbled to Jacey that the American wanted increasingly bizarre services, and did not pay a *cento* for them. When Jacey asked why not, Carmen shrugged. 'We have been told not to charge him,' she said. Jacey did not have to ask who had given the order.

Jacey knew better than to ask Nicolás for information, but she was surprised to find that Leonardo claimed to know nothing about the American either. She waited until they were lying comfortably together on her bed after a lengthy session which she had described to him as a tutorial.

This time she had made him keep his clothes on while he undressed her. But she controlled the slow strip, and controlled the order in which her clothes were removed. She made him slow down as he unbuttoned her blouse, and use his mouth and tongue on her ears, neck and shoulders as he peeled the garment off. He clearly wanted to grab at her breasts, but they were out of bounds. She also refused to let him touch her nipples when he undid her lace and satin bra.

She knew he was uncomfortably hard. Before he could do anything about it, she made him remove her skirt, unfasten her silky stockings and roll them down, unhook the lacy suspender belt, and remove her shoes, all with the minimum of hand contact, using only his mouth to pleasure her as he worked.

195

Finally, when it seemed he could hold out no longer, he was allowed to ease down her satin panties.

'And don't touch me there,' she ordered, as his finger strayed towards the glossy red bush of her pubic hair. 'That's off-limits – for now.'

'Why?' he demanded.

'Because I want to feel your hands, and your mouth, on lots of other places first,' she said. 'Diving between a woman's legs is not always the best way to arouse her.'

'It arouses me,' he muttered.

'That's because you're an impatient, sexually uneducated boy,' she said. 'And that's why I'm giving you this tutorial. It'll help you to be a much better lover.'

She guided his hands to her breasts, and made him touch her lightly, first with his fingers and then, when her nipples had tightened into little protruding buds, with his mouth and tongue. She knew he was enjoying himself, and had to push him away and order him to go to work on other places.

'No,' he protested. 'I like this. You taste wonderful.'

'Leonardo,' she said. 'You're making me sore. Now I want you to lick the back of my legs.'

'And that arouses you?' He was sceptical.

'Just behind the knees,' she said. 'It's deliciously sexy.'

She lay there with her eyes half closed, ordering him to move higher or lower, press harder or not so hard, and, as he roved over her body, stimulating many erogenous zones, one after the other, she realised that it was a very long time since a man had pleased her so much. Although Nicolás always managed to satisfy her, he was ungenerous. It aroused him to treat her like a whore, and it had aroused her, but he had never bothered to find out what other kind of treatment she enjoyed.

Would she have liked to feel his mouth moving

gently over her skin, searching for the special places that excited her? Yes, she thought, she would. But she knew it was never going to happen. For Nicolás, sex was a personal ego-trip. Could he actually perform properly if he was not totally in control? Poor Nicolás, she thought, what a lot of pleasure he's missing.

Leonardo was clutching himself uncomfortably. 'What's the matter with you?' she chided him.

'If you don't let me have you soon,' he said, 'I shall come anyway.'

'There's one more place to go,' she said. 'I've kept the best until last.'

He grunted with delight and made a grab between her legs. She slapped him sharply on the head. 'Haven't you learned anything? I meant the best for me. I'm going to teach you how to go down on a woman properly.'

She opened her legs for him, and saw the look of delight and lust on his face. The last time they had made love, she remembered, he hardly had time to look at any part of her. Her clitoris was pink and swollen, and she guessed that this was the first time he had seen a woman's sex. He muttered something that she did not catch, and she made him repeat it.

'It's not like the pictures in magazines,' he said.

'So you've looked at dirty magazines?' She pretended to be shocked.

'A few,' he muttered. 'But they didn't – I mean, I couldn't –' He floundered a moment and then dabbed a finger quickly between her legs. 'The pictures were nothing like this.'

'Of course not,' she murmured. 'This is for real. And it's just for you.' She saw him run his tongue over his lips. 'That's good,' she said. 'You've got the right idea. Only now you're going to use your tongue on me.'

197

She guided his head down, and felt his warm mouth close over her. At first, as she expected, he was in too much of a rush, nuzzling at her like a hungry animal, totally unaware of which parts were the most sensitive.

'Slow down,' she instructed. 'The bit I want you to lick is the little mound, right there in the middle, and if you learn to do that properly, you'll please every woman you ever make love to.' She pushed his head gently back, so that he had to look at her. 'Right here,' she said, demonstrating. 'It gives us the same kind of pleasure that you get from your cock. It even swells up when we get excited. The trick is finding out how each woman likes to be pleased.' She put her hands on his head again, and guided him down. 'You have to listen, really listen, and do what your partner wants, not what you think she wants. But if you start lightly, with just the tip of your tongue, you can't go wrong.'

He bent his head over her. 'Like this?'

She felt his tongue moving, and remembered how seductive she had found the shape of his mouth the first time she had seen him. Now that mouth was servicing her intimately, and the thought was almost as arousing as the smooth, stroking movements of his tongue.

'That's lovely,' she murmured, and meant it. 'But harder. Just a little more pressure. Yes, just there, right there.' She gave a groan of delight as he found her most sensitive spot. 'Oh, yes, that's it!'

She felt him squirming and knew he was having trouble controlling himself. Perversely, she forced him to pleasure her a little longer, then she took pity on him. 'All right, Leonardo. I think it's time to make you comfortable.'

He had no trouble entering her and she was so aroused that she came almost at once. His pleasure came a little while after hers, and she was glad she was able to watch the expression on his face as his orgasm rocked him. Afterwards, as they lay together, he asked her, 'Will it always be like this?'

'No,' she said. 'Sometimes you'll want to do it fast and sometimes you'll take your time.'

'Do women enjoy it fast?' he asked.

'Sometimes we do,' Jacey said. 'That's why relationships are so interesting.' She remembered Nicolás. 'But the cardinal rule is not to do only the things you like all the time. Having sex is a shared experience, a voyage of discovery.'

'Why don't you say "making love?"' he asked.

'Because I don't like lying,' she said. 'We've been having sex, Leonardo. And very nice it was, too. Let's leave it at that.'

'Have you never been in love?' he persisted.

'Once I thought I was,' she said curtly. 'I was wrong. Now let me ask you a question. Who is Curtis Telford?'

He looked surprised. 'I don't know. I was going to ask you. All I know is that my brother Carlos is angry about the American coming here. Carlos has helped Nicolás make money in the past, and now he thinks Nicolás is planning to make money without him. I also think this time Nicolás is going to exclude him, and take the profits all for himself.'

Yes, Jacey thought after Leonardo had gone, that sounds very likely. But what exactly is Nicolás planning? It has to involve the rainforest. Maybe it's a logging deal? Whatever it was she had to find out more.

One of the advantages of Curtis Telford's stay in Techtátuan was that the number of times Nicolás Schlemann called Jacey on her mobile decreased. She knew from Carmen, and from Ingrid, that the

American had an insatiable appetite for sexual experimentation, and guessed that Nicolás was too busy indulging his guest to indulge himself.

Curtis had already tried to talk Ingrid into performing for him with another woman.

'I have no objection to three in a bed,' Ingrid admitted. 'But I just don't fancy Mr Golden Boy. And he is so crass, he actually offered me money. I told him, I like sex, but I am not for sale.'

Because of her increased amount of freedom, Jacey spent more time at El Invierno. It was while she was working in the out-patients' clinic with Paloma that she noticed the number of Indian men and women who wore amulets, or had patterns drawn in red dye on their foreheads.

'It's for healing,' Paloma said, when Jacey commented on it.

'But they still come to the clinic,' Jacey observed.

Paloma laughed. 'The Indians are very sensible. They don't see why they shouldn't explore all the possibilities.'

'I daresay some of the traditional methods do work,' Jacey said. 'Not the amulets and magical things, but medicines derived from rainforest plants?'

'Oh, they work.' Paloma nodded. 'My mother was healed by a *mochtó*. She had very heavy bleeding after her first baby and there were no hospitals like this one, or doctors like you. So she went to the *mochtó* and was given a spell, and something to drink. It cured her.'

'A spell?' Jacey repeated, amused. 'Paloma, I thought your family were Catholics?'

'Oh, we are,' Paloma agreed.

'And your mother went to a witch doctor?'

'A *mochtó* is not a witch doctor,' Paloma said. 'She's a healer.'

'What does she do?' Jacey was still unable to take this seriously. 'Sacrifice a chicken?'

'Certainly not,' Paloma said. 'The *mochtó* has respect for life. Nothing is ever killed during the healing ceremonies. That would be a contradiction, wouldn't it? You can't buy life with a death.'

'You seem to know a lot about this,' Jacey said.

Paloma shrugged. 'I became friendly with some Indian women and one of them invited me to a healing ceremony. It was very interesting.' She paused. 'And I saw many cures.'

'Just from spells?' Jacey asked. 'Or from medicines?'

'Both,' Paloma said.

'I'd like to attend a ceremony,' Jacey said. 'Is that possible?'

'Oh, I'm sure it is.' Paloma nodded. 'After all, you're a healer too. If you like, I'll arrange it for you.'

The room was small, crowded and dark, with a heady aroma of herbs. Paloma urged Jacey forward, towards the tiny woman sitting cross-legged in a circle marked out by bunches of dried grass and flowers. The woman looked up at Jacey with small, bright eyes and said something in the Indian language.

'The *mochtó* welcomes you,' Paloma translated. 'She wants to know if you need healing?'

Jacey gazed into the healer's wise, kindly eyes. She felt tempted to say, Yes. Cure me of my memories, of my bad dreams. Cure me of remembering what Faisel did to me.

The *mochtó* rocked slightly, and nodded encouragement.

'No,' Jacey said to Paloma. 'Thank her, but tell her I'm fine.'

The *mochtó* nodded again, and Jacey had the

201

uncanny feeling that the old woman was aware of her problems anyway. Don't be stupid, she chided herself. No one can read minds. The darkness and the herbs are getting to you. She followed Paloma to the back of the room. When the ceremony started Paloma translated for her into Spanish.

First the *mochtó* chanted and waved burning bunches of herbs in the air.

'To placate the spirits,' Paloma explained.

Then various people came out of the crowd and sat in front of the old woman. They conversed in low whispers. Sometimes the *mochtó* simply laid her hands on the petitioner's head, or drew a pattern on their forehead with a small stick dipped in a pot of dark liquid.

'The spirits will heal that one,' Paloma murmured.

At other times assistants brought out small bags or jars, and handed them to the healer, who always opened them to check them before handing them over. This was the kind of cure Jacey could understand.

'What's in the jars?' she asked. 'Would the *mochtó* tell me?'

Paloma shook her head. 'It's secret. Indian magic. They won't tell.'

It's more likely to be Indian herbalism, Jacey thought. She wondered how many cures western science would find if they learned the Indian's secrets from the rainforest. Rather than destroy the area, they should learn from it, she thought.

After everyone who wanted to speak to the *mochtó* had done so, the old woman was helped to her feet by her assistant, and the circle was cleared. Oil lamps were lit, and Jacey realised that the room was bigger than she thought. The *mochtó* had been helped to a chair and people gathered round her, laughing and joking, without the reverential attitude they had displayed when she sat in the circle.

'Now they exchange gossip,' Paloma said. 'And drink tea. I don't recommend the tea. It's very bitter.'

Jacey had not seen any money change hands. 'Does anyone pay for their cures?' she asked.

'Only if they work,' Paloma said. 'Then you pay what you can afford. It doesn't have to be money. If you're cured, you come back here and bring a gift for the *mochtó*.'

'She trusts people?'

Paloma smiled. 'If you try to cheat her, you risk angering the spirits. No one wants to do that.'

'Spirits like the *lohá*?' Jacey remembered. 'The one that's supposed to be waiting for Nicolás?'

Paloma looked uncomfortable. 'That's what they say. The *lohá* is a very bad spirit. But I'm a Catholic. I don't believe in such things.'

Jacey smiled. 'Nicolás doesn't believe it either.' She looked idly round at the chattering crowd and saw that the attendees were not all Indians. There were far more Spaniards present than she had first imagined. 'Mind you,' she added, 'a lot of Spanish people seem to trust the *mochtó*'s spirits.'

'These people can't afford to pay a doctor,' Paloma said.

It was then that Jacey saw a face that was definitely not Spanish, a man talking to one of the Indians. He was a tall man in a white shirt and faded Levis.

Jacey nudged Paloma, and pointed at him. 'Who's that?'

'Felix Connaught,' Paloma said. 'He's an American.' She paused. 'Do you want to meet him?'

'Of course I do,' Jacey said. 'Is he a doctor?'

'No,' Paloma said. 'He's just strange.' She waved her hand and caught the American's attention. Rather too easily, Jacey thought. He waved back and then pushed through the crowd towards them.

As he came closer Jacey realised that he was older than she thought. Nearer forty than thirty, she estimated, although it was difficult to guess precisely. He had the kind of quirky good looks that did not depend on regular features. His thick brown hair was roughly but attractively cut. He was not wearing a watch, but had a narrow bracelet made of beaten metal on one wrist and, round his neck, an Indian amulet on a beaded leather thong.

He smiled at her, the kind of open, friendly smile that it was difficult to resist. 'Hi,' he said. 'I'm Felix.' He held out his hand. 'And you're Dr Jacey Muldaire, from La Primavera and El Invierno.'

'Hi,' Jacey said. 'All I know about you is that you're American, and you're strange.'

'I meant nicely strange,' Paloma said hurriedly.

Felix laughed. 'You're right, Paloma. I'm strange. And to prove it I'm going to ask you to get me a cup of Indian tea.' He turned to Jacey. 'You don't want a cup too, do you?'

'Paloma warned me against drinking it,' she said.

'Quite right.' He nodded. 'It takes about twenty years to get used to it.'

'You've been here twenty years?' she asked, after Paloma had gone.

'Longer,' he said. 'I came here when I was three. I've been away a few times, but I always come back.'

'How come I haven't seen you before?' she asked.

'At the Márquez parties, or at polo?' He shrugged. 'I'm never invited. The élite of Techtátuan don't like me. Not that it bothers me.'

'What did you do to offend them?' Jacey asked.

He laughed. 'I'm that pitiful creature, the man who has gone native. I actually prefer the rainforest, and the Indians, to Techtátuan and men like Carlos Márquez. And particularly to men like Nicolás Schlemann.' He paused. 'Is it all right to say that to you?'

'Well, you seem to know a lot about me,' she said. 'So it's hardly surprising that you know about my relationship with Nicolás.'

'Almost every beautiful woman who's ever come to Techtátuan has been in the same situation with Nicolás,' Felix said. 'If he could market whatever it is that attracts them, he'd be a multi-millionaire.' He looked at her quizzically. 'Or maybe not. I understand that the allure can wear off quite quickly?'

She looked back at him, all innocence. 'Whatever makes you think that?' she parried.

'When the beautiful woman starts to look elsewhere,' he shrugged, 'one assumes it's because she's bored? Or even afraid, maybe?'

'It could be she just likes multiple lovers,' Jacey said flippantly.

'It could be,' he agreed. 'But in this case, I don't think so.'

Paloma was pushing through the crowd, a small cup in her hand.

'I need to talk to you, Dr Muldaire,' Felix said. 'We have a lot in common.'

'Have we really?' she asked. 'I socialise with people you dislike. I sleep with a man you detest. We don't seem to have anything in common at all.'

'I think we can help each other,' he said.

'What makes you think I need help, Mr Connaught?' she asked coolly.

'Felix,' he corrected. 'You want to help the people of Guachtàl. And so do I. I know a lot about you, Dr Muldaire. We have mutual friends. But we can't talk here. Will you visit me at home?'

'I don't know where you live.' She was filled with curiosity.

'Paulo does,' he said. 'Paulo will call for you

tomorrow evening. If you're not busy, come and see me. If you are busy, we'll make new arrangements. But please come. We need each other.'

Jacey sat on the bed next to Leonardo. She had just ordered him to strip, and now he lay naked, waiting for more instructions. Simply taking orders from her gave him an erection. He had removed his clothes so slowly, in an effort to prolong the pleasure of submission, that she felt a stab of frustration.

She still found him physically desirable. His tanned body, his delicate features, his neatly defined eyebrows and his glossy shock of black hair, aroused her as much as when she had first seen him. When she saw his half-unbuttoned shirt, she wanted to open it completely, cover one of his nipples with her mouth, and tantalise the other with her fingers. It was a caress he thoroughly enjoyed.

She remembered the first time she had let her tongue travel over his smooth skin, tasting him, feeling the ridges of his bones, and then moving up to find his nipple and gently tease it. He had let out a startled yelp of pleasure, and for a moment she thought he wanted her to stop. But as her head moved away, he caught hold of her, and pulled her back.

'Please,' he said. 'Do it.' And then later: 'Is this how it feels for a woman? Is this how it feels when I touch your breasts?'

'I don't know,' she murmured. 'How does it feel?'

'It's painful, but wonderful,' he said. 'Your tongue – and your teeth nipping me – it's unbearable. But I don't want you to stop.'

'Painful? Wonderful? Don't stop? Please stop?' She laughed. 'I think you need to sort yourself out, young man.'

It became a private joke between them: don't stop,

please stop. Now she sat next to him on the bed, and let her hand stray down over over his flat abdomen towards the dark tangle of his pubic hair. She circled his upright cock in her hand, and then bent over and took him in her mouth. After a few minutes she released him, and asked: 'How did that feel?

He was panting now, his hips thrusting convulsively. He mumbled something, his eyes closed and his face contorted.

'Don't stop, or please stop?' she prompted.

'Don't stop,' he gasped.

'Don't stop, please.'

'Please.' He put his hands on her head and tried to push her down on him again. But she evaded him, and, moving with a speed that took him completely by surprise, flipped him over on his face. Then she straddled him and reached between his legs, grasping his balls roughly. He let out a strangled yelp of pain.

'Leonardo,' she said, close to his ear. 'You've been gossiping about me.'

'I have not,' he protested.

She tightened her grip. 'You know an American called Felix Connaught?'

He paused, and she shook him, eliciting another yelp. 'Yes,' he admitted.

'What have you told him about me?'

'Nothing.'

She twisted his balls a little. 'Don't lie. I met him last night.'

'I didn't tell him much,' Leonardo gasped. 'Only that you are sympathetic to the Indians. That you are a kind person. He's my friend. He would like to be your friend, too.'

She kept hold of him. 'Perhaps I'd prefer to choose my own friends, Leonardo.'

'He can tell you about Loháquin.' Leonardo was

wriggling and bucking now, and Jacey found it difficult to hold on to him. She had excited him so much that he was rapidly losing control. Taking pity on him, she loosened her hand, and grasped his cock instead. He came almost at once, with a long cry of delight. After his body had calmed, she allowed him to turn over.

'Felix Connaught is Loháquin, isn't he?' she said.

She had hoped to catch him by surprise, but he simply gave her a startled look and then smiled. 'No, no,' he said. 'He isn't.'

'How do you know?' she insisted. 'You once told me you'd never seen Loháquin.'

'Felix is not Loháquin,' he said. 'I'm certain of it.'

'Has Felix seen him?'

Leonardo shrugged. 'Why don't you ask him?' He smiled. Rather smugly, she thought. 'When you visit him.'

Jacey knew immediately from Paulo's enthusiastic greeting that he trusted her again. He chattered non-stop in the car, driving her to the outskirts of Techtátuan, then to a badly made road that led to the edge of the rainforest, and finally along a track so bumpy that she feared for the car's rickety suspension.

Felix Connaught lived in a rambling bungalow built from natural materials, with a covered veranda. It was surrounded by tall trees and tangled undergrowth, and close to a river. In an area of cleared ground around his house, he grew vegetables and large clumps of exotic flowers.

Felix came to meet them in his usual faded Levis and open-necked shirt. Jacey noted a neat patch on the shirt's sleeve. The metal bracelet gleamed on his wrist. He handed her a cool drink in a tall glass.

'Welcome to my home, Dr Muldaire.'

'Jacey,' she said, taking the drink.

Paulo left to make a quick visit his own village, which was not far away. Felix led Jacey to the veranda, where two chairs stood waiting. Jacey sipped at the refreshing, citrus drink.

'My own recipe,' Felix said, when she complimented him on it. 'The rainforest supplies the flavours, and the river keeps it cool.'

'Don't you buy anything from Techtátuan?' she asked.

'Very little,' he said. 'If I haven't already got it, and the rainforest doesn't supply it, I do without it.' He smiled at her. 'Which means I have most of the things I really need.'

'Did you build this bungalow?'

He shook his head. 'My parents built it. They came to Guachtàl thirty-six years ago, when I was three. My father was an engineer who was fed up with the rat race, and my mother was a doctor. She wanted to help people. I don't know why they chose Guachtàl, but I do know that once they made their decision, there was no going back. They sold everything, and came here with the family rocking chair – which I still have – some crockery and cutlery, and a lot of books. Everything else they obtained by barter, or made for themselves. They loved the Indians, and their culture, and the way the rainforest sustained them. My mother found that the Indians didn't need her medicine; they had their own. She spent years studying it. My father used his engineering skills to build irrigation systems, and turned himself into quite a passable farmer. He kept us alive, anyway.'

'And you're interested in medicine, too?' she guessed.

'Because I was at the healing ceremony?' He grinned at her engagingly. 'I have a confession to make. I went there to meet you. I arranged it with Paloma.'

'I get the feeling I've been manipulated,' she said rather crossly.

'Only nicely so,' he said. 'I did want to see the *mochtó* again. We're old friends.' He gave her an intense look. 'And I wanted to meet you face to face. I need to do that, before I trust someone completely.'

'And you trust me completely?' she asked.

He nodded. 'I do now.' He smiled again. It was an attractive smile, she thought. Friendly and sexy at the same time. 'I asked several people about you first,' he said. 'People whose judgement I respect. That's the way I usually play it, and it's worked for me so far.' He stood up suddenly and went inside the bungalow. When he came out he was carrying a large pottery jar. He put it on the small table next to her chair. 'Home-made biscuits,' he said. 'Help yourself. Very healthy. I think you'll like them.'

Jacey took a biscuit. It was thick and knobbly, and tasted of nuts and spice.

'So why are you so interested in Loháquin?' Felix asked casually.

'Am I?' she parried.

'Yes,' he said. 'You are.'

'He's mysterious,' she said lightly. 'A ghostly eco-warrior living in the rainforest. That's interesting.'

Felix looked at her quizzically. 'You can do better than that, Dr Muldaire.'

'OK,' she said. 'How about this? There seems to be a lot of inequality in Guachtàl. Maybe if a rebel army marched into Techtátuan they could even things out.'

'So you think Loháquin is a rebel leader, with a secret army?' He sounded amused.

'Isn't he?' she asked. She crunched her biscuit. 'These are delicious.'

He pointed to the jar. 'Keep on eating. They're very good for the intestines.' He leant back in his chair and stretched out his legs. Nice, long legs, she thought. 'I can tell you now, Jacey,' he said, 'there is no hidden army, and Loháquin isn't a rainforest Che Guevara. It's a romantic notion, and Loháquin hasn't discouraged it because it gives the poor and disadvantaged of Techtátuan something to hold on to. But he's not planning an armed rebellion. It would be a disaster for Guachtàl.'

'Because Hernandez would fight back?' she predicted. 'There'd be a civil war?'

'Sure, that too,' Felix agreed. 'But the real tragedy is it wouldn't make any difference if Loháquin won. When the dust settled, there wouldn't be any money left in the banks, or the treasury. At the first sign of trouble, the rich would run, and take their money with them. And that includes Schlemann and Carlos Márquez. Those two have their asses well covered.'

'But what about Raoul?' Jacey protested. 'He wouldn't run.'

Felix laughed. 'You've got a soft spot for the idealistic Raoul, have you? No, I guess Raoul would stay and fight like a hero. And so would Leonardo. But Carlos controls the purse-strings. He's the older brother.'

'So the winners would be losers?' Jacey said. 'Guachtàl would be destitute.'

'Right.' Felix nodded. 'You'd have a country on the poverty line and very soon also deeply in debt. So no prizes for guessing who'd move in with the tempting offers. The guys who want to slam roads through the rainforest, and cut down the trees.'

'I thought Loháquin was opposed to that?' Jacey said.

'How long do you think his resistance would last?' Felix asked. 'Environmental idealism doesn't feed babies. I think we both know what would happen when the chips were really down.'

211

'If Lohaquin knows all this,' Jacey said, 'why bother to hide in the jungle and pretend to have an army?'

'Actually, the army story grew on its own,' Felix said. 'And like I said, the idea gives people something to hold on to. But violence isn't the only way to change things. It can be done from the inside.'

'Well, Lohaquin will have to come out of the jungle to do that,' Jacey said lightly.

Felix smiled. 'Maybe he will. And maybe you can help.'

'You're really Lohaquin, right?' she challenged.

'Wrong,' he said. 'Are you willing to help me?'

'What do you want me to do?' she asked cautiously.

'Don't look so worried,' he grinned. 'Just tell me what you know about this guy Curtis Telford.'

Jacey looked surprised. 'He's American. He's sex-mad. Nicolás seems very anxious to be nice to him, and Carlos Márquez isn't very happy about it.'

'Why not?'

Jacey shrugged. 'Gossip says Carlos suspects Nicolás is planning some kind of deal, and he's not included.'

Felix stood up. 'I'll be back in a moment,' he said. Jacey helped herself to another biscuit. When Felix returned he handed her a faded colour photograph. 'Look at this,' he said. 'Is Curtis Telford there?'

Jacey looked at the picture. It showed a group of five men in suits, obviously friends, socialising in what appeared to be a large garden, with a huge swimming pool in the background. The men were not looking at the camera. The problem was, none of them looked like the golden-haired, golden-skinned Curtis Telford. She scrutinised each man in turn, rejecting three faces as being the wrong shape and the wrong age. Of the remaining two, she used her

212

imagination to alter the hair style and colour, and made her final choice.

'This one,' she said. 'He's dyed his hair, and had a crew cut, but for my money, this is Curtis Telford.'

Felix nodded. 'That's what I thought.'

'That helps you?' she asked.

'A great deal,' he said. 'More than you can imagine.'

'He's a crook?' she guessed.

Felix laughed. 'That depends on your definition of crook. Some people would call businessmen crooks. And the people who pave the way for them to make their deals.' He shrugged. 'It's all a matter of definition, isn't it? But there is one other thing you can do for me, Jacey. Keep me informed. I'd like to know when Telford goes back to the States.'

'How do I tell you?' she asked. 'You don't appear to have a phone.'

'You could come out and see me again,' he said. 'Paulo would always bring you. It gives him a chance to visit his family.' He paused. 'Would that be a problem for you?'

'I don't think so,' she said.

'You sound a little doubtful,' he said. 'If you want to, you can send a message through Paulo. Or even Leonardo.'

'It's just that Nicolás has a habit of sending for me at a moment's notice,' she explained. 'I'm not sure how he'd react if I was out here another time.'

Felix stood up, and she realised for the first time how fit and strong he looked. 'Nicolás intimidates you?' His voice was soft.

'No,' she said. 'I knew what I was getting into when I started the affair. Nicolás didn't pressure me into it. It was my choice.' She looked up at Felix. 'It's just that I don't want to get you into any trouble. He can be very jealous.'

213

The atmosphere changed between them. Felix looked down at her. 'But he's got nothing to be jealous of,' he said quietly. 'Has he?'

She had a distinct feeling that he was going to add 'yet'. 'No,' she said. 'But he doesn't need any excuses.'

Felix laughed, and the tension eased. 'Don't worry about me,' he said. 'I've survived for twenty years. I'll survive for twenty more. I've still got my American passport, and plenty of friends in the States. I can handle any trouble Nicolás Schlemann tries to hand out.'

'Do you go home often?' she asked. She wanted to know more about this man.

'This is home,' he said. 'But I go back to the States from time to time. I did my schooling there. My parents wanted me to see what life was all about in the great big world. They wanted me to be able to make my own choices about where I'd live, and how.'

'And you chose Guachtàl?' she said.

'I chose the rainforest,' he said. He reached out, and took hold of her hands. 'It's a beautiful world,' he said softly. 'A world of infinite complexity. There are so many secrets to be discovered. It deserves to be protected. To be cherished. You believe that too, don't you?'

'Yes,' she said. 'I do.'

'That's what I thought,' he said. 'I think we're kindred spirits, you and I. We've still got some time before Paulo comes back. Tell me more about yourself.'

She sketched her life history for him, but it was far from the whole truth. She said nothing about Faisel, and nothing about the work she had done, and was still doing, for Major Fairhaven. In return he told her some equally sketchy details about himself. Both his parents had been killed in a plane crash. He had

214

studied computer science in the States, and had worked there for a time, but could not stay away from the rainforest for long. He did not mention any romantic liaisons.

As she bumped home along the rutted track with Paulo, Jacey thought about Felix Connaught. Clearly he liked her, and trusted her. And if I've read the signs correctly, she thought, he'd like to be more than just good friends. Did she feel the same? She wasn't sure.

Felix was intelligent, humorous and physically attractive. They seemed to have interests in common. So why did she feel apprehensive? Was it because she had the distinct impression that he would not be interested in a casual affair? He would want commitment? The kind of commitment she was not prepared to give?

Or was it because she found it difficult to trust him emotionally? Was he too good to be true? Would he end up letting her down, just like Faisel? And Peter Draven? Would he start pressuring her into domesticity, like Anton O'Rhiann?

At least I knew Nicolás was going to be a bastard before I even met him, she thought. And Leonardo is just a pleasant diversion. I know where I am with both of them. Felix Connaught is an unknown, and that bothers me.

She gave herself a mental shake. What's the matter with you, Jacey Muldaire? she asked herself. Why concern yourself with Felix Connaught? You've got what you wanted. You know that Loháquin doesn't represent any kind of trouble in Guachtàl. You can tell Major Fairhaven that anyone who wants to invest in future logging can go right ahead. They can decimate the rainforest, and make a lot of money. No one will stop them. In fact, Nicolás Schlemann will encourage them and he's probably working on it right now, with Mr Curtis Telford.

She looked out at the trees which bordered the rough road. That's what you want to hear, isn't it, Major? she thought. Congratulations, Dr Jacey Muldaire, you've completed your mission. But she also knew that particular achievement did not make her feel happy or fulfilled.

Chapter Seven

Nicolás stretched out his legs, and smiled at Jacey across her office desk. 'Are you going to tell me what you've been doing for the last week, or shall I tell you?'

Jacey smiled back at him sweetly. 'You can tell me,' she said.

'You've been giving English lessons to baby Leonardo. And you've visited that crazy American, Felix Connaught.'

'Crazy?' Jacey repeated. 'I would call Felix Connaught intelligent and interesting.'

'I suppose he told you the Indians can solve the world's health problems with a few plants and some mud?' Nicolás scoffed. 'And the spirits of the rainforest will destroy Techtátuan if anyone cuts down the trees?'

'Something like that,' she agreed.

'You're a scientist, Jacey,' he said. 'Don't you find it pitiful when a westerner starts believing in all that superstitious rubbish? If Connaught was ill, he'd rather chew a few leaves from the rainforest than ask you for help. Does that sound intelligent to you?'

'Chewing the right leaves might help him more than I could,' she responded.

'I doubt it,' Nicolás said. 'There's nothing special about Indian medicine. If you could show me an Indian who lived for five hundred years, because of some potion or other, I might be impressed. But Indians get sick and die, just like everyone else.'

'You don't know what's in the rainforest until you investigate,' Jacey said.

Nicolás laughed. 'I know what's in the rainforest. Trees. And trees equal money.'

'And you intend to exploit that,' she said accusingly. 'You and Curtis Telford. You'll destroy the rainforest, and destroy the Indians.'

'My dear Jacey,' he said patronisingly. 'You often have to lose something to gain something. And we won't destroy the Indians, we'll resettle them.'

'And what if they don't want to be resettled?'

He smiled cynically. 'Too bad. They've had plenty of time to assimilate into our culture, but most of them won't even try to learn Spanish. The rainforest is a resource, and I intend to see that Guachtàl gets full benefit from it.'

'It isn't yours to use like that,' she said.

'I suppose you're going to tell me it belongs to everyone?' Nicolás sneered. 'That we all live in a global village? The kind of nonsense Connaught preaches?'

'It's a treasure house,' she said. 'It's the Indians' home. And it's irreplaceable. We should cherish it.'

Nicolás laughed. 'Don't be naive, Jacey. This is the real world. Phoney spiritual idealism doesn't pay national bills.' He gave her a calculating look. 'I'm surprised at you. I didn't think you cared so much about a few trees.'

'I didn't,' she said. 'Before I came here.'

'And now Mr Connaught's propaganda has persuaded you to become an eco-warrior?' He smiled but it was a cold smile. 'Well, take a little advice, Jacey. Don't go off and join Loháquin and his supporters, wherever they're hiding, because they won't have a safe haven in the rainforest for much longer. And neither will Connaught. Or the Indians. When the logging gets under way, they'll all be flushed out, and there's nothing any of them will be able to do to stop it.'

'That's disgusting,' she said.

'That's progress,' he answered.

Later, Jacey wondered why Nicolás had left her office without demanding any sexual favours. It was the kind of situation she thought he would have relished. It would have been easy to tell her to lock the door, easy to take her quickly, over the desk, or force her to pleasure him.

Perhaps he's already getting tired of me, she thought. She didn't feel any disappointment at having been denied what was usually a satisfying sexual experience. Perhaps the novelty of our affair is wearing thin for me too, she reflected wryly.

She decided that the same could be said for her liaison with Leonardo. While he still delighted in playing the submissive innocent, he was also getting more knowledgeable, and more demanding. Their sex games were no longer spontaneous journeys of discovery. She was enjoying them less and less. At their last meeting, after hinting that he had a surprise for her, he had produced a complicated piece of equipment that seemed to consist mainly of thin, black leather straps.

'Look at this,' he said proudly. 'I made it.'

'What is it?' she asked unenthusiastically. She had never been attracted to leather gear.

'It's for me,' he said. 'A restraint.' He handed it to

219

her. 'Tell me to undress, and then you can put it on me.'

She took the tangle of straps, still unclear about their purpose. She knew that Leonardo expected to be ordered to remove each item of his clothing in turn. It had become a required ritual, but now, even though he would be aroused by this enforced humiliation, it no longer excited her. It had been fun when he was an unsophisticated boy, unsure of what was coming next. It had given her a feeling of erotic power to sense his apprehension, and to know that he would do whatever she told him. Now she was no longer his teacher; she was an accessory to his games. He had lost his innocence, and with it, she thought, a lot of his appeal.

He was fumbling with the buttons of his shirt. 'Shirt first?' he asked. 'Or trousers? You must tell me.'

'Leonardo,' she said. 'Don't give me orders.'

'But I want you to use the restraint,' he said. 'I have to undress first.'

There was a note of impatience in his voice that annoyed her. 'Maybe I don't want to use any restraint,' she snapped.

'But you'll like it,' he insisted, and added, 'Please. I want you to see it.'

'All right,' she agreed. But she was unconvinced.

She went through the routine list of orders, and watched him strip, but although he had an erection by the time he was naked – as he usually did – she felt unaroused. I'm glad one of us is enjoying this, she thought.

He took the restraint from her. 'Look,' he said, demonstrating. 'This goes round my waist, and this down between my legs. Then you have these four little straps to buckle up.' His eyes were bright with anticipation. 'Do it as tight as you like. Very tight.'

220

She wondered why she had not sussed it out before. The long straps kept the gadget on him, while the short straps were designed to go round his penis, holding it upright against his stomach. As his cock enlarged, they would cause him a considerable amount of discomfort, and then actual pain.

So he had made this appliance himself. If this was the way he saw their sex games going, she wanted no part of it. It did not shock her; she simply knew she would get no pleasure out of him trussed up in an increasingly complicated selection of bondage gear. A little gentle dominance, and a little brisk spanking, was the limit of her interest in S&M.

Leonardo was already fixing the restraint round his waist, clumsily trying the buckle the straps, his hands shaking with excitement. He glanced up at her, and grinned ruefully. 'Please help me. I'm too clumsy. I want the straps very tight.'

'No,' she said.

He looked bemused. 'But why not?' Then his expression changed. 'You have a better idea?' he asked hopefully. 'Tell me.'

'No,' she repeated. 'I don't have any other ideas, and I'm not going along with this one, either.' She saw bafflement in his eyes. 'This isn't my idea of fun, Leonardo,' she said. 'I enjoyed what we had before, but if you want to go down this path, you'll have to find another companion.'

The baffled look gave way to anger. 'I didn't realise you were so old fashioned,' he said.

'Don't be stupid,' she snapped, angry herself now. 'I'm just not interested in bondage and pain.' He was about to say something, but she talked him down. 'Because that's where it's going, Leonardo. And if you want it, good luck to you. There are plenty of women out there who'll be happy to truss you up, and tighten your straps, and whip you, if that's what turns you on. And they'll thoroughly enjoy themselves doing it. But I'm not one of them.'

He looked forlorn and very young, she thought sadly, standing by the bed, still with a partial erection, the black straps dangling against his lean body. She found herself hoping that he would find a bondage companion.

'I'm sorry,' she said. 'But I can't lie to you.'

'It's over, isn't it?' he said.

'I think so.'

He pulled the restraint off. 'I expected more.' His voice was sullen.

'Be grateful for what you've had.'

He dressed in silence and she watched him, still with a feeling of regret. Was she regretting the end of their affair, or the loss of that vulnerable sexual charm that had first attracted her, and which had gone forever.

He finally pulled on his lightweight jacket. 'I am very sorry to have caused you embarrassment,' he said stiffly.

'Oh, don't be ridiculous,' she said in exasperation.

'And I think it would be best if we did not see each other again,' he added, still rigidly formal.

'Yes, if that's what you want,' she agreed.

He went to the door, and then turned. 'Thank you for the lessons,' he said. 'They were very enjoyable.'

She smiled. 'I hope the English lessons were enjoyable, too.'

She hoped he would smile, and relax, but he turned without looking back and closed the door behind him.

The next day a large bunch of flowers arrived at Jacey's apartment. The card said, in English: I learnt a great deal from all of your lessons, and of course I look forward to seeing you again. Always your friend, Leonardo. She smiled, and carried the flowers down to her office with her. She was arranging them in a vase when Curtis Telford strolled into the room.

'Very pretty,' he said.

'They're from an admirer,' she said sweetly.

'Oh, you mean the flowers?' The wrapping paper, with the card pinned to it, was still on her desk. Curtis picked it up. 'Always your friend, Leonardo,' he read. 'Little Leonardo, eh? What lessons did you give him?'

'English lessons,' Jacey said.

He sat on the corner of her desk. 'I wouldn't mind taking lessons from you, Dr Muldaire. I'm sure I could learn a lot. What would you like to teach me?'

'Manners,' she suggested.

'Like please, as in please can we fuck?' He grinned.

'Like how to knock on an office door before you come in.' She took the wrapping paper out of his hand, detached the card, and stuffed the paper into her waste basket. 'And not to read other people's correspondence.'

'A greetings card?' He laughed. 'It isn't as if I've opened any envelopes.'

'I'm sure you would,' she said, 'if you thought you could gain something.'

'Hey,' he said, 'I get it. You're one of these tree lovers, aren't you? You think those apemen in the forest ought to rule the world?'

'I think you ought to leave the rainforest alone,' she said.

He shrugged. 'This little backwater country wants cash, lady. I can help them make the right deals. I can open doors, and not just in the States. Your boyfriend likes the sound of that, even if you don't.'

'Nicolás Schlemann is not my boyfriend,' she said. She pushed past him. 'And now, if you'll excuse me, I have to do my rounds.'

Curtis followed her into the corridor. 'So, I got the wrong words. Nick's your boss, your master, whatever you like to call it. Funny, I wouldn't have put you down as the submissive type. Dressed in leather, and using a whip, that's how I see you.' He grinned. 'I don't mind a bit of that myself. Perhaps I can persuade you to change?'

She ignored him, opened the door of her first patient's room and went in, hoping Curtis Telford would be gone when she came out again. He wasn't. He stayed with her during her rounds, pestering her to indulge his sexual fantasies, and he was still close behind her when she returned to her office.

'So how about it?' He sat on her desk again. 'You and me, and a little bit of domination? Or you and the ice maiden, putting on a show? Give me some sweet memories to take home with me?'

'You mean you're going home?' she asked, frigidly polite. 'That's splendid. When?'

'Soon,' he said. 'Next few days.' He stood up and came round the desk. 'I've just got a little business to finish up first.'

'Then I suggest you get on with it,' she said. 'And let me get on with mine.'

'Part of it concerns you,' he said. His hands landed on her shoulders. 'You and I have to fuck, lady. You and the ice maiden are the only two I want, and haven't had.' He turned her round to face him. 'I'm willing to forget about the Swede. She's a dyke anyway. But I'm not going to forget about you.'

'Even if I fancied you, Mr Telford, which I don't,' Jacey said coolly, 'I wouldn't even consider it. Nicolás is the jealous type.'

Curtis waved a finger under her nose. 'You'll have to do better than that. Nick has already told me you're hot stuff, and he's given me the go ahead to check you out.' He grinned at her. 'If you don't

224

believe me, just ask him.' He moved closer, and she felt his hands tighten on her shoulders again. 'So feel free to enjoy yourself. You've got the boss's permission. We can start right now with a blow job.' Jacey tried to evade him but he crowded her against the desk. 'And don't try and pretend you're shocked, lady, because I know you like acting the whore. And that's real good, because I like whores. I like the way they get down to business, and do as they're told.' He was unzipping his trousers as he spoke. 'So get to work. You know you really want to. Do it now.'

His cock was partially erect, and partially on view, when she lifted her knee and caught him between his legs. She hardly used any force, but it still doubled him over with a yell of pain. He clutched himself and leant against the desk, his face contorted. It took him several minutes to recover.

'Bitch,' he said. 'Fucking bitch. What d'you do that for?'

'That's a very stupid question,' she answered coolly. 'I don't give a fuck what Nicolás has told you, I choose my own partners. And you're not even in the running.' She went to the door and opened it. 'And now get out. I have work to do.'

He left, his face flushed with rage. She was pleased to see that he had some difficulty walking. Her anger that Nicolás had discussed her sexual preferences with him, and offered her services to him, was tempered by the fact that Curtis Telford had told her exactly what she wanted to know.

Paulo seemed delighted to drive Jacey out to see Felix Connaught again. 'If everyone was like Señor Connaught,' he said, 'this would be a wonderful country for the Indians. Señor Connaught cares about us, and he understands us. That is unusual for a westerner.'

'Did you know his parents?' Jacey asked.

Paulo shook his head. 'No. They died before I was born. But my parents knew them. They were good people. Señora Connaught went to a *mochtó* to learn the healing magic.'

'And the *mochtó* taught her?' Jacey was surprised. 'I thought that kind of knowledge was secret?'

'It is,' Paulo agreed. 'But Señora Connaught was here for many years. The *mochtó* trusted her, and accepted her as an apprentice.'

'Would a *mochtó* trust me?' Jacey inquired.

'Maybe,' Paulo said. 'If you lived here for many years.' He smiled at her. 'So perhaps you should stay with us?'

'Perhaps I will,' she said lightly.

But she knew it was a lie. She was already considering returning to England. She had all the information Major Fairhaven needed. She was glad that Leonardo still wanted to be friends, but her affair with him was definitely over. She thought of her feelings for Nicolás as a kind of addiction. When she saw him, she wanted him, but when she was back in England that would not be a problem. There's nothing left for me in Guachtàl, she thought, except to fulfil my promise to Felix Connaught.

When they arrived at the bungalow, Felix greeted her like an old friend, led her to a chair on the veranda, and poured her a cool drink.

'So Telford's little business trip was successful,' he said, when Jacey gave him her news. 'Good.'

'What's good about it?' she inquired. 'He's made a deal with Nicolás to start logging.'

'Not quite,' Felix said. 'Curtis Telford is an intermediary. He makes sure the businessmen will be welcome. He gets rid of any opposition. And he takes a healthy cut of the profits when the deals are completed.'

'Well, he didn't have much opposition here,' Jacey said.

'Less than he expected, probably,' Felix agreed. 'I'm sure Nicolás was very obliging.'

'So the road-building and the logging will go ahead,' Jacey said angrily. 'No one's going to stop it, are they? Lohóquin will hide in the forest, and do nothing.'

Felix stared at her for a moment, then laughed. 'You do really care about the rainforest, don't you?'

'Of course I do,' she said. 'And it makes me angry to think that Nicolás and Curtis Telford have won.'

'They haven't,' Felix said. 'Trust me.'

'Why should I trust you?' she countered. 'I've a feeling you're not really trusting me.'

'I want to,' he said. 'Believe me, I want to.'

'Does my association with Nicolás bother you?' she asked. 'Because I think it's just about over.' She shrugged. 'It never was serious, anyway.'

'It did bother me,' he admitted. 'But only because I couldn't understand why a woman like you could get involved with a man like that?'

'A woman like me?' she teased gently. 'What's that supposed to mean?'

'A caring woman,' he said quietly. 'An intelligent woman.' He leant forward and took her hands. 'I know Schlemann is considered to be physically attractive, but I couldn't believe that you didn't want something deeper than that.'

'Well, you're wrong,' she said. 'That's exactly what I did want. A man with a good body, who could give me good sex. Nicolás was perfect.' Felix looked perplexed, and she suddenly felt a perverse desire to hurt him. What right had he to judge her? To decide what kind of a woman she was, and what her needs were? 'Nicolás treated me like a whore,' she said,

227

'and I enjoyed it. Does that shock you, Mr Connaught?'

'No,' he said gently. 'It makes me sad.'

'I really don't see why,' she said as offhandedly as she could.

'Because it shows that you're deeply unhappy,' he said.

'I hope this isn't going to turn into a therapy session?' she said, keeping her tone flippant.

He took her hands again, and she felt the warmth of his fingers as they held hers. 'Why do you hate yourself, Jacey?' he asked softly. 'What happened to make you hate yourself?'

She looked into his eyes and saw real bafflement, and a genuine need to understand. Suddenly her anger dissolved. For the first time in her life, she wanted to talk. To talk about her past. Why not talk to this man, she thought. It might help me. He's a kind man, a caring man. And pretty soon I'll be leaving this country, and I'll never see him again.

'I fell in love,' she said. 'A long time ago. Or maybe I should say, I thought I was in love.'

'And he dumped you?' Felix nodded.

'He married me,' she said. The memories came flooding back. 'I married, and I had a baby.' She was vaguely surprised at how easy it was to say the words. 'A son.' She paused. 'He'd be about ten years old now.'

'He died?' Felix asked compassionately.

'No,' she said. 'I'm sure he's still alive.' Suddenly, sitting there with the muted noises of the rainforest all around her, she found the words gushing out. It was as if a dam had broken, and all the pent-up rage and frustration and pain spilt out. 'I was very young, and I married an Arab boy. I went back to his country, and when my baby was born, his parents

228

took the baby, and told me that unless I did exactly as I was told, I would never see him again.'

'And your husband agreed to this?' Felix was shocked.

'My husband didn't care,' she said. 'He was gay, and his family had ordered him to give them an heir. He did. As far as he was concerned, that was the end of my usefulness. I was a westerner. I didn't matter.'

'But his parents let you see the child?' Felix asked.

'I never saw my baby again,' she said. 'They took him away the day he was born. They told me to divorce my husband, and go back to England. They told me that if I caused trouble, they'd have me deported and I'd never see my son again, but if I behaved, they'd let me come back and visit him. It was all lies. They never intended to let me see him. But I believed them; I was young, frightened and alone. I had to believe them.' She shrugged. 'Of course, when I tried to get in touch with them later it was impossible. My letters were returned unopened. I tried to get help, I tried to get my son back, but I'd married in England, of my own free will, and gone out to my husband's country willingly, and no one was interested in my case. I had the impression that some people thought I deserved everything I got for being such a gullible fool. Maybe they thought my son was better off without such a stupid mother. And I suppose that for years I secretly thought that they were right. That it was all my fault.' She drew a deep breath and smiled. 'And that's it. The dark skeleton in my cupboard. What do you make of it, Mr Therapist?'

'You decided never to trust a man again,' Felix said. 'And I can't say I blame you.' He was still holding her hands. Now he pulled her closer to him. 'But we aren't all like that, Jacey. Believe me.'

229

'Don't feel sorry for me,' she said. 'Being footloose and fancy free seems to suit me.'

He gazed at her seriously. 'And you've never wanted to settle down?'

'Never,' she said. She smiled at him brightly, trying to lighten the atmosphere. 'Perhaps my ex-husband did me a favour. I've had a good life, with no emotional ties, and no emotional responsibilities.'

'Is that really good?' he asked. 'Doesn't it make you feel rather incomplete?' Before she could answer, he let go of her hands and stood up. 'Come inside with me, Jacey. I want to show you something.'

The interior of the bungalow felt cool and the windows were shaded with bamboo blinds. Some of the furniture was western, and Jacey guessed it had probably been bought in Techtátuan, but much of it had obviously been made from indigenous materials. Felix led Jacey into a small room. It had wall-to-ceiling shelves, and they were all crammed with bulging files, books, and papers gathered into bundles. A large table was piled with documents and ring-binders and a pot of fresh, bright flowers stood in the middle of the chaos.

'My mother's workroom,' Felix said. He saw her looking at the flowers, and smiled. 'My mother always had flowers everywhere. I like to keep up the tradition.'

Jacey touched one of the thick ring-binders. 'May I look?'

'Of course,' he said. 'That's why I brought you in here.'

The binder was full of botanical drawings, annotated with meticulous neatness, a strange contrast to the untidy room.

'It's a treasure trove,' Felix said. 'For anyone who can understand it all. This represents years of research. My mother learnt from the Indians, from

230

the healers. I don't think anyone else has had that opportunity, certainly not a western doctor.' He watched as Jacey looked round the room. 'There's a wealth of knowledge here. I can't do much with it, I'm just a computer buff.' He moved closer to her. 'But if I could find a sympathetic helper, someone who was willing to dedicate themselves to a voyage of discovery, things could become exciting.'

'Are you offering me a job?' she asked gently.

'If I was, would you accept?' he murmured.

'It would take a lifetime to work through all this,' she said.

'You have a lifetime,' he answered. 'Haven't you?'

She knew he was going to kiss her, and when he did she wondered why she was allowing it to happen. Although she certainly found him attractive, he did not give her the kind of instant sexual jolt that she felt when she looked at Nicolás, or the rush of unexpected lust she had experienced when she first saw Leonardo Márquez. But she felt desire, and need, as he grasped her shoulders and pulled her close, his body pressing against her.

Telling him about her past had acted as a catharsis. She felt light-hearted, and carefree. As his lips moved over her face and down to her neck, she relaxed against him, neither encouraging nor hindering him. She guessed he would be gentle and thoughtful, and that was just what she needed. She wanted to be made love to. She did not want to do anything; she wanted to let him pleasure her.

And he seemed quite willing to do so. His kisses grew more passionate, and she felt his hands moving to her breasts. He cupped them, and explored her nipples with his thumbs while, she made soft, encouraging noises in her throat. He pressed harder, massaging the sensitive peaks into hard little buds.

She was wearing a loose, sleeveless top without

231

buttons. As he tugged the garment upwards, she helped him by raising her arms. He pulled the top over her head, and then quickly removed her bra. She felt his excitement mount. Keeping her hands linked behind her neck, and her arms bent, she raised her elbows so that her breasts were level with his mouth. His lips closed over one erect nipple, and his fingers sought the other one. He concentrated for so long on exciting her breasts with his tongue, and his hands, that in the end she felt a slight impatience. She loosened the waistband of her skirt and it dropped to the floor. Surprised, he stopped his caresses and took a step backwards.

'Oh dear,' she teased. 'I've shocked you.'

'No,' he said. 'It's just that I didn't expect – I mean, I wasn't trying to pressure you.'

'You weren't?' She reached up and linked her hands round his neck. 'Well, you could've fooled me.' She pulled his head forward and kissed him. 'Do you have a bed in this bungalow? A nice, soft bed?'

'I have a bed,' he said, his mouth still over hers.

'Then take me to it, and make love to me,' she said. 'Gently and slowly. Please.'

He lifted her into his arms in one easy movement. 'The bed isn't that soft,' he warned.

'I don't care,' she said.

The bedroom was cool and shuttered. He put her down, and then unbuckled his belt and unzipped his jeans. She wriggled out of her panties, and waited for him to finish stripping. But when he stretched out next to her, she realised that she no longer felt particularly sexy, simply drowsy and pleasantly relaxed.

He began kissing her face again, but this time he moved down towards her breasts almost at once, and then lower, to her stomach, and then to her thighs.

232

His hands moved under her body to her bottom, and raised her up. She parted her legs slightly, and felt his mouth on her, his tongue touching her gently, too gently to really arouse her.

But she did not care. She was content to lie there and let him caress her, let him enjoy his own explorations. When at last he entered her, she responded to his thrusting movements more from politeness than desire. His body felt pleasantly safe next to hers and his strength and warmth were comforting. She knew he wanted to please her, and she did not want to disappoint him by appearing indifferent. As his thrusts grew deeper and less controlled, it triggered a natural response within her, and, when he finally climaxed with a shuddering cry, her own little moans of pleasure were quite honest. Her orgasm had been so gentle, it was hardly noticeable.

Afterwards they lay together for a long time, talking. He told her about his several attempts at romance, all of which failed when each of the girls refused to leave America and return to Guachtàl with him.

'One of them actually came over here for a holiday,' he said. He laughed softly. 'When she discovered I didn't have electricity or a john that flushed, she caught the next plane back to the States.' He rolled over on his side and reached out to brush a strand of red hair from Jacey's face. 'That sort of thing doesn't bother you, though, does it?'

'No,' she said. 'I've lived under worse conditions than that.'

But she did not explain where. She did not share any more of her own past with him. Much later, when she had dressed, and was ready to leave, he put his arms round her again.

'Will you come out here again? Soon?'

'Yes, I will.'

She felt a stab of guilt because it was a lie. She felt warm towards him because he was the first man she had ever confided in, without knowing why. But he wasn't her type, she told herself; he was too damn nice. It wouldn't work. He would not let her down. Quite the opposite. He would undoubtedly be loyal, stable and devoted. But could she give him those qualities back? She was not sure. And she did not want to see the disappointment in his eyes when she explained that she could not give him a long-term commitment. It was easier to lie, to lie by keeping quiet about the fact that she had already booked her ticket to England. One way.

She told Ingrid and Dr Sanchez that a relative was getting married and she wanted a brief holiday. She lied to them, too, promising to be back after a couple of weeks. She did not say goodbye to Raoul, or to Leonardo. And she did not see Nicolás.

Two days after her visit to Felix Connaught's bungalow she was back in London.

Jacey was surprised to see how grey and colourless London looked after Guachtàl, despite the fact that the sun was shining. She also felt cold, and gratefully accepted Major Fairhaven's offer of a cup of tea.

'You've done well,' he said, after she had explained her conclusions about the situation in Guachtàl to him. 'You didn't follow the expected path, but you got there is the end.'

'What expected path?' she asked.

The major looked slightly embarrassed. 'Well,' he said awkwardly, 'we, er, thought that you and Nicolás Schlemann might get together, and that maybe he'd confide in you.'

'How sweet of you,' she said coldly, inwardly seething. 'You sent me out there as a bribe. Here you are, Señor Schlemann, here's a nice lady for you to

234

make use of, and we hope that a good fuck will loosen your tongue.'

She saw the major wince, and remembered that he hated foul language. 'Please,' he said, 'it wasn't like that at all. Do you really think we'd be so cold-blooded?'

'Yes,' she said. 'What a pity you didn't do a little research first. You'd have soon found out that Nicolás isn't the type to start whispering state secrets when he's in a euphoric post-coital daze.'

'We never intended anything of the sort,' the major said stiffly. 'It was simply a question of maybe it would happen. And maybe you could use the situation, if it did. After all –' he tried to charm her with a smile, but she stared stonily back '– you're a very attractive woman, and Schlemann has a reputation. It was just one of the options. There were others.' He was still smiling, a fixed and insincere grin. 'And you found some of them, didn't you? All's well that ends well, after all.'

'For you,' she agreed. 'And for the businessmen. But not for the rainforest.'

'My dear girl,' he said, and she heard the irritation in his voice. 'You haven't been seduced by all that green nonsense, have you? The dangers to the rain-forest have been grossly exaggerated, and countries run on money, not hippy ideals.'

Jacey stood up. 'Do you know,' she said sweetly, 'you sound just like that crook Nicolás Schlemann. Isn't that strange?' She turned to go, and then stopped and smiled. 'But on second thoughts, Major, perhaps it's not so strange after all.'

The first familiar face that Jacey saw when she returned to the Midland General was Anton O'Rhiann. He looked harassed, had a bundle of papers under his arm, and was hurrying down the corridor. If she had not spoken to him, she was sure he would have gone past without recognising her.

'Jacey?' For a moment his eyes did not seem to focus on her, and she knew he was very tired. 'What are you doing here?'

'Visiting,' she said.

'Well.' He stared at her for a moment. 'Thanks for the letter.'

For a moment she did not understand what he meant. Then she remembered the letter she had sent him, telling him she was leaving for South America, and their affair was over. 'I didn't have the courage to say goodbye to your face,' she admitted.

'Obviously,' he said.

There was a long pause, and she wondered if he felt as awkward as she did. 'You're busy,' she said. 'Perhaps we can meet later?'

'What for?' His voice was bitter now. 'So that you can tell me what a good time you had in South America? What were the men like, Jacey? All out for a good time? Sex and no strings? Did you have a lot of nice, non-permanent relationships?'

She was beginning to feel guilty. She had treated him badly, running out on him and leaving him a letter that didn't really explain much. But she had not felt able to face him, and lie to him. His increasing insistence on legitimising their relationship had been part of the reason why she had accepted Major Fair-haven's assignment. She knew her affair with Anton was virtually over. Making a clean break had seemed the right thing to do at the time.

'I went to Guachtàl to work,' she said.

'Oh, I'm sure you did,' he agreed. 'And how long were you planning it? You don't just drop everything and get a job abroad. You must have known for weeks in advance. I don't suppose it occurred to you to tell me?'

'It wasn't like that,' she said. 'It all happened very quickly.'

She knew he did not believe her, and she did not blame him. But she could not tell him the truth.

'That's what hurts the most,' he said. 'You knew that you were going to leave me. When we made love, you knew it. And you didn't say anything.' They faced each other in silence. Then he said, 'I have to go. I'm very busy.'

'I know what being a house doctor is like,' she said.

'Oh, you remember, do you?'

'Hard work, but lots of job satisfaction,' she said, saying the words more lightly than she felt.

He stared at her for a moment. 'I hope you're not planning to re-apply for a position here.' He turned away from her and started to walk down the corridor. 'Because if you do, I shall leave.'

Jacey was sitting in the lobby of her small London hotel, reading the *British Medical Journal*, when she sensed someone standing in front of her. She glanced up and saw Peter Draven smiling at her.

'Looking for a job?' he asked.

'Yes,' she said calmly, masking her total amazement. 'Why? Do you know of one?'

He grinned. 'Very good. Not even a glimmer of surprise. A good doctor can disguise her true feelings under all circumstances. Very useful when you have to tell someone they're going to die.' He sat down. 'Mind if I join you?'

'Only if you tell me what you're doing here?' she said.

'I've been back for some time,' he said.

'I mean here,' she said.

'Would you believe coincidence?'

She shook her head. 'No. I wouldn't.'

'You'd be right,' he said. 'I knew you were back. It wasn't difficult to find out where you were staying.' He grinned at her. 'Any good secret agent could do it.'

'But you're a doctor,' she said.

'So are you,' he countered.

She stared at him. 'Tell me that what I'm thinking is nonsense.'

'If you're thinking, does he work for Major Fairhaven's department too, then it isn't nonsense,' Peter said.

'Now tell me what you were doing at La Primavera,' she said.

'More or less the same as you.' He shrugged. 'But with less success. I didn't manage to penetrate Nicolás Schlemann's secret circle of friends, probably because I don't think he had a secret circle. That man is a consummate professional. I doubt if he confides in anyone.' He smiled. 'Not even in the throes of passion. Am I right?'

'Absolutely,' she said coolly.

'So it was a waste of time giving you to Nicci,' Peter said. 'I could have disobeyed orders, and kept you to myself.'

'Orders?' she repeated. 'You were told to get me involved with Nicolás?'

Peter nodded. 'You don't think I'd have been stupid enough to do it otherwise? Not after what we had going for us. Our mutual bosses were pretty certain Nicci would notice you, but I had to make absolutely sure the two of you got together. And then I was told to come home, and leave you to it. I don't mind telling you, I didn't want to. But you know how it is. Orders are orders.'

'Oh, I know how it is,' she agreed. 'Major Fairhaven wanted a Spanish-speaking doctor, attractive enough to catch the eye of Nicolás Schlemann, and willing enough to jump into bed with him, and he looked down his list and found me.' She noticed that Peter looked uncomfortable. 'And you were told to help things along. It was as cold-blooded as that.' She smiled at him humourlessly. 'Don't look so miserable. That's the way the game is played.'

'I suppose it is,' he said.

'And what are you doing now, Dr Draven? Tailing me? Making sure the major knows where I am, in case he needs me for another exciting assignment? I wonder what it'll be this time? Perhaps I'll be offered to an eastern potentate as a bribe.'

'Actually, I'm waiting to be sent out to America,' Peter said awkwardly. 'When I heard you were back, and in London, I thought I'd look you up.'

'Why?' she asked.

He looked increasingly uncomfortable. 'I thought we could spend a few days together.'

'For old times' sake?' she asked pleasantly. 'Or because it's cheaper than hiring a whore?'

He flinched as if she had hit him. 'That's unfair. I thought our affair was a mutual thing. I thought we had something together.'

'We did,' she said. 'Sex. But that was all. And I haven't forgotten that while you were fucking me in that operating theatre, you knew very well Nicolás Schlemann was watching.'

'That was his idea,' Peter said.

'I know very well it was his idea,' she answered. 'But you could have refused. And maybe you could have told me a little of what was going on.' He was about to say something but she silenced him. 'Don't say you couldn't because you were obeying orders.'

'What else can I say?' He shrugged. 'You know the rules. If it's any consolation to you, I didn't enjoy playing a double game with you.'

'It isn't any consolation to me,' she said. 'But do

you know what's even worse? I can sit here and know I've been manipulated and used, and treated like some kind of whore, and I don't even feel angry any more. I just feel numb. That's what working for Major Fairhaven does to you, Peter. And that's why I'm finished with it, for real, this time. I got out once before, and I let the major talk me back in, but this time it's over. I'm going to go away and turn myself into a nice, normal human being, with a nice, normal boyfriend, and a nice, normal life.'

'I wish you luck,' he said.

'Thank you,' she said. 'And if the major has really sent you to find me, and check out if I'm ready for another assignment, you can tell him from me to fuck off. And please use those exact words.'

She thought she saw a spark of devilment in Peter's eyes. 'If I was going to report back to the major,' he said, 'it would be a real pleasure to give him your message.'

Jacey could not really decide whether it was the rain that had sent her down to the travel agency to buy a ticket to Guachtàl, or her daydreams about Felix Connaught. She had never bothered much about British weather before, but now each grey morning made her miss the bright colours of Techtátuan. And she had never had daydreams about a man who was less than exciting in bed either, but she found herself remembering Felix Connaught's smile, his voice, his long legs in the faded Levis, and the glint of the narrow bracelet on his wrist. She could not get him out of her mind. What would it be like to work with him, live with him, share her life with him? The more she thought about it, the more she wanted to find out.

Maybe we could both give Nicolás Schlemann a run for his money over the logging, she thought.

Maybe we could drag this Loháquin out of hiding, and turn him into more than just a symbol for revolution. The possibilities were there; it just needed someone to give them impetus. And maybe, she thought, I'm that person.

As far as the staff at La Primavera were concerned, there had never been any doubt that Jacey would return. When they asked her if she enjoyed the wedding, she made up some stories to satisfy them.

Ingrid told her that Curtis Telford had returned to the States. 'And I didn't fuck him,' she said, with obvious satisfaction. 'Not once. Do you think I'm becoming a good girl at last?'

'I think you just didn't fancy him,' Jacey said. 'And I don't blame you.' She grinned. 'Did I tell you I kneed him in the balls?'

Ingrid gave a shout of laughter. 'You did not. Tell me now.'

Jacey explained briefly what had happened, and Ingrid punched the air with her fist. 'Yes! That's what he deserved. Why didn't I do it myself?'

'Because you're a well-brought-up ice maiden,' Jacey said.

After Ingrid had gone, Jacey worked through her patients' files and realised that, as usual, no one had any serious ailments. She completed her notes, and completed her rounds, and decided to go back to her apartment for a shower.

She unlocked her door to find Nicolás lounging in her armchair, wearing a smart, dark-grey suit. His jacket was undone and his shirt collar unbuttoned.

'Welcome home,' he said politely.

'Thank you,' she said, equally polite.

'It would have been nice to know in advance that you were taking a holiday.'

'I thought you already knew everything about me,'

she countered. 'And that seems to include how to get into my apartment.'

'I got the master key from the cleaning woman,' he said. 'I'm told you went to a wedding?'

'That's right.' She took off her white coat and tossed it over a chair.

'I did think you might have gone to America,' he said. 'With Felix Connaught.' She made no effort to disguise her surprise, and he smiled. 'You didn't know? How remiss of Mr Connaught. I thought he would have told you.'

'Why should he?' She loosened her hair, which had been tied back. 'It's really no business of mine where he goes.'

'I wouldn't have been very pleased if you'd gone with Mr Connaught,' Nicolás said softly.

'Wouldn't you?' she said coolly. 'It's really no business of yours where I go either, is it?'

'Yes, it is.' He had stopped smiling now. 'I don't like sharing my women.'

Jacey knew that she no longer needed to pander to Nicolás's possessive control, but as she stared at him, his long legs stretched out in front of him, she felt a surge of sexual desire. What the hell is the matter with me? she thought angrily. I was sure our affair was over; I didn't even give him a thought while I was in England. And now I walk in here, take one look at him, and all I can think about is how much I'd like to take all his clothes off. Or have him take mine off. Or go down on him. Or have him –

Nicolás interrupted her thoughts. 'I hope you missed me while you were in England.' He grinned the cynical smile that always made him look both dangerous and desirable. 'I hope you thought about me when you went to bed.'

'I didn't,' she said truthfully. And added, 'Why should I? We've never actually been to bed.'

242

'How many men did you fuck in England?' he asked pleasantly.

'None,' she said just as pleasantly, and wondered if he would believe her. 'How many women did you fuck while I was in England?'

He shrugged. 'A few, mainly to please Telford. He liked group sex.'

'And was it so very necessary to please Curtis Telford?'

He nodded. 'Yes. Financially necessary.' The cynical grin twisted his mouth again. 'But none of the whores were as good as you.'

'Well,' she said, 'that's very flattering, I'm sure. If I ever want to give up being a doctor, it's nice to know that there's another profession I'm eminently suited for.'

'You're right,' he said. 'Go into the bedroom and take your clothes off.'

She smiled at him. 'Why don't we do it a little differently this time? We'll both go in there and I'll take yours off.'

She was surprised when he stood up. 'What a very good idea,' he said.

He preceded her into the bedroom. She walked over to the window and half closed the blinds, so that the room was dappled in shadow.

'Well?' He was standing by the bed. 'Are you going to make a start?'

She sat on the bed. 'Change of plan,' she said. 'Do you know I've never seen you completely naked?'

He shrugged. 'So? Why don't you do something about it?'

'No,' she said. 'You do something. Strip.'

He looked at her for a moment, and then, to her surprise, took off his jacket slowly. He removed his shirt, turning round so that she could admire his lean musculature, kicked off his shoes, and then unzipped

243

his trousers. He took his time, letting them slide down his legs to the floor. He sat on the bed in his tight, dark briefs and pulled off his socks. Then he stood up and smiled.

'I don't think you've quite finished,' she said.

Still smiling, he hooked his thumbs under the top band of his briefs and pushed them down in a smooth movement, stretching the briefs over his erection, as he turned his back to her.

'Very neat,' she said. 'You could make a living as a stripper.'

'I thought they did it to music,' he answered.

She laughed. 'Next time I'll put on a CD. But you'd also have to learn not to short-change the paying customers. Turn round.'

He turned, unselfconsciously displaying himself, his cock rising almost vertically above his heavy balls and the thick mass of his black pubic hair. She was reminded, briefly, of Leonardo. Nicolás had the same long thighs, neat hips and small waist but his physique was more mature. He had more dark body hair, and better muscle definition. Dancer's muscles, she thought. Sinewy and strong, but not over-developed like a body builder. She had been impressed by his torso when she had given him that first medical examination. She was even more impressed now she could see his whole body. There did not seem to be an ounce of spare flesh on him.

'Lie down on the bed,' she ordered. It was a novelty to see him obey. She let her eyes move over his body for a few more seconds, then she walked to the bed and sat down next to him. She put out her hand and smoothed her palm over his chest. As her fingers touched his nipple she heard him gasp. She moved her other hand lightly over his pecs, found the other nipple, and traced a decreasing circle around that too. She felt his excitement rising, and

244

increased the pressure, catching each nipple between her fingers, and tugging. He bore it for a few minutes, his eyes closed, and his face contorted with pleasure, then suddenly reached up and caught her head with one hand. Twisting his fingers into her hair he forced her down towards his erection.

She took him in her mouth, more roughly than she intended, and heard him groan. She wanted to delay his orgasm for as long as possible, until he begged her for release, but he held her down, thrusting into her mouth and throat. He filled her; it was uncomfortable, but exciting too. She thought about moving back, out of reach, forcing him to beg her to continue. But before she could, his orgasm jolted him with an unexpected suddenness. He pulled away from her, and she watched his body thrash in uncontrolled spasms. Finally calmed, he lay on his back, panting, his face sheened with sweat. After a few minutes, he said drowsily, 'That was really good.'

'Better than usual?' she asked.

'The best,' he said. 'For a long time.'

'It can be fun to change roles occasionally,' she observed.

He smiled lazily. 'Obviously.' He tugged at her blouse. 'Why don't you take this off?'

'Why don't you undress me?' she asked.

He stretched his arms, and linked them behind his head. 'Because I feel too comfortable, and too relaxed.'

She stood up, and removed her own clothes, but without any attempt at artifice. When she was naked, she lay down next to him. He rolled over to face her, and propped himself up on one arm. Slowly, he let a hand explore her body. It started as a wandering, directionless caress, a voyage of discovery, and it reminded her that this was the first time he had ever treated her in this way. Slowly his fingers became even more exploratory, searching for erogenous zones he had never bothered to touch, and lingering on them, gauging from her reaction how long he should stay there, and how heavy or light he should make his caresses. She wondered sleepily if he had ever handled a woman this way before. Then she felt his body move. He twisted on the bed until his head was at her feet.

'Open your legs,' he said.

She parted them, and felt him edge up between them. She closed her eyes and the thought of what was about to happen gave her a sexy thrill in exactly the place she hoped he would put his tongue. He parted her thighs with his hands so that he could move more easily, and when his mouth touched her, her body shivered with pleasure. His tongue was strong and insistent: her only regret was that she would not be able to enjoy his expertise for very long, because she could already feel herself losing control.

When her orgasm came, she felt her body buck and roll on the bed so violently that he had to grasp her hips to hold her down. It took her several minutes to regain her self-control, and then she realised that Nicolás had returned to his original position next to her, and was watching her with a self-satisfied grin.

'You enjoyed that, didn't you?' he said.

'Yes,' she said simply.

'So that's both of us satisfied,' he said. 'Do you have any wine?'

'In the fridge,' she said.

She was surprised when he stood up and walked over to her kitchen, and even more surprised when he came back with a tray and two glasses.

'I thought the traditional thing was a cigarette?' she said.

'Filthy habit,' he said. He poured her a drink. 'This is much better for you.'

As they lay together, naked, drinking wine, Jacey realised that this was another first. He had never stayed with her so long after having sex. He lay next to her until he had finished his wine, and even then did not seem in any great hurry to get up. When he did, he smiled at her and asked gently, as if not to disturb her, if he could use her shower. She lay on the bed and listened to the water cascading, imagining it polishing his lean body. As she watched him dress, in her drowsily satiated state she found this reverse form of striptease arousing.

He glanced at his watch. 'The car will be waiting for me,' he said. He sounded almost regretful.

'No doubt you'll phone me when you want me?' she asked.

'Yes,' he said. Even then he hesitated, and she could see that he was reluctant to leave. He smiled, his familiar, crooked smile. 'It's been very pleasant,' he said. 'Expect to hear from me again, quite soon.'

Jacey lay in bed that night thinking about Nicolás, and wondering about the subtle change in his attitude. If I didn't know him better, she thought, I could almost believe that he had missed me, that he was glad to see me again, that he's beginning to think of me as something other than just another trophy.

But I don't really know him, she realised. I've made judgements based on what I've been told by others, and what I've seen for myself, but although we've been as physically intimate as a couple could be, we've shared very little else. A story about his first sexual experience – which may or may not have been true – and some political sparring about the fate of the rainforest.

And it hasn't mattered to me, she thought. He makes me feel as sexy as hell when I'm with him, but when I'm not, I hardly think about him. While I was

247

in England, I didn't even fantasise about him, which I usually do when someone really turns me on. I didn't wonder what he was doing, or care if he was with other women.

But she did think about Felix Connaught, she remembered, rather to her own surprise. And not about how he performed in bed, but about his ideas and his hopes for Guachtàl. It made her happy to know that someone cared about the future of the rainforest. And he was the first man – the first person – she had been able to talk to about her stolen baby. It was easy to tell him. It actually made her feel better. And since then, her horrible memories hadn't bothered her so much. Even the thought of her son didn't cause her pain. He was being brought up by a rich family, who wanted him desperately, and who were probably spoiling him silly.

She smiled sleepily. I'm halfway towards accepting what happened to me, she thought, thanks to Felix. He was the right man, in the right place, at the right time. He's decent and trustworthy, and I like him. I like him a lot.

She wondered drowsily if she could settle down with a man like Felix. Although she had told Peter Draven that she wanted a nice, normal life, and a nice, normal boyfriend, she wasn't absolutely sure that it was true. The knowledge that she was now in complete control of her life, and could make her own choices, was very attractive. She no longer had a secret agenda, and Nicolás's voice on her mobile phone could no longer summon her like a slave. She could be nice to him, but only if she wanted to.

Did she want to? That was another question she had to answer. Jacey Muldaire, she reprimanded herself, if you are going to stay in in Guachtàl you will have to sort out the men in your life. Felix first, she decided. I have to know how he really feels about me.

The next day, she telephoned Leonardo and asked him to come and see her. As soon as he walked into her office she realised that in the few weeks she had been away, he had changed completely. He had lost the innocent, vulnerable look that had attracted her when she first saw him. The awkward boy had gone forever and an elegant, self-assured young man stood in his place.

Jacey held out her hand and he grasped it. 'Leonardo,' she said. 'You look very smart.' She smiled at him. 'I'd guess that you've got a new girlfriend.'

He nodded. 'The most wonderful woman in the world.' And then he added hastily, 'After you, of course, dear Jacey.'

'Don't fib,' she said. 'I disappointed you.'

'On the contrary,' he said. 'You were my tutor. I owe everything to you. I'd never have had the confidence to approach Margaretté if I hadn't learnt about women from you.'

'So,' Jacey prompted, 'what's she like?'

'Quite a lot like you,' he said diplomatically. 'Beautiful, intelligent, and a little bit older than me.' He paused, and then smiled. 'Well, quite a bit older than me. We like the same kind of music, and the same books.'

'And the same kind of sex?'

His smile broadened. 'We have designed some equipment together. Margaretté is very inventive. She has such an imagination; you wouldn't believe the ideas she comes up with. And she is very strict. Sometimes I cannot sit down for a day after I've spent time with her.'

'She sounds just what you need,' Jacey said.

'I think so,' he agreed. He stared at her. 'But there is always room for another woman in my life.'

'Leonardo,' she chided, 'you're getting to be just like your brother. I didn't ask you to come here so that we could start up a relationship. I need to speak to Felix. When will he be back from America?'

'Soon,' Leonardo said. He paused. 'Felix was unhappy that you did not tell him you were visiting England for a wedding.'

'I didn't go to a wedding,' she said. 'I needed some space to sort out my feelings, to find the answers to some questions. I wasn't sure what decision I was going to make. I didn't even know if I was coming back to Guachtàl.'

'But you're here,' Leonardo said, 'and I'm glad.' He paused. 'I think Felix will be glad, too.'

'I hope so,' Jacey said. 'Do you think he'll contact me when he returns?'

'I'm sure of it,' Leonardo said. He smiled. 'And I think he will have something very interesting to tell you.'

It was a week before Paulo came to Jacey with a message from Felix and a date for a meeting. As she sat next to him in the car, she had a feeling he was keeping something from her. He seemed especially cheerful, and kept hinting that she was going to get a surprise, but when she pressed him for more details he suddenly became a picture of innocent ignorance.

At the bungalow Felix came out to meet them. He took Jacey's hands and held them for what seemed a long time. 'I'm glad you came back,' he said simply.

'Did you doubt it?' she teased.

'When you left without saying goodbye?' He smiled. 'I wasn't sure.'

'It was cowardly of me,' she said. 'But I needed time to think.'

'I won't ask if you're here to stay,' he said. 'But at

least promise me that if you leave again, you'll tell me before you go.'

'I promise,' she said. She smiled. 'How was America?'

'Mercenary and crowded,' he said. 'But useful.' He held out his hand. 'Do you fancy a walk? I have a couple of surprises for you. The first one is in the rainforest.'

Paulo was still standing by the car. Felix glanced across to him, and nodded. Paulo got into the car and started the engine.

'Don't worry,' Felix said to Jacey. 'He's coming back. This isn't a kidnap attempt.'

He led her into the rainforest. It was the first time she had walked under the canopy of trees and she imagined it as a green tunnel with a high roof. The air smelled warm and damp and, as she followed Felix, a myriad of noises accompanied her.

'Where are we going?' she asked.

'To Matá,' he said. 'Paulo's village. There's someone I want you to meet.'

The village was larger than Jacey expected, with neat, round huts spread over a wide area, separated by cleared ground and some cultivated plots. A group of small children ran forward to greet Felix, and they stared solemnly at Jacey. Felix spoke to them in guttural *Chachté*, and Jacey thought she heard the word *mochtó*. The children all gaped at her, open-mouthed.

'What have you told them?' she asked Felix.

'The truth,' he said. 'That you are a very powerful healer.'

He led her to a hut at the edge of the village, close to where the rainforest took over again.

'*Holé tachta!*' he called, in greeting.

Jacey was expecting to meet the elderly *mochtó* from the healing ceremony. She was totally unprepared to see a tall woman wearing native clothes, her black hair falling loosely down her back, her skin burned brown. She was obviously not an Indian.

The woman smiled, held out her hand and said in perfect Spanish: 'Welcome, Dr Muldaire. I'm Juanita Márquez. I'm glad to meet you at last. I've heard so much about you from Felix. Won't you sit down and drink *toltoc* with me?'

Jacey squatted on the ground with Felix. She felt amazed and pleased that Juanita was still alive. A young Indian girl came out of the hut carrying two gourds which were filled with a deliciously spicy-smelling liquid.

'This is a traditional welcome drink,' Felix explained. 'And it's quite safe. Just fruit juices. Drink first, and then we'll talk.'

'I'll answer all your questions,' Juanita said. 'I'm sure you have a great many.'

'I suppose the first one ought to be, what's it like being dead?' Jacey said.

Juanita laughed. 'The reports of my death have been exaggerated. Didn't someone famous say that once?'

'Most people seem to believe the reports,' Jacey said.

Juanita leant forward, serious now. 'Well, in a way, they're true. I'm not the greedy girl who married Alfonso for his money, or the silly woman who did crazy things, like redesigning that ridiculous villa. I don't regret my passionate affairs, and I love my sons. But the woman who did all those things is dead. Quite dead.'

'So who are you?' Jacey asked, quite amused.

'A woman of the rainforest,' Juanita said. 'I have been reborn.' She waved her hand round at the village. 'Everything I need is here. I'll never go back to the town. There's nothing there for me now.'

'Does anyone else know you're here?' Jacey asked. 'Apart from Paulo and the villagers, and Felix.'

'Leonardo knows,' Juanita said. 'But it's dangerous for him to keep coming out here. In the end someone will suspect. That's why I didn't tell Raoul. He's a dear boy, but so impulsive. He would have been forever checking whether I was safe, which is quite unnecessary, of course. This is the safest place in the world. No one can arrive unexpectedly, and if someone comes that I don't want to see, I simply hide until they've gone away.' She smiled. 'But I'm not isolated. I know exactly what's going on in Techtátuan.'

'So you know Nicolás has plans to let the loggers into the rainforest?' Jacey said.

Juanita nodded. 'I know all about Nicolás Schlemann,' she said.

'Do you know all about Loháquin?' Jacey asked.

Juanita looked startled, and Felix laughed. 'Jacey is determined to meet our famous eco-warrior,' he said.

Juanita looked at him reproachfully. 'Doesn't she know? Surely you've told her?'

Jacey turned to Felix. 'Told me what?' she demanded. 'What is this mystery about Loháquin?'

'There isn't one,' Felix said. He smiled. 'There isn't a mystery, because there isn't a Loháquin. There never has been. I started the rumour myself, mainly to give Nicolás some opposition, and it gathered momentum, rather like a game of Chinese whispers. Everyone made Loháquin into what they wanted him to be.' He laughed. 'I must admit, I was surprised when I first saw him on the wanted posters. I had no idea I'd created such a scruffy-looking guy.'

'Paloma has a much more flattering picture,' Jacey said. 'But didn't you feel you were raising false hopes? You've created a ghost, and ghosts can't help anyone.'

253

'They can,' Felix said. 'People brought money for Loháquin, and I always used it to help the Indians.'

'But what about the loggers?' Jacey insisted. 'A ghost can't fight them.'

Felix stood up and smiled. 'Maybe not. But I can.' He took Jacey's hand. 'Come and meet some of my friends here in the village. And then we'll go back home – for the second part of my surprise.'

Jacey enjoyed seeing the village, and felt pleasantly relaxed as she walked back to the bungalow. Paulo's car was outside.

'Good,' Felix said. 'Our guest has arrived.'

Jacey was not sure who she expected to see but it certainly wasn't the tall, dark-suited man who turned angrily to face them as they came in. Nicolás Schlemann looked at Felix, then at Jacey, and then back at Felix again. 'What the hell's going on?' he demanded.

Jacey turned to Felix. 'This is the surprise you promised me?'

'Part of it,' Felix said.

'You've brought me out here on false pretences, Connaught,' Nicolás said. 'I understood you had a business proposition for me, but if it concerns Dr Muldaire, I'm not even interested in opening negotiations. I don't share my women.' He smiled cruelly at Jacey. 'Although I sometimes give them away.'

Jacey saw Felix's expression change. 'Just leave Jacey out of this,' he said tightly. 'She didn't know you'd be here until she walked through the door. My offer to you was genuine. I have something for you. Something you need.'

'You don't have anything I need,' Nicolás said. He walked over to the door, then stopped and turned, and looked carefully round the room until his eyes rested on Jacey. 'You don't seem to have anything of worth at all.'

'I'm offering you a chance to escape,' Felix said. 'A chance to avoid going to jail.'

'Living with the Indians has got to you, Connaught,' Nicolás drawled. 'You're as crazy as they are. What makes you think I'd ever end up in jail?'

'You will,' Felix said, 'when Hernandez finds out you've filched large sums of money from the treasury and put them into a European personal account. And when Curtis Telford hears that the money he's paid out for the logging rights in Guachtàl has gone the same way.'

For a moment Nicolás looked bemused. Then he smiled derisively. 'You've been drinking too much jungle juice, Connaught. It's softened your brain. I haven't touched any treasury money, or Telford's money either. And I don't have a European account. Why would I need one?'

'Because you're planning to leave Guachtàl,' Felix said. 'You've been planning it for years, and this is the big pay-off. Why stay here for the rest of your life, when you can live like a millionaire anywhere you like?'

'You're insane,' Nicolás said contemptuously. 'I have no intention of leaving Guachtàl.'

Felix smiled. 'I know that,' he said softly. 'But no one else does.' Nicolás stared at him. 'And the evidence is going to look pretty damning,' Felix added. 'The money's been transferred, Nicci. It's safely stashed away in a numbered account. An account that I will be happy to prove belongs to you. The treasury is bare.'

For the first time Nicolás began to look nervous. 'That's impossible,' he said. 'No one can access the treasury account except me.'

'Wrong,' Felix said. 'There are friends of mine in the States who can access the Bank of England, or the White House, or the Pentagon, or any other secret files they damn well please. Sometimes they do it just to prove that they can. Other times they do it to help friends like me.'

It took Nicolás a few minutes to gather his thoughts. 'What do you hope to gain from this trickery?' he demanded, at last. 'Once I explain what's happened, you'll be the one who goes to jail.'

Felix's smile did not waver. 'Nicci,' he said, 'you've overlooked one very important point. You're not the most popular guy in Guachtàl. People accept Hernandez, because he's relatively harmless. But they don't like you. You've got too much power. If they see a chance to destroy you, they'll grab it with both hands. They won't question the evidence. They'll just thank me for providing it.'

'I'll fight,' Nicolás said, his voice thick with suppressed fury.

'You'll lose,' Felix said. 'Think about it. Who's going to support you? Hernandez won't, because his wife will order him not to. Carlos Márquez won't either, because you cut him out of the logging deal, and he's never really been your friend anyway. He used you, just like you used him.'

Jacey saw Nicolás clench his fists, and for a moment she thought he was going to punch Felix.

'Take what I'm offering you, Nicci,' Felix said softly. 'I'll give you time to run. There's plenty of space in South America. I'm sure a talented guy like you will find a niche somewhere. I'll even put some money in an account for you, enough to support you for a while.'

'Why do that?' Nicolás asked suspiciously. 'What's in it for you?'

'You might not believe this,' Felix said, 'but I'm grateful to you. You've kept this country financially stable, in your own crooked way. You've given us a base to build a future on. So I'm willing to give you

256

a chance to escape. Just don't come back to Guachtàl.'
He smiled again. 'It's your best bet, Nicci. Better than
jail.'

'How long do I have to decide?'

'Until tonight,' Felix said. 'If you want to wait that
long. I think we both know what you're going to do.'

Nicolás looked at Jacey. 'I missed you,' he said.
'When you went back to England, I actually missed
you. I was delighted when you returned. It's the first
time I've ever felt like that about a woman.' Then he
went out of the door, leaving her flabbergasted,
staring after him.

'So,' Felix said cheerfully, 'what did you think of
my surprise?'

'Hail, saviour of the rainforest,' she said flippantly.

'Well, of our little piece of it.' He looked at her
critically. 'You're pleased, I hope?'

'About the trees?' She nodded. 'Of course I am.'

'And about Nicolás?' he persisted. 'Guachtàl will
be much better off without him.'

'Let's hope so,' she said. 'Let's hope whoever takes
on the treasury can run it as well as he did.'

'I hope I'll be able to take on the treasury,' Felix
said. 'And I've already got some deals lined up.
You've heard of INBio?'

She nodded. 'The organisation in Costa Rica making an inventory of all their forest animals, plants
and micro-organisms.'

'And selling the information to pharmaceutical
firms.' He nodded. 'They've already been paid several million dollars by conglomerates in the States for
exclusive use of their research material. We could do
the same thing.' He smiled at her. 'My mother's
research will come in useful after all.'

'Have you thought,' Jacey said, 'that the *lohá*
destroyed Nicolás after all?'

257

'The *lohá*?' For a moment Felix looked perplexed. Then he grinned. 'Oh, you mean the spirit?'

'Ana Collados told me the Indians had offered Nicolás to the *lohá*,' Jacey said. 'She said it lived in the space between the worlds, and it would strike him down when he least expected it. And Nicolás has been destroyed by information that was manipulated in cyberspace.'

'Very strange,' Felix said, clearly unimpressed. 'Dear old Ana is as crazy as Juanita when it comes to Indian ghosts and spirits.'

'She said it was a cruel spirit,' Jacey said. 'And it's true.'

'You think what's happened to Nicolás is cruel?' Felix asked. 'It could have been much worse. How long do you think he'd have lasted in jail before someone knifed him? At least I've given him a chance to make another life somewhere else.' He reached for her hands and held them. 'Tell me you don't care about Nicolás, Jacey?'

Jacey smiled. 'I don't care about Nicolás,' she said. She squeezed his hands. 'But I do care about you.'

Was it the truth? Later that night, as she lay next to Felix, and listened to the constant symphony of sound from the rainforest, Jacey couldn't help wondering what would have happened if Felix had not managed to destroy Nicolás, and she had continued her affair with him. Would they have eventually found they could share something more than just sex? She would never know. If she stayed in Guachtàl, she would certainly never see him again.

Would she stay? She glanced at Felix, who was sleeping contentedly after their brief bout of love-making. He had given her an orgasm, kissed her, rolled off her, and told her she was wonderful. But she still felt unfulfilled. This is the man I'm thinking of spending the rest of my life with. Am I making a mistake?

It took six months for Jacey to confirm her doubts. It was a busy six months. She saw La Primavera become an open hospital, with Dr Rodriguez as senior physician, Ingrid Gustaffsen as his assistant and Dr Sanchez taking over as head of a newly formed interns training programme. She saw deals struck with pharmaceutical companies. She heard enthusiastic plans for eco-tourism. She saw the Indians returning to the rainforest to rebuild their villages.

And she saw Felix Connaught changing. He was still concerned with the economy and the rainforest, but now he was Generalissimo Hernandez's right-hand man. Lightweight suits had replaced his faded Levis, his hair was neatly cut, and he wore a watch instead of his metal bracelet. Jacey saw less of him, and when they met, he was often too tired to make love. She realised that he was far more interested in his work than sex. Their affair became less and less physical, until they were living together like a brother and sister.

That's when she knew she had to leave Guachtàl. She kept her promise, and told him she was going. He made her give him a contact phone number, which he tucked into his pocket as he left for a meeting, but he wasn't able to come and see her off. Another meeting with Hernandez, he explained. Ingrid and Paulo went with her to the airport. 'Behave yourself,' Ingrid said at the barrier. 'And think of us sometimes.'

'I'll do better than that,' Jacey said. 'As soon as I get a job and make some money, I'll visit you.'

'And behave yourself on the journey,' Ingrid added. 'No joining the Mile High Club.'

Jacey laughed. 'Chance would be a fine thing.'

Once inside the plane, she found her seat, and glanced across the aisle. An attractive-looking man with an angular face sat reading a book. Nice long legs, she thought. Nice hands. He sensed her watching him, and moved his hand so that she could see the book's title. *Sex in the Twenty-first Century*, she read. He moved his hand again, so that the title was covered but she could see the author's name: Gregory Ballantine.

A stewardess came down the aisle and stopped level with Jacey to speak to the man. 'I'm sorry we had to move you, Mr Ballantine. Are you sure you're comfortable there?'

'I'm fine, thanks, just fine,' he said. He smiled across at Jacey. She smiled back.

This is going to be a very interesting trip, she thought.

BLACK LACE NEW BOOKS

Published in August

LIKE MOTHER, LIKE DAUGHTER
Georgina Brown
£5.99

Mother Liz and daughter Rachel are very alike, even down to sharing the same appetite for men. But while Rachel is keen on gaining sexual experience with older guys, her mother is busy seducing men half her age, including Rachel's boyfriend.

ISBN 0 352 33422 3

CONFESSIONAL
Judith Roycroft
£5.99

Faren Lonsdale is an ambitious young reporter. Her fascination with celibacy in the priesthood leads her to infiltrate St Peter's, a seminary for young men who are about to sacrifice earthly pleasures for a life of devotion and abstinence.

What she finds, however, is that the nocturnal shenanigans that take place in their cloistered world are anything but chaste. And the high proportion of good-looking young men makes her research all the more pleasurable.

ISBN 0 352 33421 5

Published in September

OUT OF BOUNDS
Mandy Dickinson
£5.99

When Katie decides to start a new life in a French farmhouse left to her by her grandfather, she is horrified to find men are squatting in her property. But her horror quickly becomes curiosity as she realises how attracted she is to them, and how much illicit pleasure she can have. When her ex-boyfriend shows up, it isn't long before everyone is questioning their sexuality.

ISBN 0 352 33431 2

A DANGEROUS GAME
Lucinda Carrington
£5.99

Doctor Jacey Muldaire knows what she wants from the men in her life: good sex and plenty of it. And it looks like she's going to get plenty of it while working in an elite private hospital in South America. But Jacey isn't all she pretends to be. A woman of many guises, she is in fact working for British Intelligence. Her femme fatale persona gives her access to places other spies can't get to. Every day is full of risk and sexual adventure, and everyone around her is playing a dangerous game.

ISBN 0 352 33432 0

To be published in October

THE TIES THAT BIND
Tesni Morgan
£5.99

Kim Buckley is a beautiful but shy young woman who is married to a wealthy business consultant. When a charismatic young stranger dressed as the devil turns up at their Halloween party, Kim's life is set to change for ever. Claiming to be her lost half-brother, he's got his eye on her money and a gameplan for revenge. Things are further complicated by their mutual sexual attraction to each other and a sizzling combination of secret and guilty passions threatens to overwhelm them.

ISBN 0 352 33438 X

IN THE DARK
Zoe le Verdier
£5.99

This second collection of Zoe's erotic short stories explores the most explicit female desires. There's something here for every reader who likes their erotica hot and a little bit rare. From anonymous sex to exhibitionism, phone sex and rubber fetishism, all these stories have great characterisation and a sting in the tail.

ISBN 0 352 33439 8

If you would like a complete list of plot summaries of Black Lace titles, or would like to receive information on other publications available, please send a stamped addressed envelope to:

Black Lace, Thames Wharf Studios,
Rainville Road, London W6 9HT

BLACK LACE BOOKLIST

All books are priced £4.99 unless another price is given.

Black Lace books with a contemporary setting

PALAZZO	Jan Smith ISBN 0 352 33156 9	☐
THE GALLERY	Fredrica Alleyn ISBN 0 352 33148 8	☐
AVENGING ANGELS	Roxanne Carr ISBN 0 352 33147 X	☐
COUNTRY MATTERS	Tesni Morgan ISBN 0 352 33174 7	☐
GINGER ROOT	Robyn Russell ISBN 0 352 33152 6	☐
DANGEROUS CONSEQUENCES	Pamela Rochford ISBN 0 352 33185 2	☐
THE NAME OF AN ANGEL £6.99	Laura Thornton ISBN 0 352 33205 0	☐
SILENT SEDUCTION	Tanya Bishop ISBN 0 352 33193 3	☐
BONDED	Fleur Reynolds ISBN 0 352 33192 5	☐
THE STRANGER	Portia Da Costa ISBN 0 352 33211 5	☐
CONTEST OF WILLS £5.99	Louisa Francis ISBN 0 352 33223 9	☐
THE SUCCUBUS £5.99	Zoe le Verdier ISBN 0 352 33230 1	☐
FEMININE WILES £7.99	Karina Moore ISBN 0 352 33235 2	☐
AN ACT OF LOVE £5.99	Ella Broussard ISBN 0 352 33240 9	☐
DRAWN TOGETHER £5.99	Robyn Russell ISBN 0 352 33269 7	☐
DRAMATIC AFFAIRS £5.99	Fredrica Alleyn ISBN 0 352 33289 1	☐
DARK OBSESSION £7.99	Fredrica Alleyn ISBN 0 352 33281 6	☐

COOKING UP A STORM £7.99	Emma Holly ISBN 0 352 33258 1	☐
SEARCHING FOR VENUS £5.99	Ella Broussard ISBN 0 352 33284 0	☐
UNDERCOVER SECRETS £5.99	Zoe le Verdier ISBN 0 352 33285 9	☐
FORBIDDEN FRUIT £5.99	Susie Raymond ISBN 0 352 33306 5	☐
A PRIVATE VIEW £5.99	Crystalle Valentino ISBN 0 352 33308 1	☐
A SECRET PLACE £5.99	Ella Broussard ISBN 0 352 33307 3	☐
THE TRANSFORMATION £5.99	Natasha Rostova ISBN 0 352 33311 1	☐
SHADOWPLAY £5.99	Portia Da Costa ISBN 0 352 33313 8	☐
MIXED DOUBLES £5.99	Zoe le Verdier ISBN 0 352 33312 X	☐
RAW SILK £5.99	Lisabet Sarai ISBN 0 352 33336 7	☐
THE TOP OF HER GAME £5.99	Emma Holly ISBN 0 352 33337 5	☐
HAUNTED £5.99	Laura Thornton ISBN 0 352 33341 3	☐
VILLAGE OF SECRETS £5.99	Mercedes Kelly ISBN 0 352 33344 8	☐
INSOMNIA £5.99	Zoe le Verdier ISBN 0 352 33345 6	☐
PACKING HEAT £5.99	Karina Moore ISBN 0 352 33356 1	☐
TAKING LIBERTIES £5.99	Susie Raymond ISBN 0 352 33357 X	☐
LIKE MOTHER, LIKE DAUGHTER £5.99	Georgina Brown ISBN 0 352 33422 3	☐
CONFESSIONAL £5.99	Judith Roycroft ISBN 0 352 33421 5	☐
ASKING FOR TROUBLE £5.99	Kristina Lloyd ISBN 0 352 33362 6	☐

Black Lace books with an historical setting

THE SENSES BEJEWELLED	Cleo Cordell ISBN 0 352 32904 1	☐
HANDMAIDEN OF PALMYRA	Fleur Reynolds ISBN 0 352 32919 X	☐

Black Lace non-fiction

------------✂------------------------------

Please send me the books I have ticked above.

Name ....

Address ....

....

....

.... Post Code ....

Send to: Cash Sales, Black Lace Books, Thames Wharf Studios, Rainville Road, London W6 9HT.

US customers: for prices and details of how to order books for delivery by mail, call 1-800-805-1083.

Please enclose a cheque or postal order, made payable to **Virgin Publishing Ltd**, to the value of the books you have ordered plus postage and packing costs as follows:

UK and BFPO – £1.00 for the first book, 50p for each subsequent book.

Overseas (including Republic of Ireland) – £2.00 for the first book, £1.00 for each subsequent book.

If you would prefer to pay by VISA, ACCESS/MASTER-CARD, DINERS CLUB, AMEX or SWITCH, please write your card number and expiry date here:

....

Please allow up to 28 days for delivery.

Signature ....

------------✂------------------------------